GW01043795

Maddie The Baddie

A Lottie Baxter adventure

ALAN BARBARA

DEDICATION

To Mum and Dad who taught me to believe in the idea,
that one day, shoes with Velcro strips would be the
next best thing since sliced bread. How right they were!

ACKNOWLEDGEMENTS

Many thanks to Russell Scott for the brilliant cover artwork, and Clay Kelly for her help with the editing of this book.

CHAPTER 1 – ANOTHER ONE BITES THE DUST.

It was lunchtime. 12.37 to be precise. Lottie Baxter dropped a jar of her favourite Seltsam's Hot Chocolate into her shopping trolley next to a multi-pack of Leben's crisps. Lottie (like nearly every other 12-year-old) loved crisps, and she also loved collecting the empty packets (*unlike* nearly every other 12-year-old). She had six scrapbooks full of different crisp packets under her untidy bed at home.

Collecting 'stuff' was her thing – crisp packets, thimbles, feathers, purple buttons and anything else she could put in an album or trinket box. The only thing she had trouble collecting were friends her own age.

Lottie was shopping in the Verdi supermarket in Alum Bay with her great grandad, Cheddar George. He stood hunched in the middle of aisle five, trying to decide if he preferred the red or the green wetsuit that Verdi had on offer this week. Before he could make up his mind, Mrs Fish came wandering up to him.

"Going swimming, Cheddar George?"

"Kalispera, Mrs Fish. I can't *actually* swim, but these wetsuits are cheap as chips, and you never know when

7

they might come in handy," said Cheddar George (who could never resist a bargain).

"Righty-o. I wanted a fishing rod for my nephew, but they've sold out," said Mrs Fish.

"Fishing. Now you're talking. I have 'shark fishing' on my bucket list along with 'having one of those baths with a door in the side'."

Mrs Fish chuckled and patted Cheddar George's hand. "Hope to see you at the bingo later. We're due a win, don't you think?"

"Agreed indeed. I'll be there for 'eyes-down' with Vera and Frank at about six. Or 'Tom-Mix-Six' as we say in bingo lingo," said Cheddar George, as Lottie joined them and picked up a set of spanners from a large metal basket.

"Righty-o. I'm off to spend some of my pension and treat myself to lunch," said Mrs Fish and wandered off.

"Red or green, Lottie?" Cheddar George asked, studying the wetsuits again.

"Red," said Lottie.

"Tickety-boo! Pop one in the trolley for me would you. What other delights are on our list?"

Lottie pulled a piece of paper from her back pocket. "Tea bags, mints, Pontefract Cakes, plain chocolate, Piccalilli, Marmite, carrots…"

"Cheese?" asked Cheddar George, hopefully.

"No cheese," said Lottie.

"Better get some though. Just in case, and it is the food of champions," said Cheddar George. "Lead on Macduff."

*

While Lottie and Cheddar George were strolling up and down the food aisles, filling their shopping trolley with groceries from the list Nanny Vera had given them (with strict instructions *not* to buy anything else), Mrs Fish went to the self-service restaurant at the back of the store. Today's 'specials' were cod and chips with mushy peas, or sausage and mash. But by the look of the contents slopped in the heated trays on the counter, there was nothing 'special' about either of them.

She'd had sausages yesterday, when her old friend Binky Dupont came to dinner (after collecting her new teeth). So today, as it was Friday, Mrs Fish decided on the cod and chips with mushy peas.

Once she'd paid and put the change in her purse, she slipped the handle of her battered handbag over her arm, picked up her tray of insipid food and headed for an empty table. The cashier, wearing a fake smile and a grubby badge with 'Zoe' etched across it sniffed and waited for the next customer to slide their tray of lukewarm sludge towards her.

The restaurant in the Verdi supermarket was nearly empty. A Pic-A-Pasta had just opened next door and taken all their regular customers. Mrs Fish had tried it last week with Binky Dupont. But for her, the place was too dark, and she struggled to read the menu and see what she was *actually* eating. She might try it again if Pic-A-Pasta were to use some brighter lights or a larger font.

BING-BING-BONG

The noise blasted from the shop's loudspeakers above the aisles, making Mrs Fish jump. Nosey Rosie

Saunders' voice bellowed around the store (she'd just started working at Verdi and spent her day picking up bits of juicy gossip from the staff and customers).

"Good afternoon, super shoppers. Today's Star Deals at Verdi are a pack of 12 Luxy-soft toilet rolls in aisle three for just six pounds, or why not nip to aisle eight and treat yourself to a welder's helmet for only nine pounds. And finally, congratulations to Tracey from Maintenance who's just got engaged."

BING-BING-BONG.

Mrs Fish took a seat near the window and placed her tray onto the freshly smeared table. She sat at this end of the restaurant for two reasons – it was nice and light, and it didn't smell of pee (like the tables near the toilets). As a person from the older generation, she certainly didn't want to be linked to *that* smell.

Mrs Fish sat and stirred her mug of frothy coffee. It wasn't the brown, muddy sludge Verdi usually served, which was a bonus. She waved out the window at Binky Dupont, who's smile was greatly improved by her new teeth.

Binky hurried across the road, on her way as usual to the Burlington Bingo Hall by the promenade. Mrs Fish was planning to go that evening. She hadn't won a penny in ages but enjoyed meeting her old friends there for a chat.

Binky disappeared around the corner of the Pavilion Theatre and Mrs Fish stirred her coffee again, as a thin middle-aged lady, dressed in the standard orange and grey supermarket tabard, tidied away plates of half-eaten sausage and mash from the tables around her.

As she knocked the spoon on the side of her mug, Mrs Fish noticed two odd things about the lady. Firstly, her name badge said 'Colin' and secondly, she had a small tattoo of a mermaid's tail on the back of her left hand.

Mrs Fish's thoughts then wandered from the tattoo to a pink crimplene dress she'd seen in Lara's Womenswear opposite the Post Office (where she'd go and collect her pension later). She'd been invited to her great nephew's wedding next month, and the dress would be just perfect. She might even squeeze into a size 10 (if she could somehow breath in for the entire wedding ceremony).

"I'd put your handbag on the seat next to you if I were you, my love," said the clearer-upper, picking up Mrs Fish's handbag from the floor by her feet. "Just in case some oik nicks it while you're not looking."

Mrs Fish's thoughts of a new dress melted away and she smiled.

"Righty-o. Mind you, there's nothing in it that's worth stealing. It's just full of fluff from my knitting, a shoehorn, bunion cream and my bus pass."

She chuckled and took the handbag from the clearer-upper and turned to place it on the empty seat next to her. The distraction was just long enough for the clearer-upper to drop a small red pill into Mrs Fish's mug of coffee.

The clearer-upper smiled at Mrs Fish, showing teeth like gravestones and ambled with a noticeable limp across to another table and began smearing it with a soggy grey cloth. Mrs Fish chomped on a mouth full of her tasteless battered cod. Then she lifted the mug to her lips. The cleaner-upper watched closely as Mrs Fish took a slurp.

BING-BING-BONG

"Staff announcement… spillage in aisle seven. Tracey, bring your mop and bucket," Nosey Rosie Saunders' voice droned.

BING-BING-BONG.

A second later, Mrs Fish's chin (which contained more than a few old-lady-whiskers) buried itself in the middle of her cod and chips special. Blobs of mushy peas splattered the table as if she'd done the world's wettest sneeze.

'Staff announcement… spillage in the restaurant" should have echoed from the loudspeakers – but it didn't.

The clearer-upper glanced around, checking that nobody had seen Mrs Fish face-plant her mushy meal. She limped over to the pensioner, who groaned into her plate of food.

"You've had a funny turn, my love. Let me help you," said the clearer-upper, lifting Mrs Fish's head from her pile of mushy peas, and wiping her face with her grey cloth. She hoisted the limp woman from her seat and draped her floppy arm around her neck. The clearer-upper had another glance around, and then picked up the handbag and dragged Mrs Fish through a door into the staff break-room.

The small room was empty. Most of the staff were in Pic-A-Pasta next door, making use of their 25% off Friday deal. The clearer-upper eased a drowsy and confused Mrs Fish onto a chair.

"Sit there and don't move."

She then tugged open the metal door to a tall locker, and a pair of terrified eyes stared from within. The eyes belonged to Colin Thomas – the rightful owner of the uniform and name badge. He'd been squashed so tightly into the locker he might not get out again without the help of the local fire brigade. It was his first day working at Verdi, and he'd already decided it would be his last.

"Thanks, Colin. Not a *word*," hissed the clearer-upper, tossing the orange and grey tabard at the petrified man, who let out a "WAAAA!" from his gagged mouth.

The clearer-upper grabbed a duffel bag from Colin's lap and slammed the locker door, sending the poor chap back into his terrified darkness.

"Cod liver oil and washing up liquid," mumbled Mrs Fish, chanting random things from her shopping list, as she began to recover a little from the effects of the strange red pill.

"We can get you those in a second, Olive," said the clearer-upper, removing the set of fake teeth from her mouth.

She opened her duffel bag and slipped on a pair of glasses (which were missing the lenses). She put on a brown jacket and a green beanie hat then pushed a blonde wig over Mrs Fish's blue-rinsed hair.

"Rice pudding," mumbled Mrs Fish.

"Sure. Why not," said the clearer-upper, suddenly hearing voices in the restaurant, as some of the Verdi staff returned from their lunch at Pic-A-Pasta. Quickly, she helped Mrs Fish stand.

"This way, Olive. Let's go and do your shopping. They've got Spam on offer," said the clearer-upper.

"Spam… Righty-o," mumbled Mrs Fish.

Still dazed, the clearer-upper walked the old lady through the fire-escape door that led onto the rain-soaked street.

Mrs Fish's plans to buy her basket of groceries and the pink dress from Lara's Womenswear (probably a size 12 to be on the safe side) were scuppered.

The clearer-upper ambled with Mrs Fish into St Anne's Road and then disappeared amongst the elderly crowd coming out of the Burlington Bingo Hall. The clearer-upper grinned as she held Mrs Fish by the arm and walked at a pace that wouldn't attract attention – there was no longer *any* sign of her limp.

CHAPTER 2 – WITH A LITTLE HELP FROM MY FRIENDS.

Lottie Baxter sneezed. It was the dust. Whipped up by the constant wind that seeped into every corner of the crumbling building. The Pavilion Theatre had been derelict for 20 years, so there was plenty of dust to swirl around, which meant Lottie sneezed an awful lot.

Some roof tiles had blown off in a storm 15 years ago. And since then, the rain had worked its way down, rotting everything in its path, bringing with it the smell of damp and decay.

But a month ago, the theatre near the Verdi supermarket was bought by Lottie's friends, SooTed and BooTed and the two men (along with their entire life savings) were slowly bringing the old Pavilion back to life.

SooTed and BooTed weren't their real names (they were Thaddeus and Edward.) But as a Showaddywaddy Rock 'n' Roll tribute band who wore suits in a rainbow of colours along with black creeper boots, everyone knew the two men by their stage names, SooTed and BooTed.

The first thing SooTed and BooTed did was to pay for the damaged roof to be fixed. As the inside of the theatre dried out, dust had taken over from the damp and decay as the main problem for anyone working inside.

It was early September and Lottie was helping SooTed and BooTed with the renovation work before the new term started at Cringle Park school. It was the least she could do after the part they'd played stopping Timothy Pinkerton from swindling Lottie's family and all the other residents of Alum Bay out of their homes.

That was two months ago and much had happened in that time. Timothy Pinkerton was in prison (and rightly so) and Cheddar George had passed his first yodelling exam to earn his brown feather badge (which he'd proudly sewn on the front of his favourite Panama hat next to his old Scouting badges).

Lotte had started two new hobbies – riding a unicycle (which wasn't going very well) and collecting old train tickets. She hadn't given up her other hobby of playing the bagpipes (even after complaints from a neighbour, Mrs Lacey, about Tiddles her cat going berserk and hiding amongst the begonias in her greenhouse every time she played them).

Lottie sat alone in the auditorium on the edge of the dusty stage with her feet dangling in the old orchestra pit. Her laces were untied, but that was how kids today rolled. Her Nanny Vera couldn't understand that and was forever warning Lottie she'd trip over and lose a tooth.

On Lottie's lap sat Casey, her dog-shaped pencil case

where she kept her collection of extraordinary stationery. Lottie's great uncle Walter had invented the British Railway Espionage Crew (or BREW Crew for short), in 1941, and now Lottie owned the pencil case and the amazing collection inside. She spent ages in her bedroom, reading about their daring adventures in Arnhem, Berlin, Dunkirk and other places they were deployed during WWII to sabotage German troop trains using their incredible skills.

"What's next on the list?" Lottie asked.

A piece of paper from Paddy, the blue notepad, and the Duke, a shiny fountain pen, rose out of Casey's soft belly. The paper, with a long list of jobs, settled on Lottie's hand while the Duke's silver lid slid off and the nib glided across the paper, as if held by an invisible hand.

"Sitrep. BooTed has finished painting the kitchen and it looks top-ho."

"Amazeballs. We can cross that one off," said Lottie.

The Duke nodded and drew a neat line through that item while Lottie read the remaining tasks.

"We can mend the extractor fan in the loo. That's an easy-peasy job for you, Spike."

A rusty compass whizzed from inside Casey and zoomed through the air towards the exit at the rear of the auditorium.

"Wait, Spike. Come back!" shrieked Lottie just as the compass was about to dart through the newly renovated opening to the lobby.

The compass did a U-turn in mid-air and returned, hovering in front of Lottie's eyes.

"You're supposed to be a secret, remember," said Lottie and nodded at Casey on her lap.

Spike floated back inside the pencil case and settled next to an old wooden ruler. Lottie was right. Only her family and SooTed and BooTed knew about the BREW Crew's amazing talents and Lottie was desperate to keep it that way.

"More haste, less speed," said Lottie, quoting one of Cheddar George's favourite sayings (though she didn't really understand what it meant).

Cheddar George was in the office having a nap in a comfortable (or uncomfortable) chair and probably making a terrible smell from his rear end by 'letting Tommy out of prison'. Then, no doubt, he'd live up to his nickname by putting his false teeth in properly and scoffing a cheese sandwich or two. His idea of a balanced diet was a cheddar cheese sandwich in each hand.

Lottie headed for the ladies' toilet (without tripping over her laces). She pushed open the squeaky door and tried to ignore the terrible smell of damp and decay inside. She had a quick look to make sure nobody was around and then opened Casey.

"*Now* you can do your magic, Spike."

The old compass eagerly shot out of Casey again, morphed into a screwdriver and began taking the EX-AIR-360 extractor fan to pieces. Lottie stood by the door, watching in case one of the builders turned up to fit the new wash basins stacked in the corner.

Five minutes later, Spike flicked a switch on the wall and the EX-AIR-360 hummed into life.

"Amazeballs," said Lottie as Spike tightened the last screw on the front cover.

Lottie sneezed again and checked her list of jobs and then went backstage where the BREW Crew got to work once more. Ledley the black pencil inscribed fancy new signs on the dressing room doors and Penny the felt tip coloured them blue, green and orange – SooTed and BooTed's favourite colours.

*

In the box office, just inside the theatre's entrance, an old Sony CD player, covered in brick dust belted out *You Got What It Takes* (SooTed's favourite Showaddywaddy tune).

SooTed scratched his dusty bald head. His massive frame filled the cramped space behind the wooden counter. He wasn't alone. He stood with a skinny man, who wore clothes splashed with paint of every colour. On the man's head sat a yellow hard-hat with 'Nick the Gaffer' scrawled across the front in black marker pen.

"You've certainly bought a money pit here, mate," said Nick. "There's dry rot in all those purlins and joists holding the old ceiling up," he added, pointing vaguely above his head into the dusty darkness.

"But you can sort it, right?" asked SooTed, towering over Nick, the owner of Alum Bay Construction.

"Sure. Anything's possible if you throw enough money at it," chuckled Nick.

"OK. If you can put the new joists in today, I'll carry on clearing the rest of the room," said SooTed.

"No problem-o. You're the boss," said Nick, shoving his hands into his paint-splattered pockets and trudging off to his van to fetch a ladder and a tape measure.

SooTed turned up the volume and happily sang along to the Showaddywaddy tune blaring from the CD player. He began shovelling rubble by his feet into a wheelbarrow and once full, he pushed the heavy barrow towards sunshine, blazing through the battered doors at the entrance. The wheelbarrow squeaked as SooTed made his way over to what was once a carpark at the side of the theatre.

Parked in one corner under a tree was SooTed's car – his old American Hudson Hornet (known as 'the Huddy'). It was mint green with glinting chrome everywhere and inside, a welcoming cracked leather interior.

On the far side of the car park was a massive pile of rubble. BooTed stood beside it in the warm sunshine, hurling old seat cushions onto the ever-growing heap as if it was an Olympic sport. So far, he'd removed the seats from rows 'A' to 'H' in the auditorium and had cuts on four of his fingers to show for his efforts. Once the last cushion had been launched, he puffed hard and picked flakes of magnolia paint from his quiffed hair and wiped his filthy hands down his shirt.

"We should get the new sign ordered for above the entrance," he called to SooTed. He watched his good friend shove his barrow up a long wooden plank and tip it on the pile, creating a cloud of dust as if the rubble volcano had erupted.

SooTed sneezed into his hand. "Happy-as, buddy," he said, unwrapping a boiled sweet and flicking it into his mouth, not bothered that it was covered in his own dusty snot.

After its expensive renovation the old Pavilion would no longer be a theatre. It would have a new use and a new name (and a new sign over the entrance). In eight weeks, according to Nick the Gaffer, his army of builders would complete their huge task and the Pavilion Theatre would open its doors on October 18th and be reborn as 'The Trocadero' – SooTed and BooTed's brand new Rock 'n' Roll club.

The two men couldn't wait for the opening night and finally perform their Showaddywaddy act on the large stage. Their Rock 'n' Roll dream was just weeks away.

Lottie had finished the new dressing room signs and now appeared from the rear stage door carrying a black bucket. Stagnant water sloshed over the lip. She had Casey tucked in the pocket of her yellow dungarees which were now too short.

"The tap still drips by the stage door," she said and emptied the bucket onto a flower bed, now home to a jungle of stinging nettles. "I'll add it to the list of jobs for the BREW Crew."

"Happy-as," said SooTed, crunching his snotty boiled sweet.

Cheddar George slowly tottered out to join them in the sunshine. In his wrinkly hands, he gripped a battered tea tray with three chipped mugs. He was dressed in red corduroy trousers, a yellow shirt and an orange and pink tie. A red hard-hat was perched on top of his purple beret. He looked as if he'd dressed himself in the dark, but this colourful mix of clothes were normal for him.

On his left foot he wore a sky-blue flip-flop and, on his right, a brown slip-on (because he'd lost his big toe on that foot many years ago and couldn't keep a flip-flop in place). He referred to his footwear as 'flip-flips'.

"Kalispera, Lottie. How's your belly off for spots? I've made builder's tea for the workers. Tash-hag kettle's boiled."

"Kalispera, Cheddar George. I'm OK," said Lottie.

Unfortunately, the mugs on the tray were half empty due to Cheddar George's trembling hands, which had managed to slop tea all over his flip-flips during the walk from the kitchen.

"You're a good lad," said SooTed.

"I put six sugars in your tea as usual, SooTed," Cheddar George said. "But I can't remember which mug is yours."

SooTed chuckled. "Happy-as. Can you mix up a barrow of concrete next?"

"Young man, I'm 90-11," said Cheddar George (he was actually 101 but told everyone he was 90-11, as that sounded a lot younger). "And sadly, my concrete mixing days are *well* and truly over. Blimey, all I can manage to mix these days is builder's tea and a Whisky-Mac after my supper."

BooTed chuckled. "You'll be glad to know we've *finally* chosen the paint for the walls in the box office."

"Wickedoolie. What colour did you pick?" asked Lottie.

"It was a tough choice. Your Nanny Vera suggested

a nice beige as usual, but in the end, we went for sea-green," said BooTed.

"Thrilled-as. Can't wait to finally get some paint on the walls," said SooTed.

"Tickety-boo. It will be emulsional," said Cheddar George, slurping his tea and then letting 'Tommy out of prison'. "Parpon me."

BooTed chuckled, glad they were outside, and it was a breezy morning, so he wouldn't get a stinky whiff of that one.

"Do you think your BREW Crew can take the old sign down, Lottie?" asked SooTed, taking a slurp of tea and nodding at the rusty PAVILION THEATRE sign which hung above the entrance. His expression soured showing he'd picked the wrong mug of tea.

"Nick has just nipped off in his van to get some eight by twos and none of his guys are here yet, so it's quite safe," he said, swapping his sugar-less mug with BooTed.

"Sure," Lottie said, opening the zip on Casey's back.

Spike emerged and as he flew upwards, into the cloudless sky, he turned into a screwdriver for the job of disconnecting the power cable that snaked into the sign above the old entrance.

More of the BREW Crew helped with the task. A chunk of Rob the eraser was cut by Sharpy, the blade of a pencil sharpener and the rubber stretched to make a length of rope which looped around the sign. Rula, the strong wooden ruler bent in half and held the rope, hovering high above the entrance and taking the weight of the old sign.

"It still amazes me how they can do that," said BooTed.

Cheddar George chuckled. "Agreed indeed. Tickety-boo, I'd say."

Spike then transformed into a three-eighths spanner to undo eight rusty bolts and the heavy sign creaked and finally swung free from the wall. Rula flew slowly across to the rubbish volcano where Sharpy cut the rope and the sign crashed on the heap, causing another cloud of dust.

"Another job off the list," said Lottie.

SooTed nodded. "This building lark is easy-as when you have the right tools!"

BooTed looked at the crumbling brickwork and rotting wood around the entrance and frowned. "I'm not sure. There's *bound* to be a few surprises along the way before our opening night."

"Mate, poz-not-neg, remember," said SooTed.

*

In a dark corner of the basement of the theatre, hidden behind a wall of wooden crates containing forgotten theatrical costumes, a hand decorated with a mermaid's tail tattoo struck a match to light a stumpy candle.

In the dull yellow glow from the candlelight, Maddie Mainard opened a tin of Boomer's Tuna chunks, wiped a fork on her grubby sleeve and ate noisily.

Maddie wasn't happy at all. For months, the deserted Pavilion had been her perfect hideout. Nobody had bothered her while she went about her business of kidnapping the old people. But with the builders crawling all over the place, she'd now have to be careful to stay out of sight. Very careful.

Alan Barbara

CHAPTER 3 – TICKET TO RIDE.

Maddie Mainard tossed another empty tin of Boomer's Tuna chunks onto a growing pile in the corner of her hideout. The fishy pong coming from the heap didn't bother her. She'd got used to it. Maddie didn't really like tuna, but she needed to scrimp and save every penny and last month Boomer's Tuna chunks were on special offer in Verdi. She'd bought one hundred and forty-four tins.

Maddie wiped her hands on a filthy towel and pulled an old Samsonite suitcase from a wardrobe. She placed the case carefully on a dusty table and flicked the rusty metal catches, easing the brown lid open. Inside was her collection of dolls. Roxy dolls to be precise, made by the Ratello Toy Company. A total of 19 dolls, each one dressed in a different outfit, still in their original boxes and looking as shiny and new as they day they'd been made.

Maddie's doll collection would be complete if she could get her hands on 'Astronaut Roxy'. Only 11 of these dolls were ever made by Ratello – the same number as NASA Apollo missions to the moon.

A pristine Astronaut Roxy was to be auctioned at

Sotheby's in London next month and Maddie was desperate to own it and finally complete her rare collection. She was saving hard for the auction (which is why her diet consisted of tins of Boomer's Tuna). She slipped on a pair of white cotton gloves and picked up 'Doctor Roxy' from the suitcase and smiled.

"Just a little longer, Doctor Roxy. I'm going to earn a bucket-load of money soon and then I'll have a new friend for you all," Maddie said, carefully laying the doll on the seat of her camping chair.

"You need a shower, Mainard," she muttered, noticing her grubby reflection in a mirror she'd stolen from one of the six dressing rooms above, before the new owners had bought the theatre.

But a hot shower would have to wait. Maddie took her duffel bag from a shelf and pulled out the disguise she'd worn to kidnap Olive Fish. She put the fake teeth in a small box and the clothes went in a drawer containing a dirty chef's outfit and a pile of wigs of different colours and hairstyles.

"A place for everything and everything in its place," said Maddie, who often talked to herself. Working for the PCS was a very lonely job and there were times when she didn't speak to another person for days.

"Time to go, Roxy" she said, returning Doctor Roxy carefully to her place in the suitcase and storing it in the wardrobe.

Maddie removed her white gloves and grabbed a small torch from a shelf next to the mattress where she slept and her old walking stick (hand made by Carmichael's of London). She snuffed out the candle on top of an old filing cabinet and shoved the heavy unit aside to reveal a hole in the wall and a dark tunnel that led to the quiet alley behind the theatre. Maddie bent and squeezed through the hole and walked quickly and quietly along the tunnel. The light from her torch danced eerily off the walls and she saw at least a dozen rats scurry into the darkness ahead.

Halfway along the tunnel, Maddie pressed a tiny button, hidden in the curved top of her walking stick to expose a two-inch spike at the other end. She came to a stop by a heavy wooden door with a sign inscribed 'BEER CELLAR'.

She unlocked the old door and heaved it open. The door used to squeak badly, but Maddie had oiled it (with Boomer's Tuna oil) when SooTed and BooTed began poking about in the theatre upstairs. She was desperate to avoid her hideout being discovered.

The windowless cellar stank of stale beer and mildew. Grey-green mould festered on every wall and water dripped constantly from the black ceiling, making a puddle by the door. Empty barrels lay abandoned on the floor and huge spiders had made them their home. Maddie was sure this was where the rats lived.

She shone her torch into a corner of the cellar. "Move," she said, brandishing her Carmichael walking stick like a sword.

Mrs Fish sat on a barrel with her head leaning against the damp wall. She'd been asleep, but an enormous rat scurrying across her foot a second ago had woken her with a start. She shielded her petrified sunken eyes with a shaky hand to block the bright torchlight.

"I said move," Maddie ordered, whacking the walking stick on a broken wooden barrel by her feet, startling the old woman.

Mrs Fish, exhausted and terrified, stood and shuffled across the cellar.

"Out," said Maddie.

Mrs Fish trudged through the door as ordered, shoulders hunched, staring down at the uneven floor. Maddie prodded her bum with the spikey end of her walking stick to force her down the tunnel to the alley at the back of the theatre. It was four o'clock in the morning and the alley was deserted, just as Maddie expected.

She led Mrs Fish through the menacing shadows to a row of lockup garages where she took a key from a chain around her neck and opened one of the doors. Inside was Maddie's white and blue VW Campervan. Built in 1972, the van had been rotting in a scrapyard in Dorset before Maddie spotted it last summer. She'd worked tirelessly to restore it and now loved it *almost* as much as her collection of Ratello dolls.

"Wait," hissed Maddie and in the still night air, she slid open a door in the side of the van. "Get in."

Mrs Fish was unable to argue, due to the strip of black Gaffa tape stuck across her mouth. She felt another prod in her posterior from the old Carmichael stick. Having no choice, Mrs Fish did as she was told. The hours sitting on the barrel in the cold, wet cellar meant her troublesome back was now more painful than usual and the climb into the van was a struggle.

She let out a feeble "EEEEK" as she felt another painful poke in the bum from the walking stick.

Mrs Fish sat gingerly, and Maddie took a thin rope and tied a reef knot to secure Mrs Fish's thin and pale wrists to the handle of a kitchen stove in the back of the campervan. She then drew the red and yellow striped curtains.

Mrs Fish closed her eyes, hoping it would help block out the horrifying nightmare. The whole terrible business made no sense at all to Olive Fish. Why had she been taken? Who was the evil kidnapper poking her bum? She heard the side door close and felt the van rock as Maddie climbed into the driving seat.

The engine fired and Maddie drove from the garage and left the shadows of the Pavilion Theatre. The van chugged passed the rear of the Verdi supermarket and the Pic-A-Pasta, onto Connaught Road and headed for Ryde, a town 20 miles away on the east of the Isle of Wight. Empty tuna tins clattered around Mrs Fish's feet as Maddie drove along the winding roads, carefully keeping to the speed limit.

When she reached the village of Wooton Bridge, they passed a lay-by and Maddie bit her lip when she noticed the red and blue markings of a parked police car. She looked in her mirrors, deeply worried when the headlights came on and the car pulled out behind her.

"Steady, Mainard," Maddie muttered, her eyes flitting between her rear mirror and the speedo in the dashboard. The police car followed Maddie's campervan for over a mile towards Ryde and then suddenly, the blue lights came on and the siren blared.

Maddie felt her heart thumping. This was her worst nightmare. If the police found Mrs Fish trussed up in the back, then she'd get arrested and locked up. That would surely be the end of her PCS career *and* her quest to get her hands on the Astronaut Roxy doll.

Questions swirled in Maddie's head. Like how did the local police find out about Mrs Fish so quickly? Had Colin Thomas at the Verdi told them. And how did the police know Maddie owned this campervan?

The road ahead snaked through the dark countryside and Maddie considered ramming her foot hard on the gas pedal to try and outrun the trailing police car, but she knew that was a waste of time in her old and sluggish VW.

"No. You're built for comfort and not for speed," she muttered. "Don't panic, Mainard and trust Caruthers' training."

Maddie spotted a lay-by two hundred yards ahead and quickly hatched a better plan to deal with the troublesome police officer.

The campervan chugged into the deserted lay-by, followed by the police car. Maddie killed the engine and turned to Mrs Fish. "Not a sound. Do you hear."

Mrs Fish's eyes, empty and terrified, just stared at the floor.

The police car's tyres crunched across the loose gravel and came to a stop behind the campervan. The sirens and blue lights went out, plunging the lay-by into darkness. The only glint of light came from the summer moon's waning gibbous.

Maddie opened the door and was quickly out of her

seat. Take the initiative. That's what Major Caruthers had drummed into her on her PCS training. In her head, she could hear Major Caruthers' hard-as-nails voice. *"Always take the initiative, Mainard. And handle the situation your way."*

She waited in the shadows near the back wheel, watching the police officer in his car talking on the radio. Then he opened his door and climbed out. The man was huge. Maddie knew she'd have trouble overpowering him. Still, with her expert training from Caruthers and his team, she could do it. She was focused and ready.

"I thought you weren't going to stop and I'd have to chase you all over the island," said the police officer in a high-pitched voice which didn't match his muscular body. He kept his eyes on Maddie and opened the boot of his patrol car.

Maddie slid her hand behind her back and pulled a short length of nylon rope from her pocket. She held it out of sight as the police officer grabbed something long and thin from the boot and approached. Maddie guessed he was taking no chances with her and holding some sort of baton. Her hands tightened round the rope, and she waited for him to get within striking distance.

"I don't want to use this," the voice squeaked.

In the soft moonlight, Maddie could just make out a metal bar, clutched in his huge hand.

Maddie's PCS training kicked in. She moved her left foot to stand side-on to the enormous police officer. For a split second she thanked Caruthers for being so thorough with his arm-to-arm combat training, hearing his gravelly voice in her head listing her next moves.

One step quickly towards the target, pivot on the left foot and swing your left arm, using the rope in your dominant hand to disarm the target's weapon. Then, right hand on their shoulder and spin the target round, left hand on the back of their elbow and shove as hard as you can.

According to Major Caruthers, this would get Maddie behind the target with their hands behind their back, and the whole movement would take less than two seconds. Then the rope would be tied in a double bowline, a knot she could tie one-handed with her eyes shut.

Maddie's eyes locked on the metal bar, and she took the step towards the target.

"I bought it for my old banger but she's a 1971 model and it won't fit," squeaked the police officer.

Maddie stopped, just before pivoting her left foot and swinging her arm with the rope.

"Yours is the '72, with the newer gear box," said the police officer, now just a yard from Maddie.

"Sorry?" asked Maddie, confused.

The police officer nodded at the metal bar in his hand. "It's a gear stick from a Vee-Dub campervan. I bought it on eBay last week but it's not the right one for my van."

"Gear stick?" asked Maddie, even more confused and still suspecting a trap.

The police officer grinned. "I know how hard spares are to get for these old campers. When you drove past me, I noticed you had the '72 model, so wondered if you wanted it."

"Erm… yes… please," said Maddie, now understanding the situation and relaxing a little.

The police officer handed Maddie the gear stick and shone a torch, admiring the rear of her van. "She's in great condition. Mine's in a sorry state, but I'm hoping to have her up and running before Christmas."

He went to walk along the side of the van and Maddie knew she needed to take control again and not let the police officer open the door and spot Mrs Fish.

She moved to stand by the driver's door, her hand resting on the chrome door handle. "Thanks for the gear stick. But I'll be late for the ferry if I don't get a move on."

"Of course. I hope she runs smoothly for many years yet," said the police officer, gently patting the rear light of her campervan and then his huge ten-to-two feet crunched back across the gravel to his car.

Maddie watched the police officer like a hawk while she climbed back into the driver's seat. The police officer swigged from a Coffiesta takeaway cup, waved and drove off back towards Wooton Bridge.

"That was close," muttered Maddie, wiping her sweaty palms on her jeans and letting out a sigh of relief.

The journey to Ryde took another five minutes, and in that time, Maddie didn't see another vehicle on the roads. Just what she needed to settle her nerves. She drove into the quiet town and headed for the deserted seafront, turning right into the entrance to Ryde Pier.

The wooden structure, which stretched half a mile

out to sea, had closed suddenly at the beginning of the summer. Large red signs swung in the sea breeze above the entrance, warning that parts of the wooden pier were rotting and unsafe to enter. The rides and amusements scattered along the pier now lay abandoned and falling apart.

The rats and seagulls had made it their home. The fences along the sides of the pier were edged with barbed-wire and every 50 yards, tall metal poles held CCTV cameras aloft. In the darkness, the pier looked like a scene from a horror film.

Holiday makers could no longer enjoy the thrill of the Ellis Brother's Dodgems, or the lighthouse helter-skelter, or amuse the little ones in the Old Macdonald soft play. Ryde Pier was no longer a fun place for the public to spend a day.

But Maddie knew the pier was perfectly safe. The sinister warning signs across the entrance were to keep the general public out. And they worked. The VW drove onto the pier and chugged across the thick wooden planks, making a DUD-DUD-DUD noise.

Halfway along the pier, far away from prying eyes, a red and white security barrier blocked Maddie's path. Next to it was a wooden hut, the inside lit by a faint light. The CCTV cameras whirred, focusing on Maddie's VW as it rolled to a stop.

"ID," barked a man's voice from the shadows. He'd appeared from nowhere. Caruthers had trained him well. He was dressed completely in black and as he came closer, Maddie noticed he was missing half an ear. A military radio was clipped to his waist with a wire trailing up to an earpiece attached to his good ear. The voice reached the driver's door and Maddie flashed her PCS security pass and pulled up her sleeve to show the mermaid's tail tattoo on her wrist.

"Secret passphrase," said the guard.

"They've Got an Awful Lot of Coffee in Brazil."

The man nodded once.

"Busy night?" asked Maddie.

"Nope. But you're late," said the man, adjusting his black beret and the gold PCS badge on the front caught the moonlight.

"Spot of bother with the law," Maddie said and smiled.

The man said nothing else, but raised the barrier and Maddie drove on. The barrier lowered with a clunk behind her, and the man disappeared back into the shadows.

Maddie drove on to the end of the pier. She stopped the campervan beside a metal gangplank that led to a door in the side of an enormous rusting battleship, securely moored to the pier with ropes as thick as Maddie's wrist. HMS Chichester had been officially retired from British naval duties in 2010, but the ship now had a new use - a *secret* use.

Another guard appeared, dressed identically to the first at the security barrier.

"Just the one today," Maddie said, smiling politely.

The guard nodded and opened the van's sliding door.

"Welcome to the Guest House Paradiso," he said, untying Mrs Fish and helping her climb out. The cool breeze coming off the sea ruffled Mrs Fish's blue-rinsed hair and she looked at the ship, her eyes full of tears.

"Come on, love," said the guard and he slid the door closed and thumped twice on the roof – the signal for Maddie to depart.

Maddie Mainard craned her neck to watch through her side window as the guard took Mrs Fish up the narrow gangplank. They disappeared through the steel door which locked behind them with a CLANG.

Happy with her day's work and the money she'd bank towards her Astronaut Roxy doll, Maddie drove carefully back to Alum Bay. She filled up with fuel (Caruthers drummed it into the PCS agents to always be prepared) and then hid her campervan in the lockup behind the Pavilion Theatre. Exhausted, she crept back down to the basement where she forced down another tin of tuna chunks. After eating, she took her laptop and filled in a PCS Handover Report to claim the payment for delivering Mrs Fish safely (and nearly on time) to HMS Chichester.

It was now six o'clock in the morning. Maddie yawned and picked up a sleeping bag laying in a heap by her fold-up camping chair. A cloud of dust erupted as she shook the sleeping bag and unzipped it.

"Bloomin' dust," Maddie muttered and climbed inside the bag and quietly zipped it up.

She shuffled across the floor like a large caterpillar and clambered onto a mattress on the floor.

"Busy day tomorrow with any luck, Mainard," she muttered, yawning again and snuggling further into the warmth of the sleeping bag. PCS Control were due to call at nine o'clock for their daily update. She hoped they'd assign her yet another well-paid collection and she needed to sleep.

Alan Barbara

CHAPTER 4 – DON'T STOP 'TIL YOU GET ENOUGH.

Emelia Douthwaite sat at her cluttered desk and looked out of her office at her team of PCS Managers. She sighed when Ken Oliver came over. He knocked on her door and entered without waiting to be asked. Emelia knew Ken was *never* happy unless he was miserable and moaning about something or other (even Ken's blood type was B negative).

"The LAD system is down *again*," Ken groaned as he slumped in the unremarkable chair opposite Emelia.

LAD stood for Logging and Dispatch and was the troublesome computer system that Ken and his team needed to do their job. It had crashed three times already today and it wasn't yet ten o'clock.

"These things happen all the time. They're just teething problems, Ken. Do we have any more to collect yet?"

Emelia knew she was in for another tale of Ken's doom and gloom, but she needed to know.

Ken leant back in his seat and stared back through the open door at a large screen hanging on the far wall behind his desk. It showed graphs and charts with numbers changing every few seconds.

"Nobody yet," Ken said, sighing again, louder than necessary.

"Pity. I have a meeting with the Home-Sec in five minutes and he *won't* be happy, that's for sure," said Emelia, checking her watch.

"It's a crazy idea, if you ask me. I'll let you know when the flipping LAD system is back up," moaned Ken, as he stood and trudged back to his desk.

Emelia searched her government-issued desk for her mobile phone. She found it under a chicken and bacon sandwich she'd bought for her lunch the day before, which she hadn't had the time to eat. As she left her office, she stopped by a cluster of desks, which some of her PCS managers occupied, including Ken Oliver. He now had his head in his hands (his 'doom-omitor' was off the scale due to the fact that IT had just told him the LAD system would be down for the rest of the day).

"I'm going upstairs. If I'm not back in half an hour, trigger the 'Boss Evacuation Process', said Emelia.

Her order was met with blank looks from the group.

"Call my phone and *pretend* there's an emergency."

"Yes, Ma'am," said a young man sitting opposite Ken, who wore a suit which still had the price label dangling from the sleeve.

"Don't call me Ma'am. This isn't MI5, Neil," said Emelia. "It's *far* worse," she muttered.

"Sorry, Emelia. But my name's not Neil, it's Hugo."

Emelia didn't hear. She was already off, hurrying up the stairs to the ninth floor. One thing you *didn't* do was keep the Home Secretary waiting.

Now out of breath, Emelia stood outside the panelled door to room 51 and took a bottle of Pierre Thabaut perfume from her jacket pocket. She sprayed a generous dose of the expensive scent over her head and shoulders; an invisible shield to mask the terrible aroma she knew awaited on the other side of the door. Emelia took two deep breaths to allow the sweet smell of perfume into her nose and then knocked.

"Ter!" came a booming voice from within.

Emelia turned the handle and entered the large office to find Sir Charles Oakley, the Home Secretary, sitting in a leather chair with his feet perched on a handmade antique desk.

Sir Charles had a massive head, topped with hair as black as coal and parted in the middle. He kept his neatly trimmed hair and thick moustache in place by smearing them every morning with Lugo Cream, made from peanut oil and the sap from the Yoshino cherry tree.

He wore an expensive three-piece suit in blue with a white pinstripe and a white shirt with a green and gold tie, carefully tied in a neat Windsor knot. Sir Charles Oakley was a toff, that fashion had left behind, and he looked very much like a detective from an old black and white film.

Sir Charles had been Home Secretary for four years and although he was in his sixties, he still had ambition. Ambition to become Prime Minister, believing he could do a much better job than Jarvis Bertrand, the current PM. Sir Charles knew that if he continued doing well at his job as Home Secretary, he'd surely get promoted to the post of Prime Minister when old 'Jammy Jarvis' retired in a few months.

An old telephone was jammed against Sir Charles' ear, and he listened intently. He peered over the top of a pair of half-moon spectacles he'd used for 30 years and gestured at an empty chair before him.

Emelia sat, feeling she was about to be interviewed as a murder suspect.

On the wall behind Sir Charles' oversized head was a framed painting showing the Oakley coat of arms in royal blue and gold. An ornate mermaid's tail wrapped around the family motto, etched in Latin at the bottom - 'Ad infinitum, et ultra'.

Grubby oak-framed portraits of family members covered every inch of wall space. Emelia wondered if they might all be related to Ken Oliver, as every one of them had his same miserable expression.

Although it was a non-smoking building, that rule certainly didn't apply to Sir Charles and his pipe. Emelia's eyes watered. The office smelt as if a bonfire had been lit in a pile of pig dung. She made a mental note to spray herself with even more Pierre Thabaut when summoned again to see Sir Charles. Half a bottle should do it.

Everyone who entered his stinky office had their own way of dealing with the smoky stench which oozed from every wall and piece of old furniture. Emelia heard a rumour yesterday that Katie Harmsworth from Immigration actually filled her nostrils with mint toothpaste.

While Emelia waited, Sir Charles' expression changed from uninterested to anger, and his cheeks turned red as he cradled the black phone in the crook of his neck. He picked up his old pipe with a silver shaft and black bowl from a glass ashtray. The angry look remained, and he struck a Swan Vesta match and tried to light the brown tobacco, rammed into the small bowl.

"Darn thing," mumbled Sir Charles, knocking the pipe on the side of the ashtray and showering the surrounding area with blobs of thick black gunk. He opened a leather pouch, took a fresh pinch of his favourite Cornell tobacco and rammed it in the bowl. Then he struck a second match and managed the task of lighting his pipe.

Satisfied, he leant further back in his chair, looked up at the brown, stained ceiling and took a deep puff. The tobacco in the bowl glowed bright red and the smoky stench got even worse. Emelia sat patiently opposite, waiting for him to finish his phone call and feeling sorry for whoever was on the other end of the phone.

"Howard, that's *not* good enough. It will have to be much sooner. The Oakley motto is 'ad infinitum, et ultra'," Sir Charles said, looking expectantly at Emelia.

"Ad infinitum," said Emelia, performing the PCS salute by pointing her index finger upwards and wagging it as if telling someone off.

"And I won't accept *average*, Howard. I need an update first thing tomorrow," barked Sir Charles and he slammed the phone down. "Ahhhh, Emelia. How are

45

you, my dear?"

"I'm fine, Sir Charles," replied Emelia, trying to ignore the disgusting burnt tobacco stink, teasing her nose. Pierre Thabaut was fighting a losing battle.

Sir Charles puffed again, took his feet off his desk (which usually meant he was about to say something important) and his head disappeared behind a plume of grey smoke. Emelia wafted a hand to clear a peephole in the foggy cloud.

"I see the number of collections is down. That's *deeply* worrying, Emelia. Explain, do," said Sir Charles, studying a piece of paper with a graph he'd picked up from his desk, now peppered in black gunk from his pipe.

"Actually, the collection numbers are *up*, Sir Charles. You have my report upside down," said Emelia.

Sir Charles frowned and turned Emelia's collection report around. "Ahh. *That's* better! Now, what's the latest with the Coffiestas. Explain, do," he said, his cheeks losing a little of their redness.

Emelia checked her notepad perched on her lap. "The Coffiesta in Alum Bay is now open, and we have PCS agents on site, listening to the customer's conversations. And next week, we are expanding across the Isle of Wight and opening the coffee shops in Ventnor, Shanklin, Bembridge and Yarmouth. Which means we'll have five Coffiestas in total on the island."

"Good. And what about collections? Explain, do."

Emelia turned a page of her notepad and cleared her throat. "So far this week we've only collected three senior citizens."

Sir Charles frowned and wagged a finger. "Three collections aren't enough. And I'll remind you not to refer to them as 'senior citizens'. They are 'pensioners', Emelia. *Pensioners* that take a *pension* from taxes paid by you and me.

"Yes, Sir Charles," said Emelia, looking down at her lap as if she'd been told off by the headmaster.

"And what about customers?" asked Sir Charles, clearly not happy with just three collections.

"We only had 28 customers in our Alum Bay Coffiesta yesterday. And 21 of these were senior… erm… I mean *pensioners*," said Emelia.

"Only 21? We need more, Emelia. *Lots* more," said Sir Charles.

"Yes, Sir Charles," said Emelia once more.

Sir Charles lit his pipe again and puffed a huge grey cloud of smoke. "The Home Office have spent a fortune. A *fortune*, I say, setting up Coffiesta coffee shops on the Isle of Wight to deal with all the ruddy pensioners. If my plan goes well on the island, we'll open Coffiestas all over Britain and collect thousands of pensioners and save millions. So, explain, do, Emelia. How are you going to entice more and more Silver Cuppa Suppas into our new Coffiestas?"

"Well, my team had a brain-storming session yesterday and came up with a few ideas that might appeal to pensioners," said Emelia, flicking through her pages of notes.

"Explain, do," said Sir Charles.

"Well, *pensioners* enjoy things from 'the good old days',"

"That's true," said Sir Charles. "Mrs Oakley and I still enjoy the Basil Brush show to this day."

"So... We could name all the food and drinks on our menu after famous people from their era. From their 'good old days'," said Emelia.

Sir Charles looked confused. "For instance?" he asked.

"Well, take the name 'Mick Jagger', we could call our white coffee a Milk-Jagger. I think pensioners would be more likely to visit our coffee shop which sold a Milk-Jagger, than one offering drinks called Latte or Americano."

"Who's Mick Jagger?" asked Sir Charles, curious to know more.

"The lead singer of the Rolling Stones," said Emelia, surprised Sir Charles needed reminding who he was.

"Ahh, yes... Or Rolling *Scones*," said Sir Charles with a smug look.

"Yes, Sir Charles. Very good. And our cups of tea could have names like Tea-Vee-Wunda or Tea-Ner-Turner.

Sir Charles' eyes lit up. "Or... Paul-McCart-Tea and Fred-Tea-Mercury!"

"Exactly. And we could do the same for our biscuits and cakes. Like... Bour-Bon-Jovi-Biscuits or Laurel-And-Lardie-Cake," said Emelia, delighted that Sir Charles looked pleased with her idea.

"Agatha-Crispy-Cakes," squealed Sir Charles, clearly enjoying himself. "And how about a Fred-Éclair and Ginger-Nut-Rogers as well, for the *really* old ones!" said Sir Charles excitedly.

"Exactly, Sir Charles," Emelia said, writing his suggestions down on her pad.

"A Custard-Dolly-Tart-On and… Bob-Marley-And-The-Wafers or… John-Lennon-Drizzle-Cake!" shrieked Sir Charles.

"Very good," said Emelia, adding these to her ever-growing list. "And for hot meals, we came up with Fleetwood-Mac-And-Cheese and Soup-Waddywaddy?"

"Excellent idea, Emelia. But let's not have anything *healthy* like… a UB-Fruit-Tea… or Ryvita-Franklin."

"Yes, Sir Charles," said Emelia.

"Well," said Sir Charles, rubbing his hands together. "That should get loads more of the oldies on the island coming in our coffee shops for a chat. I'll get the marketing team on it right away. What else?" asked Sir Charles.

"We could also hang cat and dog calendars on all the walls and turn the heating right up. And have regular games of bingo and offer free vitamins with every tea or coffee."

"I like it, Emelia. I like it *a lot*. Pensioners love all that," said Sir Charles, puffing on his pipe and then his face turned serious once more.

"Our new Coffiestas need to be *full* of Silver Cuppa Suppas for my plan to work."

"Of course, Sir Charles, but are you sure what we are doing to the British public is… *legal?*"

"Legal? Why, Emelia, my dear, of course it's legal! And if it's not, it jolly well should be," laughed Sir Charles and then his serious face returned.

"As you know, there are now over sixty-six million

people in Britain. Jammy Jarvis' government is running out of money to pay for all the pensions, healthcare, hip replacements and what-not caused by the huge increase in the number of old folk. And as for that ruddy winter fuel allowance, that's just puffle-huff," barked Sir Charles slapping the desk with his fist, making Emelia jump.

"But Sir Charles, listening to the pensioners' conversations in our Coffiestas… that's surely not allowed? And locking them up just because—"

"Nonsense," barked Sir Charles, his cheeks turning red once again. "I have to do something to save money and your department, the *Pensioner* Collection Service was created to do just that — save *oodles* of cash."

Sir Charles believed that if he could reduce the amount of money his government department spent (while all the other departments were spending billions more to keep the country running) it would prove he was surely the right person to succeed Jammy Jarvis as Prime Minister.

Another cloud of smoke came from his pipe, and he continued.

"Pensioners love sharing their fond tales of yesteryear and the job of the PCS agents in the Coffiestas is to listen to pensioners chit-chat while they slurp their… their Milk-Jaggers and what-nots. The agents listen and *if* the oldies confess to their chums about a crime from their past that's gone unpunished, then that gives us the right to collect them and lock 'em up for good. Then it's goodbye Norma Jean and we no longer pay their pensions and what-not and I save a bucket load of money."

"But Sir Charles, some *pensioners* have been collected and locked up by us for admitting very minor wrongdoings," said Emelia.

"I very much doubt it. Explain, do," said Sir Charles, frowning.

Emelia pulled a piece of paper from her jacket pocket and unfolded it. The paper was a printout of a Collection Report (spat out by a printer in her office before the LAD system crashed).

"Well, last week, we collected Olive Fish from Alum Bay. She went to the Coffiesta with her friend Binky Dupont. Our agents listened to Mrs Fish telling Binky she'd taken four ounces of pick n' mix sweets from Woolworths in 1978. Mrs Fish explained that it wasn't on purpose, as she thought her husband had paid for them. It sounds like Olive Fish made an *honest* mistake. Isn't being locked up for the rest of your life for forgetting to pay for a few sweets a bit *harsh*?"

"Harsh? Certainly not, Emelia," barked Sir Charles, puffing again on his pipe. "Theft is theft in my book. And with her locked up, how much do I save by *not* paying her pension and what-nots?"

Emelia checked the bottom of the Collection Report. "Errrm… Nine hundred and seven pounds a month."

"There you go. Excellent. And it only costs 19 pounds 27 pence a week to keep a pensioner locked up, so you see, my plan *is* working, Emelia. You need to lock up loads more pensioners and save me even more money."

Sir Charles then pointed at the coat of arms behind him. "Ad infinitum, et ultra, remember."

"Ad infinitum, Sir Charles," sighed Emelia, wagging her finger and shifting awkwardly in her chair.

"Who is your top Collector?" asked Sir Charles.

"We now have a team of seven Collectors who've been trained by Major Caruthers and his team. Out of that seven, Maddie Mainard has collected the most pensioners. She grabbed six last week," said Emelia, taking a sneaky glance at her watch. She'd only been in the stinking office ten minutes, so it was far too early to expect the 'Boss Evacuation Process' to trigger.

"Ah, dear Maddie. Feisty little 'un is our Maddie. A true 'ad infinitum'."

"Ad infinitum," replied Emelia, saluting with her finger again though finding the ritual a little tedious.

Sir Charles puffed happily on his pipe. "She'll be in line for a bonus if she carries on Collecting at the rate she is.

"Yes, Sir Charles," said Emelia.

"But your team needs to work *smarter*, not harder and get the ruddy pensioners into our Coffiestas. I need results. Emelia, I need evidence that the PCS is making progress. I will show Jammy Jarvis and the other ministers at the cabinet review next month that I, the Home Secretary, can save money. And the Pensioner Collection Service is a critical part of that," barked Sir Charles and disappeared behind another cloud of acrid smoke.

CHAPTER 5 – I HEARD A RUMOUR.

Lottie bent over, steadied herself and waited for the gust of wind to ease. If she could sink this putt, she'd win the game *and* reclaim the Baxter Crazy Golf cup (which Lottie had made from a plastic water bottle covered in tin foil and her collection of spare seashells).

Lottie's Grandad Frank won the cup last time they played. He'd proudly sat it on the mantlepiece in the beige lounge at their home in Rose Crescent where Lottie lived with Grandad Frank, Nanny Vera and Cheddar George.

The wind stopped. Lottie held her breath and swung the putter like a pendulum from an old grandfather clock. The club head struck the golf ball, sending it on its way, bobbling over a ridge and disappearing down a drainpipe. A second later, it reappeared further down the course. It bounced off a concrete treasure chest, then a plastic alligator (that was missing the end of its snout) and rolled slowly back towards Lottie and finally dropped into the hole.

"Who-hoo. Hole in one!" Lottie shrieked, holding her putter triumphantly aloft.

The Duke wrote the score down for the final hole on the scorecard.

"Top-ho. Lottie won the tournament by one shot."

"I only lost because I couldn't see with my one eye and ball of fat," chuckled Grandad Frank, pretending to snap his putter across his knee. "OK I admit defeat. You win the Baxter cup. Remind me, what's the extra prize for the winner?"

"A hot choc from the new Coffiesta," said Lottie.

"Good idea, darling. I've never been there, but Nosey Rosie Saunders told me all about it yesterday. Mind you, that's an hour of my life I won't get back."

Lottie grinned at Grandad Frank victoriously, taking his putter and putting them both in a tall plastic bucket by the exit to the Pirate's Galleon Crazy Golf course.

"Right. Let's go and get that drink," said Grandad Frank. "Before it rains."

They walked along the promenade under a cloudy sky. Lottie tucked Casey under her arm and picked up a crisp packet that blew across the path in front of her.

"Bacon SnackNacks. I haven't got this one!" she said, folding the packet carefully and putting it in her pocket. "They only sold SnackNacks in these purple packets for a couple of months, so I'm well happy."

"You never know when treasure might find you," said Grandad Frank, holding the door open to the Coffiesta.

They stepped into the coffee shop and the first thing Lottie noticed was the beige walls, beige seats and beige carpet and the smell of lavender. It reminded her of their lounge at home and Nanny Vera's love of beige (which Grandad Frank described as 'granouflage').

The Coffiesta was full (thanks to Emelia Douthwaite's suggestions for attracting more pensioners). Groups of old people sat and chatted happily at the tables while drinking and eating. Another lot crowded around a large TV next to the toilets. It was playing a detective show from the 70s called Murder By The Book.

Lottie sat at a table while Grandad Frank queued behind a long line of pensioners. *Fly Me To The Moon*, an old Frank Sinatra tune, gently echoed around the bustling coffee shop and Grandad Frank 'Do-Bee-Doo'd' along to the familiar tune.

Coffiestas were opening all over the island in the coming months and Lottie had decided to visit as many as she could and collect a napkin from each one to stick in yet another album. Collecting Coffiesta napkins would be a new hobby to replace keeping stick insects (which wasn't going at all well).

On every table was a large brown plastic box in the shape of a coffee bean. The boxes held the Coffiesta menus (printed in a very large font), a copy of Gardening Today magazine, a bus timetable and a blood pressure monitor (which Lottie found a little odd).

Lottie sat with her elbow on the table and her chin cradled in her palm and checked her phone for messages. There were none, as expected, so she amused herself while waiting for Grandad Frank to be served by counting the number of cat and dog calendars hanging on the walls. She lost count at 33.

Guz Sharma was the manager of this new Coffiesta. He was five hours into his 12-hour shift and had drunk far too much of his own coffee in that time. His new beige uniform was already splattered with drink and the rim of his trilby hat was wet from where it had fallen off his head and into the sink.

Grandad Frank reached the front of the queue just as a Matt Munro tune began playing over the speakers A couple of old ladies near Lottie began singing along.

"Do you sell hot chocolate, young man?" asked Grandad Frank.

"Abso, dude. We call it a Choc-Berry," said Guz Sharma (one of Sir Charles' suggestions to the marketing department at the PCS).

"Perfect. I'll have one of those and a white coffee," said Grandad Frank.

"No wuzzies, dude. A Choc-Berry and a Milk-Jagger coming up," said Guz. "And we have slices of Tart-Garfunkel or Banana-Rama-Cake for just a pound?" he nodded at the beige plates, piled high with cakes, sitting on the glass counter.

"No thanks. But I'll have an Elton-Scone and an Iced-Ozzie-Oz-Bun," said Granddad Frank while Guz poured steaming milk into two mugs, scorching his fingers.

Grandad Frank paid and carried the tray over and sat opposite Lottie (his mug control was far steadier than Cheddar George's and he hadn't spilled a drop).

"There you go, Lottie. Two mugs of froth. I like it in here. It's very 'homely'. They even have bingo on a Friday, so I'll have to bring your Nan."

Lottie sipped her Choc-Berry and bit into the Elton-Scone. "This is totes lush, Grank, but the music is dull."

"Dull! Cheeky stick. That's Matt Munro. Known as 'The Man With The Golden Voice'. Me and Nanny Vera love a bit of Matt Munro. And look, a blood pressure monitor. That's handy. I haven't checked it this week."

Grandad Frank strapped the pad to his arm, and it began inflating. "I can see why these Coffiestas have suddenly got so popular with us old folk."

At that moment, Guz Sharma bent and picked up some litter by the entrance. As he did so, his shirt parted company with the waistband of his beige trousers and he flashed his hairy bum crack. Unfortunately, Lottie got an eyeful. She winced and turned to face her grandad.

"A hundred and thirty over eighty. A little higher than normal," said Grandad Frank, pulling the blood pressure pad from his arm. "This is where the Greasy Spoon café used to be, where many years ago, Cheddar George met your Granny Doris."

"I don't remember Granny Doris," replied Lottie.

"No, she died before you were born. They did some crazy stuff in their day! In the 80s, Granny Doris used to go on Cheddar George's bus, and he'd drive her around the island with Angus Dixon and Rob Owzess. Amazes me how they got away with it," said Grandad Frank, taking a spoon from his mug and licking the froth from it.

Guz Sharma stopped sweeping the floor by their

table and suddenly snatched Grandad Frank's spoon from his hand. "Finished with this?" he asked.

"Well… I suppose so, young man," replied Grandad Frank, somewhat surprised.

Guz smirked. It was a truly evil smirk.

He then rushed to his office at the rear of the Coffiesta and jammed a broom under the door handle to stop anyone disturbing him.

"I've caught another one," Guz shrieked excitedly, shoving half a Snickers bar into his mouth.

He used one finger to type his password into the computer that sat humming gently on his desk and then clamped the other half of the Snickers between his teeth. Guz selected 'TABLE 32' from a list on the screen and clicked the 'PLAY' icon to replay the last ten minutes of CCTV footage from his coffee shop.

The screen showed an empty table and a view of the door and the promenade behind. Guz pressed the 'FAST FORWARD' icon and the screen showed people rushing in and out of his Coffiesta.

Watching the video at eight times the normal speed never failed to amuse him. He'd *never* seen pensioners move so fast. He giggled like a naughty schoolboy, allowing dribble to drip from his mouth, down the melting chocolate bar onto his shirt.

There they were – a girl rushing over to sit at the table and a few seconds later, an old man holding a tray of drinks, joining her. Guz Sharma slowed the video footage to normal speed and turned the volume up. He sucked in the spit-laden chunk of warm chocolate and gazed at the screen, listening carefully to the conversation captured by the tiny microphone hidden inside the blood pressure monitor on table 32.

In the 80s, Granny Doris used to go on Cheddar George's bus, and he'd drive her around the island with Angus Dixon and Rob Owzess. Amazes me how they got away with it.

"PCS will be *bangin'* chuffed," Guz shrieked as he clicked the icon labelled 'PCS REFERRAL' and completed the form which popped up on the screen.

STATION ID: C040763
TABLE : 32
DATE: 1 September 2019
TIME: 11:34

Guz took a bunch of keys and unlocked a metal cabinet at the back of the office. Inside was a SureSign TB94 – a machine used to analyse DNA and identify its owner within seconds from the vast amounts of data held in Government databases.

Trembling fingers selected a cotton-bud from a tin and Guz wiped it along Grandad Frank's coffee spoon and then he transferred a tiny smear of frothy spit onto a small glass plate at the front of the machine. He took a deep breath and flicked the power switch.

"OK. Who are you," muttered Guz as the SureSign TB94 beeped, and a red LED blinked on the top panel.

Guz gazed at his watch as the time ticked by. After 30 seconds, there was another beep and the LED turned green. 'ID=AN126682D' showed on the control panel.

"Gotcha!" shrieked Guz.

He typed this into the 'DNA FOR IDENTIFICATION' field on the form and giggled again as he clicked the large red button at the bottom of the screen labelled 'SUBMIT TARGET'.

CHAPTER 6 – I ONLY HAVE EYES FOR YOU.

"Identify yourself," said a gruff voice on the phone from PCS Control in London.

"Yo, Dude. It's Agent Sharma coming to ya loud 'n' clear from the bangin' Alum Bay Coffiesta… C040763."

"Secret passphrase?" barked the voice, as if in a hurry.

"Errrm… hang on, Dude-o… Brazil Has Lots Of Coffee?" replied Guz.

"Incorrect!" barked the voice.

"Wait, wait. I am a mush-head, dude… I got it now… They've Got an Awful Lot of Coffee in Brazil."

"Correct," said the voice. "I see your new target in our LAD system, Agent Sharma. What is the proof of criminal activity?"

"The dude at table 32 was talking about an old relative called Cheddar George. He said that back in the 1980s, this Cheddar George guy would go and *rob houses*. It's as clear as day on the recording, dude. And he *never* got caught!"

"Interesting. Forward the CCTV clip to us using the secure channel and we'll review it," said the voice and the line went dead.

Gus Sharma sent the CCTV footage to PCS Control as directed. His phone rang 15 minutes later, while he stood behind the counter cleaning the vast array of stainless-steel pipes that coffee machines always have (but nobody knows what they actually do).

It was the same gruff voice from earlier.

"We've identified the DNA as Frank Jenson, who lives at the same address in Alum Bay as a pensioner known as Cheddar George. Target verified and accepted. Congratulations, Agent Sharma. Keep up the good work."

Guz smiled and bit into a Raspberry-Donut-Osmond. "Bangin' perfect-o, dude. When will this Cheddar George bloke be collected?"

"That's classified, Agent Sharma. Goodbye."

*

Two minutes later, Maddie Mainard's phone chirped while she was storing two dozen tins of Boomer's Tuna chunks in a cupboard in her campervan.

"Got a collection for you, Maddie," said Ken Oliver.

"OK. No peace for the wicked, Ken. Who's the target?" asked Maddie.

"It's a George Hardwick. An ancient wrinkly who goes by the name 'Cheddar George'. His son-in-law just grassed him up for robbing houses on the Isle of Wight. He's one hundred and one, so old Georgie Boy is likely to cost the NHS a *fortune*. The Home-Sec will save some big bucks with him permanently out of the way.

"I'm on it," said Maddie, delighted to earn another payment towards her Astronaut Roxy.

"Glad to hear it," sighed Ken in his 'doom and gloom' voice. "Do me a favour and grab him quick to get him off my books."

"No sweat," said Maddie.

"His address is 25 Rose Crescent in Alum Bay. Nice and local for you. I'll send all the details to your phone. By the way, I saw the Collection Report for Olive Fish. Nice work, Maddie. Those red DTH pills are really something, eh?"

"Thanks Ken. I'm proud of that one. Not even a whisper in the newspaper about her going missing," said Maddie, as she poured a cup of Earl Grey tea. "As I said, no peace for the wicked. I best get a move on. See ya, Ken."

"You take care now," said Ken and he hung up.

On his computer, Ken Oliver logged into the LAD system (that had only crashed once today) and changed the status of the record for George Hardwick from 'PENDING' to 'COLLECTOR DISPATCHED' and assigned it to Maddie Mainard's collector ID '7-1'.

Maddie stacked the last tin of Boomer's Tuna in the small cupboard then drank her Earl Grey tea while she waited for the Collection Report to come through to her phone from Ken.

"Time to go to work," she muttered to herself as her phone dinged and she studied the report.

Maddie had collected a lot of pensioners since she'd qualified to join the PCS. Emelia Douthwaite set the

PCPW (Pensioner Collections Per Week) target at three and Maddie was *well* ahead of that. She was the department's top performer by a mile and if she stayed at the top of the leader board, she'd get another nice fat bonus (minus Income Tax and National Insurance of course). It would all help raise the money for the auction at Sotheby's when her beloved Astronaut Roxy would be sold.

Maddie climbed into the driving seat and turned the key to start the campervan's engine. The 28-year-old VW chugged unnoticed from the lockup garage behind the Pavilion Theatre and headed for Rose Crescent.

It was late afternoon when Maddie pulled into Rose Crescent and found number 25. A house with a neatly trimmed lawn and an old beige Volvo parked with precision on the drive. Maddie parked close enough to watch the house and see the comings and goings, but far enough away to avoid suspicion. She sat and watched through her pair of Magni-view binoculars and waited; a part of her job she liked the least.

Later that evening, Lottie was in Cheddar George's bedroom playing Uptown Funk (badly) on her bagpipes. Cheddar George's bedroom looked very much like it belonged to a teenager. A single bed with a Tottenham Hotspur quilt cover and matching curtains and clothes of every colour under the sun piled on a stool and likely to topple off any second.

Lottie had been playing her bagpipes for over half an hour, blowing hard into the mouthpiece and using her fingers to cover the chanter's holes to produce the melody.

Cheddar George sat in a comfy armchair (the only piece of furniture in the room which matched his age).

He wore tartan slippers and a matching dressing gown. On his face he'd smothered a Magic Moment Moisture Bomb (a face mask he used once a week to keep his skin smooth).

His trembling hand clutched a mug of tea which was just the right temperature to drink. He'd turned his beige hearing aid down to the minimum setting but could *still* hear the awful din Lottie created.

As Lottie finished the final chorus to Uptown Funk, Cheddar George clapped and turned up his hearing aid.

"Coming along nicely, Lottie. Goodness, is that the time? The older I get, the earlier it gets late!" he said, drinking his tea through a straw to avoid tasting the pink goo smeared around his lips.

"Goodnight, Cheddar George," said Lottie and headed for her bedroom where the BREW Crew were ready to clean and adjust her bagpipes while Lottie fed her two remaining stick insects (called Dipstick and Nonstick).

At 9.27, Maddie looked through her powerful binoculars and noticed an old man appear at a bedroom window at the front of the house. She was surprised to see his face covered in pink gunk, so couldn't tell for certain if this *was* her target. But she was pretty sure this person would be her next collection for the PCS. The old man yawned, removed his teeth and drew the curtains.

"Sleep well, Cheddar George. You'll be an easy collection," muttered Maddie.

At midnight, Maddie finished another mug of Earl Grey tea and quietly left her VW. She crept silently along the footpath and up to the house. She'd watched the bedroom lights snuff out two hours ago, so was sure everyone inside 25 Rose Crescent was now asleep.

The front of the house was like all the others in the road. Upstairs were two bedrooms and downstairs, a kitchen window next to a front door, though this house had a sign below the doorbell:

'WE DON'T NEED ANY MORE AVON OR TUPPERWARE' (Grandad Frank's handywork).

The streetlight outside the house was broken, making it easy for Maddie to hide in the shadows and wait, checking the road was quiet. After 20 minutes, she was happy everyone nearby was tucked up in their beds. Maddie crept up the drive and peered through the kitchen window. The wooden table was set ready for breakfast. Maddie guessed it would be a tea and toast.

"Perfect," muttered Maddie.

She knew that old people sat and talked for hours in their kitchen's, and she needed to hear every word to plan the perfect way to collect old George Hardwick. During her training, Major Caruthers told her time and time again that planning was the most important part of the job.

From her pocket Maddie took a Boomer's Tuna tin. She'd eaten the fishy contents earlier and replaced them with an Eagle Security-12HS listening device.

Maddie stuck the tin to the wall next to the kitchen window and flicked a button on the side. A red LED flashed once.

"I do love a good chat," she muttered.

Maddie then expertly climbed an old oak tree in the front garden to reach the windowsill of Cheddar George's bedroom above. She slipped another tuna listening device behind the wooden trellis next to the window.

With the house bugged, Maddie returned to her van and turned on the radio. The sounds of Cheddar George snoring and a hooting owl, nesting in the oak tree, came clearly through the speaker in the dashboard.

"All set, Cheddar George," Maddie muttered and promptly fell asleep in her seat.

Maddie spent the next three days cooped up in her van near Lottie's house, listening to the specially-tuned radio and living off tuna chunks and Earl Grey tea. In those three long days, she learnt an awful lot about the residents of Rose Crescent from the chatter coming from inside number 25.

At breakfast on the first day, Grandad Frank reported that Nosey Rosie Saunders at number 46 took Half-Pint, her three-legged sausage dog, for a walk twice a day and it always piddled up the wheel of Sherman the German's BMW (who lived at number 52). Sherman *wasn't* happy about it at all and was now busy installing CCTV to gather evidence to complain to the Neighbourhood Watch Committee (which Nosey Rosie Saunders was of course the leader of).

On the second day, Maddie heard Nanny Vera fill the kettle to make tea and mention that Heather the Weather at number six predicted a very bad winter with heavy snow from next month (on account of her swollen knee which ached more than usual). Even though it was still late summer, Heather had rushed out and bought six sacks of salt and enough soup and tinned peaches to feed an army.

On day three, Maddie was just about to tuck into a tin of Boomer's Tuna chunks for her breakfast when she heard a *very* interesting conversation from the kitchen.

"I bumped into Heather the Weather yesterday. She said it will be nice today, Frank," said Nanny Vera, stuffing a pile of her granouflage clothes into the washing machine.

"In that case, I might mow the grass this morning," replied Grandad Frank. He sat at the kitchen table and opened his Daily Mail newspaper that had been delivered at dawn.

"Well, remember to mind your toes," said Nanny Vera (not wanting a repeat of Cheddar George's accident many years ago, when he chopped off his big toe with the lawn mower).

"They do say 'There's *toe* fool like an old fool'," said Cheddar George, sipping his tea.

"I'll try and finish the job with the same number of fingers *and* toes as I have now," said Grandad Frank, turning the page of his newspaper.

An advert started playing on the kitchen radio perched on a shelf next to Nanny Vera's cookery books (which she'd never opened).

"Pop in to your local Coffiesta today for a rich, smooth coffee. Why not try a Milk-All-Jackson for only one pound eighty and get a free packet of vitamins? How's *that* for a brew-sea bonus?"

As the advert ended, Nanny Vera reached for a plastic tub on a shelf next to the cooker and peered at the contents. She was forever putting left-overs from jars, tins and packets of food in her vast collection of plastic tubs, but never bothered to label them. When it came to eating the contents, it was always pot-luck what was *actually* stored in them. "I think this is marmalade. Would you like some on your toast, Lottie?"

"Please," said Lottie, who sat at the table, inspecting an old train ticket she'd been given for her collection by Mr Theakston at number 17.

"Crikey, you're brave," said Grandad Frank. "There could be anything in there."

There was a THLUP as Nanny Vera removed the lid and sniffed the contents. She still had no idea what the tub contained but spread it on Lottie's toast anyway.

"Cheddar George is playing bowls this afternoon and I've got a lot of old paperwork that needs shredding. Do you want to go with him to keep him company and make sure he gets there and back safely?"

"Roger that," said Lottie (as she had nothing else planned).

"It's a big game today. We're playing the dirty dozen from Ventnor," said Cheddar George.

Maddie stopped forking chunks of tuna into her mouth and grinned. "Thank you, George Hardwick. That's *very* interesting."

CHAPTER 7 – YOU'RE THE ONE THAT I WANT.

Old Bob Sanchez, the greenkeeper at the Alum Bay Bowls Club locked his shed and slipped on his old tweed jacket. His bike ride home today would be tricky, as a strong easterly wind was blowing, scattering the leaves from the trees around the car park.

As Bob was about to get on his pushbike, Cheddar George rode in on his brand new red and gold mobility scooter. It was a Ranger 200EV and it was Cheddar George's first trip out in it. Lottie sat in a sidecar attached to the scooter, which the BREW Crew had built from an old pram and wooden pallets. Bob gave a friendly salute as the Ranger 200EV came to a stop next to him.

"Kalispera, Bob," said Cheddar George, removing a pair of swimming goggles and a black bandana adorned with white skull and crossbones from his head and replacing it with an orange beret.

"Afternoon, young man. Love the new wheels," said Bob.

"She's a real Bobby Dazzler, isn't she? I call her my

Oldie TT. Nought to sixty in a little over a millennium," said Cheddar George, patting the polished speedo (which only went up to eight miles per hour).

"Isn't it amazeballs?" asked Lottie, climbing out the sidecar.

"Certainly is," said Bob.

Cheddar George was very proud of his new ride and keen to show Bob Sanchez the special extras he'd installed.

"She's had a custom paint job and we've fitted a radio cassette player *and* a fax machine. And what do you think of this? It's called a sat nav. A young lady talks to me and tells me where to go," said Cheddar George, poking the 'HOME' button on the Route Master sat nav strapped beneath a wicker basket by the handlebars.

"Turn right in 50 yards onto Ventnor Road," said a woman's voice from the Route Master's speaker.

"Thank you, love. I'm not going home yet, but if you're free later, that would be just tickety-boo," said Cheddar George.

Lottie giggled. "You do know she's not *actually* listening to you, Cheddar George, and it's only a recording."

"Ahh, you never know, Lottie," said Cheddar George knowingly.

Bob Sanchez chuckled when he noticed a sign stuck to the rear of Cheddar George's seat:

'NO BUTTERSCOTCH SWEETS ARE STORED IN THIS VEHICLE OVERNIGHT'.

"You playing in the match today?" Bob asked, taking

Cheddar George's walking stick while he eased himself from the tartan cushioned seat (fitted with extra padding).

"Yes, it's all part of my fitness training for my over 90's leapfrog display team," joked Cheddar George, taking a few seconds to assume his upright position.

"A word of warning," said Bob. "Be careful of the large brown smear on the far side of the bowling green. That ruddy dog has been doing its business there again. I needed a *shovel* to clear up its pile of poo."

"Ah, the Grim Heaper strikes once more," said Cheddar George.

"If I ever find the owner, there *will* be trouble! Anyway, I think it'll be a close match and I hope you win," said Bob, tucking the bottom of his trousers into his socks, so they wouldn't catch in the well-oiled bike chain.

Bob returned the walking stick to Cheddar George and continued his team talk.

"I'm sure you can beat them. Ventnor are a strong squad, but they *hate* losing – *especially* their captain. He complained about the length of the grass the last time they played here. He even measured it! Measured it with his own flipping ruler. Blooming cheek. I just hope you thrash them *again*. Anyway, places to go, things to do and spuds to peel," Bob said and rode off, wobbling as the wind blew him across the car park.

"Didn't realise bowls was like this," said Lottie.

"It is when we play Ventnor," said Cheddar George as he shuffled down a neatly mowed path (thanks to Bob's efforts) to the clubhouse.

Lottie followed, carrying Casey in one hand and Cheddar George's leather bag containing his four bowls in her other.

"You didn't need to come with me today, Lottie. I *am* old enough to go out on my own, despite what your nan says," said Cheddar George. "And that lovely young lady on my new sat nav will tell me how to get home. Heaven knows how she finds the time to help everyone."

"I don't mind," said Lottie as they reached the clubhouse. "If I get bored, I can look for some more feathers to stick in my album."

The clubhouse was a low brick building, freshly painted white. A collection of elderly people with silver and blue-tinged hair mingled outside. A woman called Edna Biddle (known to everyone as Old Biddy Biddle) was thrusting a photo of her latest great grandchild under everyone's nose.

"A 21-minute labour and the bonny chap weighed four point eight kilograms," Edna reported.

She measured in metric units because she'd voted 'Remain' in the BREXIT poll, (as her husband had helped dig the channel tunnel) and Edna still considered herself to be very much European.

Unfortunately, most of the gathering of pensioners only saw a pinkish blob on the photograph because they'd left their reading glasses at home. They had no idea if four point eight kilograms was a weight to be worried about or not, as they were from the era of pounds and ounces. Jim Atkins (a retired accountant) did a long-winded conversion in his head and came up with three stone and a bit, but didn't say anything as he was *sure* that wasn't right and didn't want to look a fool.

A tubby man called Sid de Sousa with a bulbous nose hurried over to Cheddar George. Deep concern was etched on his face. Sid was the captain of the bowls team, and everyone called him 'Skipper' (but Cheddar George found it funny to call him 'Skidder' every now and then).

"Ah, Cheddar George, just the chap. I sent the *official* playing order to the Ventnor team captain on Wednesday, giving them 48 hours' notice as per rule 24 of the British Bowls Association, open bracket Southern Region, close bracket, but I need to swap you with George Peacock. He has gout *again* and only just told me that he needs to leave early today. As it's a medical emergency, we *are* permitted to swap players around, as per rule 44, as long as clause D is met, which of course it is."

"Of course, Skidder. Tickety-boo," said Cheddar George (who'd never even opened his copy of the rule book Skipper quoted all the time, so had *no* idea if clause D was met or not).

George Peacock (or Gouty George as he was known) limped over and pulled up his trouser leg to reveal a bandaged ankle and no sock.

"I've a hospital appointment, so must shoot off sharpish. Then the current Mrs P and I are off to Spain – if I can find my flipping passport. Looked everywhere for it. Two things go when you get old. The first is your memory and I can't remember the other one!"

"And how is Mrs Peacock?" Cheddar George asked.

"Better than nothing," sighed Gouty George. "We plan to do a little bird watching while in Spain. I'm hopeful to spot a Horned Screamer. Or rather a Natalensis Fluvicola to give it it's official name."

"Sounds fun," said Cheddar George, convinced that Gouty George made up all his Latin sounding bird names.

"I've put you on first instead of Cheddar George, Gouty, but you need to give me more notice next time," said Skipper, looking flustered.

Gouty George nodded. "Aye, Skipper."

Skipper scribbled the team change on his piece of paper. "So, Cheddar George, you'll *officially* now play in match five after Wendy's afternoon tea, with Celia Murphy and Gouty here will play in match one with Old Biddy Biddle."

Cheddar George liked Celia Murphy. She called everyone 'duck', had a lazy eye and wore an eyepatch, but still managed to bowl pretty well.

"Thanks for swapping, Cheddar George," said Gouty.

"Not a problem, young man," said Cheddar George. "It gives me more time to limber up and do my squat thrusts."

"Would you like a job sorting out our lost property bin, young Lottie?" asked Skipper. "Edna's mislaid her false teeth and I've no idea whose gnashers she's got in today. And if you find a pair of red socks, they're mine – my *official* lucky ones.

"OK," said Lottie, wondering what stinky delights she'd find in the festering dustbin that was always full of random stuff.

A white minibus with Ventnor Bowls Club emblazoned on the side rolled into the carpark. Smoke billowed from its exhaust and a terrible rattle came from under the bonnet.

"Here come the enemy. The dirty dozen," muttered Skipper to nobody in particular.

The doors opened and the smoke cleared as if an alien spaceship had landed next to Bob Sanchez's shed. Cheddar George watched the opposition team slowly climb out. He'd been playing bowls against Ventnor for years and easily recognised 11 of their team. But their arch-rivals had a new recruit – a woman he'd never seen before.

"What *are* they playing at?" huffed Skipper, checking the *official* list of Ventnor players on his sheet of paper.

The woman was tall, with long ginger hair. Huge sunglasses covered most of her pale face, making her look like a barn owl. The group of 12 wandered down to meet the Alum Bay team at the clubhouse, led by their captain, a man called Bernard Barnes and known as B-Squared. He was a wiry man with bandy legs that would never stop a pig in an ally.

"Wasn't sure we'd make it. I think the big-end is on its way out," said B-Squared. "I'm referring to the minibus, of course," he added.

"I did wonder," chuckled Edna Biddle, staring at B-Squared's backside. She had a soft spot for B-Squared.

"You've brought a player that's not on your *official* team sheet, said Skipper in a fluster. "That's in violation of rule 13, clause A of the British Bowls Association, open bracket Southern Region, close bracket," he said, prodding a tatty page of his rule book with a finger.

"Calm down, Skipper," said B-Squared. "Poor old Camila Delgado went down with a sudden bout of food poisoning earlier and sadly can't venture more than ten feet from her loo. I got special permission from the league secretary to bring a sub at short notice and Dorothy kindly offered her services. Here, Old Boy, a copy of the email from Archie the league secretary, no brackets."

B-Squared handed over a piece of paper and while Skipper carefully studied it (as if it was an important legal document), B-Squared marched onto the perfectly flat bowling green where he knelt and measured the length of the grass with a metal ruler.

"All in order, *this* time."

Polite handshakes between the teams then ensued and an excited Edna Biddle shoved the photo of her new great grandchild under Dorothy's nose. "Four point eight kilograms," she announced.

"Gosh!" was all Dorothy said from behind her massive sunglasses.

"Right," said Skipper, tucking his rule book into his blazer pocket. "Everything seems to be in *official* order, so shall we begin and 'up sticks'?"

"Let battle commence, Old Boy!" B-Squared announced triumphantly and a clattering echoed around the bowling green as a forest of walking sticks were shoved in an old umbrella stand outside the club house.

Six players from each team then ambled onto the playing area. All were dressed in white shirts and trousers as per rule nine clause C of Skipper's rule book. Coins were tossed and the first three games of mixed doubles began.

Lottie went to a small room off the main clubhouse and found the dustbin marked 'Lost Property'. It was overflowing with clothes that had seen better days.

"Yuck. This stinks!" said Lottie, holding her nose and using Rula to pick out a white string vest (unnamed, smelly and size XXL, so she guessed it belonged to Big Stan).

The Duke wrote on a piece of Paddy paper.

"Smells foo-foo."

"Totes," said Lottie, placing the vest to one side and fishing out a brown sock with a hole in the toe.

The Duke wasn't keen on the smell coming from the reeking garments, so he switched off his SSDS (Sensitive Smell Detection System), which Lottie's great uncle Walter had built into the lid of the old fountain pen.

*

Cheddar George stood outside the clubhouse and limbered up for his bowls game by marching on the spot for ten seconds. When the wind nearly blew his beret from his head, he decided to skip the rest of his warm-up routine (taking a few deep breaths) and tottered inside to help Wendy de Sousa, the Skipper's wife, prepare the refreshments for the afternoon tea (to be served at half-time).

The rest of the players, waiting for their game of bowls after tea and sandwiches, sat in deckchairs. The ones who hadn't fallen asleep in the sunshine were clapping politely when a winning bowl was dispatched along the bowling green, expertly cut to the required length by Bob Sanchez (as per rule three clause F of Skipper's rule book).

Dorothy, the new Ventnor player was teamed with B-Squared. They were up against the Alum Bay pair of Edna Biddle and Gouty George (who's limp didn't affect his bowling performance).

"That Dorothy isn't very good," said Wendy de Sousa, watching the game through an open window while arranging Fondant Fancies on a paper plate into a Jenga tower.

Cheddar George watched Dorothy's bowl roll into the small ditch that edged the bowling green.

"Agreed indeed. Skipper wasn't happy when she turned up, but Gouty George could get an easy win and be early for his hospital visit if she carries on bowling like *that*!" he said as Dorothy's next bowl went so far astray, it clunked Skipper's ball on the opposite side of the bowling green. Skipper swiped his rule book from his pocket and hastily thumbed the pages.

"Sandwich?" asked Wendy, offering a silver platter of triangular bread, stacked with military precision.

"I've no idea what the fillings are. Jurassic Clarke made them, and you know Jurassic and his 'sense of adventure'".

Cheddar George sniffed the plate and turned his nose up. "Not a clue. I'll stick to my own thanks," he said, patting the bulging pocket of his purple and yellow striped blazer. "Mature and cheesy. Just like me."

Two minutes later, Gouty George and Edna Biddle

finished their match, thrashing the Ventnor pair 21 - 3. B-Squared refused to shake hands and was on his hands and knees, brushing his hand over the brown patch caused by the Grim Heaper, to see if he had a case to complain to Archie the league Secretary about the state of the playing surface.

He looked fuming when he marched back to the clubhouse sniffing his fingertips.

"I'll be sending a report to Archie about the state of the lawn," he barked, grabbing his ruler from his blazer pocket to take more measurements.

"Tea or coffee?" asked Wendy de Sousa, wiping her hands on a yellow tea-towel.

"Sadly, not for me, Wendy. I'm off to see the Gout Doc and then *hopefully* I can track down my passport and Spain, here I come. Olé," said Gouty George.

He dropped his bowls in his leather bag and his face winced as he lifted the handle.

"Here, let me help you to your car, George," said Dorothy, taking the heavy bag from Gouty George's hand.

"That's very kind, Dorothy," Gouty said. "See you in a fortnight, Wendy. And give my regards to Skipper."

*

Lottie had almost emptied the lost property bin and the Duke listed the items on a piece of Paddy. So far, they'd identified the owners of four things – Big Stan's string vest, a moth-eaten pullover belonging to Jurassic Clarke, a grubby cap, which belonged to Noel Atkins (who wasn't playing today because he'd had a fall in the week and was waiting for a new hip) and just one of

Skipper's lucky red socks. Rula disappeared inside the bin and fished out the final piece of moth-eaten clothing from the bottom.

"Brown jacket. Size large," the Duke wrote.

The jacket smelt musty and had a button missing from the front and a stain on one sleeve. Lottie slid her hand slowly into the pockets – fearful of a snotty handkerchief or worse still, Edna Biddle's missing false teeth. "The pockets are empty."

"And there's no label, so we have no idea who owns this," the Duke noted.

"OK. Let's put all this stinky stuff back and go and watch the rest of the game," said Lottie, relived the smelly chore was finally complete.

As she folded the jacket, Lottie felt something trapped within its lining.

"Perhaps it's a treasure map," she joked.

"Or a ration book."

"We don't have *them* anymore," said Lottie.

Sharpy cut the neat stitching that held the jacket's lining in place and Lottie pulled out a small book. She opened it and recognised the ghostly photo inside. "It's George Peacock's passport. He'll be well-happy. Quick. Let's tell him!"

"Roger that."

The BREW Crew flew inside Casey and Lottie tucked the pencil case under her arm and headed back into the main clubhouse.

"I've found Mr Peacock's passport," Lottie called, waving the small red book under Cheddar George's nose.

"Tickety-boo! Gouty's just left," said Cheddar George, munching on his cheese sandwich. "But if you hurry, you should catch him," he added, nodding towards the car park at the top of the path.

*

Gouty George limped with Dorothy to the line of cars by Bob Sanchez's shed. A small bird with a yellow beak landed on the tartan seat of Cheddar George's Oldie TT.

"Oh look, Dorothy. A Validas Plory," said Gouty George and opened the boot of his red Ford. A gusty wind blew a few leaves into the boot as Dorothy placed his bowling bag inside, next to a picnic blanket, a first aid kit and a large thermos flask.

"Could you do me a big favour, George. I've lost an earring and I think it fell under my seat on the way here in the old minibus. My eyesight isn't what it was, so would you take a quick look for me?" asked Dorothy.

"Sure, Dorothy," said Gouty George. "I may have a grotty gouty foot, but there's nothing wrong with my eyes."

"That's very kind. My daughter gave me the earrings for my birthday, so I'd hate to lose one," Dorothy said as she opened the door of the minibus and stood aside.

Gouty George limped across, bent down and peered under the seat.

"I can't see anything, Dorothy. I'll grab a torch from my car. Your earring might have dropped down the…"

Gouty George didn't feel the thin needle of a syringe prick his backside through his white bowling trousers. Seconds later he was slumped across the seat of the minibus.

Lottie hurtled up to Bob Sanchez's shed and she was just about to call out to Gouty George when Dorothy hoisted his legs into the minibus. A sudden gust of wind blew the ginger wig from Dorothy's head, and it fell to the ground, looking like roadkill.

Maddie Mainard, wearing her 'Elderly Bowls Player' disguise, scooped up the wig and slapped it back on her head and climbed in the minibus.

Confused, Lottie ducked behind the shed and watched the woman slam the door and clamber unladylike over Gouty George's limp body, into the driver's seat.

The engine clattered and threw out another plume of grey smoke and the minibus eased out of the parking space, heading for the exit.

"I said you'd be easy to collect, Cheddar George," Maddie muttered.

But there was no reply from the old man slumped in the seat behind her. He was out cold.

CHAPTER 8 – COME FLY WITH ME.

"What just happened here?" shrieked Lottie.

"A kidnapping. Textbook execution of a Distract and Snatch operation. In 1944, we thwarted an identical attempt by a German spy to kidnap Charles de Gaule."

"Who'd want to kidnap poor Mr Peacock?"

"Let's find out! Get eyes on the target vehicle to see which direction it goes while we sort out some transport."

Lottie clambered on a dustbin and then onto the shed roof and while she watched the minibus, Rula pressed the power pedal on the Oldie TT and Spike steered the scooter to face the exit.

The minibus reached the main road and turned left. "They went towards my school. Quick! They're getting away."

"Roger that. Let's go."

Lottie jumped onto the Oldie TT and pressed the power pedal with her foot, but as the scooter's top speed was only eight miles per hour (and somewhat less with the weight of the sidecar and all the other weighty extras), it crawled at little more than walking pace across the carpark.

"Nik-nacks. How can we go faster?" asked Lottie.

"Hold tight. We'll do something we tried at Dunkirk in 1942 to save an RAF pilot in a downed Spitfire."

"OK. Quick as you can," Lottie said, trundling passed the line of parked cars.

Suddenly, a piece of Paddy stretched to the size of a bed sheet and chunks of Rob were cut by Sharpy and pulled to make four ropes which tied themselves to each corner of the paper sheet. The other ends wrapped around the handlebars of the Oldie TT and Spike tied them with a clove hitch knot.

The strong wind blew the paper sheet and it lifted above Lottie to create a sail.

"Come on… come on," said Lottie, watching the sail fill with air above the scooter.

The paper sail caught a gust of wind and the Rob rope snapped tight. Lottie felt a sudden jerk as the Oldie TT shot off across the carpark at way more than eight miles per hour.

Lottie turned the handlebars to steer out the exit, narrowly missing an oak tree on the far side of the road. The Oldie TT's tyre's screeched and two wheels lifted off the tarmac, nearly tipping the scooter onto its side. Luckily, the wind dropped for a second and Lottie straightened the handlebars and the wheels crashed back on the road.

"That was close," Lottie shrieked as the wind blew again and the scooter picked up speed.

Lottie hurtled down the road and as she got used to kite-scootering, she caught up with Maddie and Gouty George in the minibus. If she needed to slow down, the paper sail above the Oldie TT shrunk a little, so less wind filled it and blew her along. To speed up again, the paper sail simply grew to catch more wind. Lottie hurried through the streets and kept the minibus in sight as it headed east along Cowes Road towards Freshwater.

Maddie drove the minibus passed Cringle Park school and glanced over her shoulder. "I'm afraid you won't be playing bowls again, George," she said, turning left at some traffic lights into St Paul's Road and then left again onto Vincent Road.

"Is that a Martinica Rustica?" mumbled Gouty George from his seat before passing out once again.

Just after the Red Lion pub on Vincent Road, Maddie turned right and pulled into a small industrial estate. She pressed a button on a remote control in her pocket and a roller shutter door to a large workshop in front of her clanked open.

Maddie drove the minibus into the workshop, filled with tools and bits of old cars. The sign above the door read 'BOB BELL AUTO REPAIRS'.

Cardboard cut-outs of Bob Bell, dressed in blue overalls and clutching a large spanner, hung on the walls on each side of the roller shutter, which lowered and clanked shut behind the minibus.

The paper sail shrunk to nothing and Lottie rolled the Oldie TT behind a blue tow-truck.

"What do we do now?"

"Hold your position. We'll recon the building and get eyes inside."

Spike and Rula flew to the metal roller shutter and

Rula levered the bottom slightly off the floor. Spike squeezed through the gap and disappeared inside and hid in the middle of a stack of old tyres.

Gouty George began to stir again on the back seat of the minibus.

"Edna, that's an Albus Palumabus," said Gouty George, pointing at a blob of bird poo on the window.

"Stay still, George. You'll feel much better soon," said Maddie, grabbing a brown envelope from her handbag. She pulled out the Collection Report (sent to her by Ken Oliver) and her eyes scanned the printed details on page one.

"Well, George… You don't look much like your photo," she muttered.

"Photo? Say cheese," mumbled a confused Gouty George.

Maddie turned to page two. "Ah. Distinguishing marks… Four toes on right foot. I'd better check. Just to be on the safe side."

She removed Gouty George's right shoe and peeled off his sweaty grey sock. "Five toes! *Five*? That's not right!"

Maddie quickly checked Gouty George's left foot with the bandage, just in case it was an admin error. It wasn't.

"Darn. You're the *wrong* George!" she hissed, thumping her fist on the dashboard.

"Wrong Georgie Porgy," mumbled Gouty George.

Maddie frowned while looking at the dazed pensioner, trying to work out how she'd got it so wrong. She was furious. All her planning and effort to give Camila Delgado a bad stomach and taking her place at the last minute in the bowls team had been a waste of time. She'd easily collected George Whoever-he-was but would now miss the collection payment she was desperate for if she was to stand a chance of winning the upcoming auction for the Roxy doll.

Maddie wondered what Caruthers might say about her failed Distract and Snatch operation as she grabbed her handbag and paperwork. She had to get away from the crime-scene quickly.

"So long, George," sighed Maddie and she jumped from the minibus and hurried across to her powerful Yamaha FS 500 motorbike which she'd hidden in Bob Bell's workshop earlier. The roller shutter door clanked as it rose again and from behind Bob Bell's tow-truck, Lottie watched the powerful motorbike shoot out and roar off back towards Alum Bay.

Spike and Rula returned to the tow-truck and the Duke wrote frantically.

"Sit rep. Hostage found safe and well inside, but a little groggy. Unsure why kidnapper has scarpered. Let's follow."

"OK," said Lottie and she jumped onto the Oldie TT again just as Gouty George emerged from the workshop. He staggered barefoot across the entrance of the warehouse to stand in front of the cardboard cut-out of Bob Bell.

"Is this the hospital? Which way to the Victoria Ward, young lady?"

"We can't leave Mr Peacock," said Lottie, as the blustering wind began to fill the Paddy paper sail overhead. "It's too dangerous."

"Roger that."

The sail shrunk again as the noise of the motorbike's engine tailed off. Lottie ran across to Gouty George and took him by his elbow. "Mr Peacock, the Victoria Ward is this way."

"Thank you, nurse. Oooh look, a Tersina Zosterops," said Gouty George, pointing into the empty sky.

"That's nice," said Lottie and led Gouty George over to sit on the back of the tow-truck.

"Er… Let's wait here for the Doctor, shall we?" asked Lottie, not daring to look below Gouty George's knees, as the sight of bare feet always made her feel queasy.

"OK, nurse, said Gouty George and he put his hand in his pocket. "I was told to bring this," he said, handing Lottie a small bottle filled with his wee.

CHAPTER 9 – STAYIN' ALIVE.

"Stellula Porzana," said Gouty George, pointing again at an empty sky and rubbing his non-gouty ankle. "Is the doctor going to be long?"

"He's still do-lally and needs a medic ASAP."

"Nik-nacks. What do we do? It won't be safe to move him in the sidecar," said Lottie.

"Where is the nearest hospital?"

"Newport, I guess," replied Lottie. "I went there last year when Cheddar George got his tongue stuck to a mug that Grank tried mending with superglue."

"Roger that. We'll have to take him there. Can you drive?"

"No!" said Lottie.

"It's easy. We'll help."

"OK. Let's get going," said Lottie, surprised at how brave she sounded.

"When will the doctor be here?" asked Gouty George again.

"Er… he'll see you soon, Mr Peacock," said Lottie, taking Gouty George's hand and leading him back to the minibus.

"Lay down on the couch please, Mr Peacock," said

Lottie, helping him into the back and onto a bench seat.

"Thank you, nurse," said Gouty George. "You're very kind."

He yawned and stretched out on the seat. His glazed eyes stared at his feet and he tugged at the bandage on his gouty ankle.

"The current Mrs P *won't* be happy if I'm late home. Olé."

"You'll be home soon, Mr Peacock. I'll go and find the doctor for you now," said Lottie, climbing across the seats to the front of the minibus.

Spike unscrewed a panel below the steering wheel and Sharpy delved into the tangle of wires and snipped a red wire and then a yellow one. He spliced a red end to a yellow end causing a tiny spark and the engine fired, smoke billowing from the exhaust.

Rula plonked an old tyre on the driver's seat for Lottie to use as a booster cushion and allow her to see through the windscreen. A sheet of Paddy paper stuck to the centre of the steering wheel. The Duke wrote quickly.

"We can work the pedals and gears, so all you have to do is steer."

"Roger that. I'll try," said Lottie.

"OK. Let's go."

Ledley and Rula pressed the pedals beneath Lottie's dangling feet and Penny eased the gearstick into reverse. Spike revved the engine and the minibus edged backwards. Lottie turned the wheel, but steered the wrong way, smashing into the stack of old tyres and sending them rolling across the workshop.

"Whoops!"

"Steer to the left."

"Which way is left?" asked Lottie.

Penny drew 'L' and 'R' on the back of Lottie's hands.

"OK. Got it," said Lottie and the engine revved again and she managed to safely steer the old minibus under the roller shutter and out of the workshop.

"Electus Cardellina," groaned Gouty George, mistaking a scuff mark on the minibus' roof for some exotic bird.

"He's getting worse. We need to hurry," said Lottie.

"Roger that."

Penny put the minibus in first gear and Rula released the clutch pedal and they chugged forward, kangarooing along the road with Gouty George bouncing up and down in the back.

"The doctor is on his way, Mr Peacock," shouted Lottie.

They'd only driven a few yards when disaster struck. A loud BANG came from under the bonnet and thick smoke engulfed the front of the minibus. B-Squared had been right about the engine having a serious problem. A piston ring had shattered, sending a drive rod bearing through the crankshaft, spewing thick black oil onto the road. The minibus rolled to a stop.

"Oh no. Can you fix it?" asked Lottie, as Spike disappeared under the bonnet to perform a sitrep. Seconds later, the Duke wrote.

"Negative. The engine has Panzernacked itself."

"Nik-nacks, what do we do now?" asked Lottie.

"Ask Skipper to check his rule book," giggled Gouty George.

Suddenly, a roaring came from the sky overhead. Lottie looked up to see a yellow and green Westland helicopter. It was Heli-Med-five-one, the Isle of Wight's Air Ambulance, with Captain Joe Keller at the controls. Also on board was Annie Walker, a Paramedic who'd joined the Heli-Med team a week ago. Captain Keller was taking Annie on a training exercise. It was her first ever helicopter flight.

The relentless din inside the helicopter meant both Annie and Captain Keller wore helmets with headphones and microphones, which allowed them to talk to each other by radio. However, Annie was in no mood to talk. She held a cardboard vomit bowl under her chin and was sure she'd fill it to the brim with sick any second and couldn't wait for the helicopter to land.

Annie heard the calming voice of Captain Keller in her headphones.

"Keep your eyes on the horizon, Annie, and you'll feel much better. We'll head back to base now."

"OK," said Annie, her face drained of colour, but she was thankful her terrifying flight would soon end.

Captain Keller pushed the control stick right. "ETA five minutes. Hold tight."

As the helicopter turned above them, Spike, Penny and Sharpy shot out of Casey and flew back up the road to the workshop.

"What are they doing?" asked Lottie.

"Change of plan. Hold tight."

Spike unbolted a cardboard cut-out of Bob Bell

from the wall next to the roller shutter door and laid it on the ground by the tow-truck. Sharpy hacked Bob's foot off and Penny drew a pool of fake blood on the ground.

*

In the sky above, Annie Walker gripped a thick handle above a door as the helicopter banked sharply and she looked down at the rooftops below. On the ground, she spotted the 'body' of Bob Bell outside his workshop.

"Captain, there's a person laying near that tow-truck down there with a lot of blood coming from their lower leg, which seems to be missing!"

Annie heard Captain Keller calmly reply in her headphones.

"Copy that. Hold tight and I'll take us down and land on the grass opposite."

The helicopter dropped like a stone and Annie fought to control the contents of her stomach. This was no longer a training exercise.

When it was six feet from the ground, Captain Keller expertly pulled the control stick to slow their drop and landed his helicopter softly on the grass. He pressed a button by his knee to kill the engine that drove the roaring rotor blades overhead.

*

"That's our lift to the hospital"

"Roger that. Don't let Mr Peacock leave," said Lottie and as the wind from the rota blades died, she jumped off her booster cushion and ran for the helicopter.

Annie Walker grabbed a backpack full of medical

'stuff' while Captain Keller spoke over his radio to the hospital in Newport.

"This is Heli-Med-five-one. We're dealing with a possible RTA on the Churchill East industrial estate. One casualty with a serious lower leg injury. Medic will be assessing shortly. Stand by."

Annie slid open the door and swung the backpack onto her back just as Lottie reached her.

"Can you help Mr Peacock in the minibus? He's not well," Lottie blurted.

"Is he breathing?" asked Annie.

"Yes, but he's-"

"I'll take a look in a second, treacle. First, I need to deal with the patient over there who's losing a lot of blood," said Annie, pointing in the direction of Bob Bell's workshop.

"But that's just-" said Lottie.

"Wait with Mr Peacock, treacle and I'll come as soon as I've dealt with the leg trauma, OK?" asked Annie and she ran towards the workshop.

"But that's just a cardboard cut-out," shouted Lottie, but Annie didn't hear her.

As Annie Walker dashed towards the workshop, her mind quickly went through the steps to treat the injured patient. ABC. Check their airway, then breathing, then pulse. Then apply direct pressure to the wound to stop the bleeding.

As Annie reached the tow-truck, she noticed the cardboard cut-out of Bob Bell smiling up at her. "What the...."

"Everything OK, Annie?" asked Captain Keller,

calmly through her radio. He sat in his pilot's seat in Heli-Med-five-one, ready to fire up the rotors at a moment's notice for a speedy flight to the hospital in Newport.

"False alarm," replied Annie, puffing hard.

She'd be the laughingstock of the Heli-Med team is *this* ever got out.

"I'm just going to check another patient in the minibus. It's probably another false alarm and just kids messing around. Stand by."

She jogged back to the minibus to find Lottie and Gouty George standing next to it. Gouty George stooped and bowled an imaginary bowl along the footpath.

"That's a winner, Edna," said Gouty, clapping his hands. "And look, a Gularis Muticus".

"This isn't a false alarm after all. Standby," Annie said into her radio. "Are you OK, sir?"

"It's your turn, Edna. One good bowl and then we'll see if my teeth fit you better," said Gouty George.

"Let me have a look at you. Mr Peacock, isn't it?" Annie asked, opening her medical rucksack.

"I saw him faint at the bowls club. Has Mr Peacock been drugged?" asked Lottie.

"He might have been. Or it could be his blood sugar level," replied Annie.

Before she had time to do anything else, Gouty George bowled another imaginary bowl and then fell face-first into the gutter.

Annie turned to Lottie. "Help me get him into the chopper and I'll check him over on the way to hospital."

Annie and Lottie grabbed Gouty George's hands, pulled him to his feet and helped him stagger to the helicopter and eased him into an empty seat.

"Ready for transit," said Annie into her radio, climbing into the helicopter with Lottie. She strapped Gouty George into his seat and closed the door.

"Buckle up, treacle."

Captain Keller started the rotors and waited for them to reach 500 RPM and then eased the control stick towards him. Heli-Med-five-one's engine roared as it took off and the captain spoke over his radio to the medical staff at Newport hospital.

"This is Heli-Med-five-one. We are on route to you with an elderly gentleman. Condition unknown. ETA five minutes."

The helicopter hit air pockets blowing in from the sea and rocked violently as it thundered towards Newport. Annie Walker felt sicker than ever while she tried her best to examine Gouty George.

Annie frowned. Gouty George's sugar levels were fine, so he'd need more blood tests at the hospital to find out what was wrong with him. All she could do was wind a bandage around his head to stop the blood oozing from where he'd face-planted the gutter.

Gouty George just sat in his seat, mumbling about getting his torch to look for Dorothy's lost earring.

As they approached Newport, the helicopter banked right.

"Ready for landing, Annie?" asked Captain Keller, flicking two switches above his head.

"Ready," said Annie, clutching her vomit bowl again as if her life depended on it.

"Is this Madrid airport? Eviva España," mumbled Gouty George.

"No, we're at the hospital, Mr Peacock. You've had a fall," said Annie, taking a deep breath.

Seconds later, the helicopter dropped and landed on a large yellow 'X' painted on a landing pad on the hospital's roof. Captain Keller killed the power to the rota blades and a nurse rushed out, followed by a doctor. They helped a groggy Gouty George from his seat and into a wheelchair.

"Are you Doctor Zimmerman?" asked Gouty George, yanking up his trouser leg. "My ankle is still sore. Why do you have an Alba Prunelba on your shoulder?"

"No, mister. I'm Doctor Dunn and this is Nurse Hurst. Do you remember what happened?"

"Bowls," mumbled Gouty George.

"Charming!" said Nurse Hurst.

"No. He was playing *bowls* and was kidnapped by Dorothy," explained Lottie, jumping from the helicopter.

"His pupils are odd sizes, his pulse is racing, and he has a temperature of 39 degrees. It's possible he's been drugged," Annie Walker managed to say, before filling the vomit bowl with Minestrone soup, which she'd eaten at lunchtime (not one of her better ideas).

Doctor Dunn shone a torch into Gouty George's eyes. "You're right. "Get him into Resus."

The doctor grabbed the wheelchair's handles and

shoved hard, wheeling Gouty George through a door marked 'CASUALTY DEPARTMENT' with Nurse Hurst and Lottie hurrying after them.

"Will he be OK?" asked Lottie, as Doctor Dunn hurtled past the reception desk with his patient, narrowly missing a child wearing a Spiderman costume with a Lego brick jammed up his nose.

"Don't worry. We will do everything we can," said Nurse Hurst, giving her standard reply to Lottie's question (which she was asked at least a dozen times every day).

"The police are on their way and will want to talk to you, so please sit over there, my love," said Nurse Hurst, offering a reassuring smile and pointing to an empty chair in the busy waiting area.

Lottie sat anxiously next to a woman wearing a wedding dress. She had tears streaming down her cheeks and blood dripping from a broken nose. The distraught bride was deeply regretting her decision to not wear her glasses for the earlier walk down the aisle.

Gouty George was wheeled through a door to a room marked 'RESUS ROOM 1', crammed with medical equipment. Nurse Hurst took his pulse and Doctor Dunn shone his torch in Gouty George's eyes again.

"No change. Are you allergic to anything?"

"Pain," mumbled Gouty George, as three more medical staff hurried in, and the door closed.

Minutes later, a police car with its sirens blaring screeched to a halt outside the hospital. Lottie recognised the man who scuttled into the waiting area.

Detective Inspector Sergeant-Constable was the nerdy policeman who solved the case earlier that summer and arrested Timothy Pinkerton for trying to swindle the residents of Alum Bay out of their homes.

"Lottie Baxter! Trouble has a nasty habit of finding slash locating you lately," said Detective Inspector Sergeant-Constable.

Lottie quickly explained to the policeman what had happened at the bowls club and Bob Bell's garage.

Detective Inspector Sergeant-Constable filled six pages of his notebook and then scratched his chin.

"And the woman suddenly rode away on a motorbike?"

"Yes. She just left poor Mr Peacock in the minibus. said Lottie.

"Sounds to me like a kidnapping that didn't go well slash to plan."

The door to RESUS ROOM 1 opened and Nurse Hurst hurried out.

Detective Inspector Sergeant-Constable opened a leather wallet and showed his Isle of Wight Police badge.

"I'm Detective Inspector Sergeant-Constable."

Nurse Hurst looked confused.

"All *four* of them?"

"Detective Inspector is my police rank, my surname is Sergeant-Constable. How's the victim? Can I interview him yet?"

"Mr Peacock's pulse and breathing are now under control and we've sent his blood off to the lab to try and find out what he's been given. You can talk to him, but only for a minute, as he needs to rest."

Detective Inspector Sergeant-Constable nodded and scribbled some more in his notebook and scuttled into the room. Gouty George laid on a bed with wires and tubes poking out everywhere.

"Hello, Sir. How are you feeling?"

"My leg is so sore, Doctor Zimmerman. It's spreading up to my knee. Look," replied Gouty George, undoing his trousers.

"I'm a police officer, Mr Peacock. You've had a nasty slash bad turn. Can you tell me what happened at the bowls club?" asked Detective Inspector Sergeant-Constable, notebook and pencil in hand.

"Bowls," said Gouty George closing his eyes.

"Did someone give you something today?"

"Yes," slurred Gouty George. "Before lunch. By the Post Office. A voucher for a cheap eye test at Vision Mission."

"No, did a woman give you something to eat or drink?" Detective Inspector Sergeant-Constable asked.

"My wife's sister, Mavis. She told me gout can be cured by drinking pints of nettle and banana tea."

Gouty George beckoned the Detective Inspector closer and whispered in his ear. "She's a right berk. It doesn't work."

He belched loudly and spewed all down Detective Inspector Sergeant-Constable's jacket; undigested banana dripped on the floor by his feet.

"Better out than in," sighed Nurse Hurst, passing the unimpressed policeman a paper towel while taking Gouty George's blood pressure.

Detective Inspector Sergeant-Constable screwed his nose up and wiped the smelly sick from his sleeve. "When will he be more compos mentis?"

"I've given him a dose of BNT162B2. Hopefully the drowsiness will wear off in a few hours," said Doctor Dunn, holding a stethoscope to Gouty George's hairy chest.

"I'll come back later and see what he remembers," said the Detective Inspector closing his notebook.

"Thank you, Doctor Zimmerman. These Colma Pipilods are so annoying, aren't they," mumbled Gouty George pointing at the lights in the ceiling, as Detective Inspector Sergeant-Constable threw the sticky sicky paper towel in a bin and left.

Out in the waiting room, Lottie jumped from her seat. "How's Mr Peacock?"

"He should be fine. Unlike my jacket. I need to investigate what happened at the bowls club and see if anyone there knows slash recalls anything useful. Come along, I'll give you a ride."

Alan Barbara

CHAPTER 10 – I CAN'T GET NO SATISFACTION.

The bowls match had ended in a draw. Both teams sat outside the clubhouse in deckchairs. Half the group drank tea from china cups and saucers and the other half were asleep. Edna Biddle had the photograph of her great grandchild out again, showing it to Jurassic Clarke, but unfortunately, he'd just nodded off; having mastered the trick of falling asleep with his eyes open.

"My team should have won, Old Boy," said B-Squared.

"That's *utter* claptrap. You lot were lucky to even get a draw," shrieked Skipper, his mouth full of a potted meat sandwich.

B-Squared stood and put his hands on his hips. "Then how about you and I play a decider. Sudden death!"

The mention of 'sudden death' wasn't a good phrase to use amongst a group of over 70s. Edna Biddle panicked and poked Jurassic Clarke in the ribs with a bony finger.

Jurassic woke with a start. "What did you do that for?"

"Just checking you hadn't gone to join God's bowls team in heaven," said Edna.

"Alright. You're on," said a flustered Skipper. "Although it's *officially* against rule 9 clause B but I'm feeling lucky. Four bowls each and the winner takes the whole match."

But before they ambled onto the lawn (avoiding the Grim Heaper's handywork), Lottie and Detective Inspector Sergeant-Constable arrived. The policeman announced he needed to urgently speak with all the players, so Cheddar George woke the snoozers up by yodelling the national anthem.

Once everyone was fully awake, Lottie sat next to Cheddar George, sipping a milky tea with four sugars. Wendy de Sousa had given it to her, as she said it was good for shock. It wasn't working. An afternoon of kidnapping, kite-scootering, helicoptering and a hospital visit while dealing with Gouty 'the Birdman' George, had taken a lot out of her and all she wanted to do was go home.

Detective Inspector Sergeant-Constable stood before the pensioners and opened his notebook. He could still smell the banana-sick on his crusty jacket sleeve.

"If I could have your attention."

Cheddar George and at least a dozen of the others turned up their hearing aids.

"At around 15:30 today, George Peacock from Alum Bay was drugged and kidnapped by a woman slash female from the Ventnor bowling team calling herself 'Dorothy'."

"Good grief! I'll brie dammed," muttered Cheddar George.

"It's the French. That bloke, Sacha Distel from the 70s always looked shifty to me. You can never trust the Frenchies," said Jurassic Clarke, wagging an angry fist at Detective Inspector Sergeant-Constable.

"You're dead right, Jurassic. And you can blame BREXIT for *that*. There's nothing working with umlauts," said Edna Biddle, crossing her arms in defiance.

"You need to set up roadblocks and close the ferry port *immediately*," announced Henry Waddle, a retired traffic warden from the Ventnor team.

"All in good time, sir. I need information first. Does anyone have any more details slash description of this 'Dorothy'?" asked Detective Inspector Sergeant-Constable.

"Well," said B-Squared, "poor Camila Delgado phoned me this morning to say she'd gone down with the squits and couldn't play. She said it was probably a dodgy corned beef and piccalilli sandwich she'd bought from her corner shop. Then a minute later, I got another call from this 'Dorothy Gale', or whoever she was, asking to join our club. As we were a player short *and* she was free, I asked her to come along this afternoon. I'd say she was in her late sixties and had ginger hair and big glasses."

"She wouldn't have been here if you'd stuck to rule seven clause A," said Skipper, brandishing his rule book.

"Oh, pipe down, Skipper. Mind you, to say there

was something fishy about her is an understatement," said B-Squared. "Her breath stank worse than an Icelandic fishing trawler and she was *diabolical* at bowling. We would have won easily if it hadn't been for Dorothy *and* the state of the playing surface."

A few mumbles and nods of agreement came from other members of the Ventnor team sat in the deckchairs.

"Poppycock," Skipper muttered and put his rulebook away.

"I never trust a woman with hairy knuckles," said Jurassic Clarke.

"And did Dorothy Gale *have* hairy knuckles?" asked Detective Inspector Sergeant-Constable.

"Nope," said Jurassic.

"I'd say she had *no* knuckles, by the way she bowled," said B-Squared.

"So, I'm looking for a ginger haired, French female slash woman with hairless knuckles and a fishy aroma. Anything else?"

"She wasn't good at bowls due to her small hands," said Cheddar George. "And I think there was a tattoo on the back of one of them."

"Excellent. Now we're getting somewhere," said Detective Inspector Sergeant-Constable. "Can you remember slash recall the design of this tattoo?"

"Young man, I can hardly remember slash recall what day it is," said Cheddar George.

"Thursday!" called Jurassic Clarke. "Oh bum. I forgot to put the bins out."

Cheddar George shut his eyes, trying to think. Lottie

wondered from his expression if he might be trying to let 'Tommy out of prison', as she'd seen that look many times.

"It was on her wrist… on her bowling hand. Left, I believe," said Cheddar George, opening his eyes again.

"I didn't like her sunglasses," said Edna Biddle.

"OK," sighed the Detective Inspector, knowing he wasn't going to get any other useful information about the kidnapper out of the group. "If you remember slash recall anything else *useful*, then please call the station."

The puzzled policeman closed his notebook and scratched his chin.

"What *on earth* is happening slash going on?"

Alan Barbara

CHAPTER 11- PAPA DON'T PREACH.

Maddie climbed the steps leading to the entrance of the tall grey building. There were no signs above the door indicating what went on in secret behind the windows – grubby from the bustling city traffic.

At the top of the steps, Maddie pushed open the door and stepped into the lobby of Trafalgar House in Godliman Street, central London. The Georgian building was the headquarters of the Pensioner Collection Service and she'd been summoned for a meeting.

A security guard sat behind a grey desk. He studied an unfinished crossword puzzle on a neatly folded newspaper and held a half-eaten bacon sandwich to his lips, deep in thought.

"I have an appointment with Sir Charles Oakley," said Maddie, her mouth-watering as the smell of bacon teased her nose. How she'd love a bacon sandwich smothered in ketchup, but that would cost her money. Money she couldn't waste if she was to win the auction for Astronaut Roxy. Maddie would have Boomer's Tuna chunks *again* later for lunch.

The security guard looked up and tutted his

annoyance for being interrupted while trying to solve the crossword clue to seven across.

"ID?" he asked, fishing a piece of bacon from a gap in his back teeth with his tongue and detecting an unpleasant fishy pong.

Maddie handed over her ID and pulled up a sleeve to show her mermaid's tail tattoo. "They've Got an Awful Lot of Coffee in Brazil," she said nervously.

The guard slipped on a pair of glasses, sniffed and peered at Maddie, then her wrist and finally the photo on her PCS badge.

"Waiting Room 51. Ninth floor," said the security guard and he pushed a button by his knee releasing the electronic lock on a pair of heavy doors to his left. The doors slowly opened, and he returned to the task of finishing his bacon sandwich and battling with his crossword.

Maddie walked past the guard and through the open doors; her footsteps echoing in the empty lobby. She stepped into a lift and pressed the button for floor nine. The doors closed and the lift clattered its way to the top floor. When the doors parted, Maddie found herself in a narrow corridor, which she walked along until she found the door to Waiting Room 51.

She turned the handle and stepped into the wood-panelled room containing rows of chairs along three of the walls. Emelia Douthwaite sat on one chair. She was nervously cleaning her glasses with a tissue, rubbing the lenses so hard, she was in danger of shattering them.

"Hello Agent Mainard," said Emelia, as she stood. Her high heels clomped on the polished wooden floor as she approached. "Thank you for coming," she added, shaking Maddie's hand.

"I don't think I had much choice," said Maddie.

"I know, Maddie. Sir Charles will see us now," said Emelia, her nose detecting the pungent aroma of tuna on Maddie's breath. "Oh, and we *will* need this," she added and sprayed an entire bottle of Pierre Thabaut perfume over the two of them, hoping the perfume would mask tuna breath just as well as pipe smoke.

"Take a few deep gulps of the lovely Pierre. Trust me, you're going to need it," said Emelia and then she clomped across the waiting room and tapped on a wooden door.

"Ter!" Sir Charles Oakley bellowed from within.

"Welcome to Fogwarts," muttered Emelia as she opened the door and Maddie followed her into the smoky stench.

Sir Charles sat in his chair with his feet up on his desk, reading the Times newspaper.

"Ah, Emelia and Agent Mainard. Ad infinitum, et ultra."

"Ad infinitum," Emelia and Maddie chanted and saluted with a circular wag of a finger, as expected.

"Come... come sit. Maddie... good to see you."

Sir Charles nodded at two chairs in front of his desk and peered over the rim of his half-moon spectacles.

"Let's have a quick chat."

Emelia and Maddie sat and waited as Sir Charles took his feet off his desk, folded the newspaper and filled his pipe with fresh Cornell tobacco from his leather pouch. He took a deep breath and spoke without lighting it.

"The PCS has been up and running for a while now. Plenty of Silver Cuppa Suppers have been visiting our Coffiestas on the island for a cup of Tea-Vee-Wunda and dunking a Bour-Bon-Jovi. And they've been confessing to *all sorts* of wrongdoing, which gives us the right to take them off the streets and lock them in prison. Recently, we've ramped up the number of pesky pensioners being collected and we're saving a *fortune* in pension pay-outs. Everything was going exceedingly well… until yesterday, Maddie, when *you* put the cat amongst the Columbidae with your shenanigans. My country residence is near Alum Bay, and I *don't* see the town bursting with Olympic athletes. How hard can it be to grab one of the wrinkly old folk?"

"I can explain, Sir Charles," said Maddie.

"Explain, do, Agent Mainard," barked Sir Charles, finally lighting his pipe (much to Emelia's disappointment).

"The target switched bowls games with another gentleman named George. I didn't know I'd collected the *wrong* one until I counted his toes," said Maddie.

"Toes?" barked Sir Charles, looking confused while puffing out a dreadful stink.

"Distinguishing mark on the target – medical records reported a missing toe on his right foot," said Emelia Douthwaite. "An easy mistake to make."

Sir Charles puffed hard on his pipe and the two women knew he was annoyed.

"Puffle-huff. A mix up over an old codger's phalanges? Collectors are *not* supposed to make mistakes. It tarnishes the whole department. I'm *not* happy."

Sir Charles was also deeply worried that if word got out about this mistake, his dream of taking over form 'Jammy Jarvis' as Prime Minister would be well and truly over.

"Maddie understands the graveness of her error, don't you, Maddie," said Emelia.

"Of course, Sir Charles. It *won't* happen again. I'll collect the correct George… the correct target before the end of the week."

"See that you do," barked Sir Charles. "I don't want the three strikes rule to be applied. Not on my watch."

"Three strikes rule?" Maddie asked. Her eyes flitting between the faces of Emelia Douthwaite and the angry Home Secretary, bathed in a foggy mist.

Emelia Douthwaite sighed. "It is a rule I persuaded Sir Charles to agree to when the PCS was created. If a Collector fails to take their target in three attempts, then the slate is wiped clean, and the target is spared."

"I can't believe I agreed to that piff-paff," said Sir Charles, his cheeks turning crimson.

"Well, you *did*, Sir Charles. You fully agreed to it, so you *must* honour the three strikes rule," said Emelia Douthwaite, sounding agitated.

Maddie looked Sir Charles in the eye. "It won't come to that."

"Excellent. Failure is *not* an option, Agent Mainard. 'Ad infinitum, et ultra'," said Sir Charles and he pulled a face at Emelia Douthwaite just visible behind the smoky fog.

Alan Barbara

CHAPTER 12 – ONE WAY OR ANOTHER.

Maddie turned the black dial to switch on the campervan's radio. While she waited for the residents of 25 Rose Crescent to wake, she boiled a kettle on her stove to make a flask of Earl Grey tea.

Bored and depressed, she scoffed two tins of Boomer's Tuna chunks for breakfast and listened to Grandad Frank singing 'My Way' in the shower (with a few rude words added of his own). She finished her tuna and tossed the tins on the floor and monitored the chit-chat now coming from the kitchen. Information which might come in handy. You never knew with Maddie's job.

Nanny Vera emptied the dishwasher and mentioned that Heather the Weather's swollen knee was now a lot better, and she was no longer predicting a cold snap. Heather declared the south of England would now have an Indian summer, so she'd returned the tins of soup and sacks of salt to Verdi and instead, bought 30 tubs of Neapolitan ice cream to fill her freezer.

Grandad Frank reported that Owen the postman had retired after 35 years and was off on a cruise to somewhere that sounded like a medical complaint. He also reported that Sherman the German at number 52 had installed his CCTV but hadn't yet caught any dogs piddling up the wheel of his BMW. And there was concern for Mrs Fish, who hadn't been seen at the Burlington Bingo Hall for a while (Maddie could obviously explain that one).

Nosey Rosie Saunders also reported to Cheddar George (when she cornered him in Verdi) that the council were going to change the collection day for their rubbish bins. There was uproar from the entire street and the AABBCC had been formed (the Angry Alum Bay Bin Collection Committee) with Nosey Rosie a natural choice for its leader.

Grandad Frank wasn't happy about the council's plan either, as he'd only just finished colouring the days for the *current* bin rota for the whole year on their Pampered Pooches calendar which hung in the kitchen.

But just after breakfast (while Nanny Vera ironed Cheddar George's Batman underpants), Maddie heard what the family planned for the weekend. She grinned and punched the air, knocking over her cup of Earl Grey.

"Got you, George Hardwick. I'll not mess it up this time," she muttered. She quickly rescued her phone from the puddle of spilt tea and dialling Ken Oliver's number at PCS Control.

"Hi Ken. I need an RC-3 for the weekend. The long range one with the extra power-pack."

"We probably don't have any. Let me check what's in stock," replied Ken in his usual 'doom and gloom' voice.

Maddie heard Ken's keyboard clatter. "Hang on. You're in luck. We have one in the Portsmouth warehouse."

Suddenly the sound of bagpipes erupted from Maddie's radio, followed by Cheddar George's yodel (sounding like a whale in considerable pain).

Maddie killed the volume. "Great. When can you get it to me?"

"That was tuneful, Maddie! I can get the RC-3 shipped on the Isle of Wight ferry that leaves at three o'clock, and delivered to the Coffiesta in Alum Bay. You can pick it up tomorrow morning. That's if the Shipping Department pull their finger out."

"Perfect. Thanks, Ken."

Maddie stayed in Rose Crescent for the rest of that day and overnight, glued to the radio, but there wasn't any more useful chit-chat from the house. She left mid-morning to buy another crate of Boomer's Tuna from Verdi. After eating two tins for lunch, Maddie collected the RC-3 from Guz Sharma at the Coffiesta.

She then called in at the Pavilion Theatre to collect her toolbox from the basement. As dusk fell, she returned to Rose Crescent and waited in her campervan with the curtains shut, looking through a thin gap with her Magni-view binoculars.

At midnight, the street was quiet as expected. Maddie took her toolbox and crept up the driveway and around Grandad Frank's Volvo. The old Yale lock on the garage door was simple to pick (thanks to Major Caruthers' training) and Maddie eased the wooden doors open and slipped inside. She waited in darkness for a minute, listening for movement from the house. All was quiet, so she switched on a torch strapped to her head and found Cheddar George's Oldie TT under a shelf stretching the entire length of the garage stacked with tins of beige paint.

Maddie installed the RC-3 beneath the Oldie TT's tartan seat and connected the six wires, making sure everything was well hidden. By 12.15, she was back in her VW, fast asleep. She left Rose Crescent well before dawn.

CHAPTER 13 – HIGH HOPES.

The beige Volvo drove along a narrow country road between Alum Bay and Freshwater. Attached to the towbar at the back was Cheddar George's Oldie TT and sidecar. Nanny Vera sat next to Grandad Frank and in the back sat Lottie and Cheddar George.

Grandad Frank slowed the Volvo as he approached a hand-painted sign nailed to a tree next to a wooden gate.

The sign read 'ALUM BAY SUMMER FETE CAR PARK' with an arrow pointing left into a field, which was part of Pennywell Farm. Nosey Rosie Saunders, wearing baggy shorts and a t-shirt with 'NO FLIPBIN CHANGES' printed across her chest, stood at the entrance. Grandad Frank wound his window down and stopped the car.

"There's plenty of spaces over on the left, Frank," said Nosey Rosie Saunders, thrusting a leaflet about her next weekly meeting of the AABBCC under his nose. "And did you know Amanda Nelson will be here? She went to the same girl's boarding school as me *and* the Queen's second cousin."

Grandad Frank nodded. "Oh really," he said, as if showing some interest and then took the leaflet and drove into the field.

Nanny Vera loved coming to the Alum Bay fete. It was held every year on the second Sunday of September. Grandad Frank disliked the afternoon as he always ended up carrying all the weird stuff Nanny Vera won on the stalls, which she'd then display proudly on her shelves at home. Last year, the most notable item she won was a sculpture of Carisbrooke Castle made from painted fir cones and the inside of toilet rolls.

"This will ruin the suspension," Grandad Frank muttered as the car wallowed across the grass and the gentle rocking caused Cheddar George to let 'Tommy out of prison'.

"Stop moaning, Frank," said Nanny Vera as the Volvo eased into a gap between a tree and a van belonging to an electrician whose business was called 'Socket and See'.

Cheddar George gave a gentle snore from the seat next to Lottie. He'd dozed off on the short drive from their home and sat with his head tipped back and a half-eaten cheese sandwich resting on his good knee (he no longer referred to his knees as 'left knee' and 'right knee', but 'good knee' and 'bad knee'). His top set of false teeth hung out his mouth at an angle and the window next to him was open an inch to allow the aroma of 'Tommy' to escape from the car.

"Give him a little nudge to wake him, Lottie," said Nanny Vera as she lifted a gingham tea-towel to check the beige plate of home-cooked treats on her lap.

Nanny Vera's 'Rock Cake Surprises' were her entry for the baking contest. Hetty Edwards judged the fiercely contested baking contest every year and also did Morris Dancing at the fete (although not at the same time). The 'surprise' being that Nanny Vera's jam was made with pickled red cabbage instead of strawberries (which of course came from one of her unlabelled plastic tubs).

Lottie tapped Cheddar George's hand gently. "We're here Cheddar George. Time to shine."

Cheddar George opened an eye and his wrinkly thumb reset his false teeth.

"Kalispera, Lottie. I'm looking forward to this."

Grandad Frank looked over his shoulder. His face wore a confused look.

"Quick question… Why are you two dressed as Woody from Toy Story?"

"These are traditional Bavarian outfits made by that fashion designer Dolce and Banana. Rather fetching don't you think?" replied Cheddar George.

"And what's that all over your face and hands, Dad?" asked Nanny Vera.

"Ah, well. I did a DIY spray tan after breakfast. Made it myself from orange juice, peanut butter and a spoonful of Marmite. I call the colour 'burnt waffle'."

"You never cease to amaze," chuckled Grandad Frank.

Cheddar George tapped his head and then pointed at his feet. "Up here for beauty treatments, down there for dancing."

"Totes. We've entered 'The Bay's Got Talent' again, Grank," said Lottie.

"And we're going to do *much* better than last year," said Cheddar George, looking at Lottie and they both nodded in agreement.

"Yes, I remember the look of terror on that judge's face when your plate spinning act got out of hand. I'm *sure* he didn't expect to end up in casualty," said Grandad Frank.

"I hope you're doing something less dangerous this year," said Nanny Vera.

"Yes, Vera. We're playing it safe. Lottie's doing her thing with the bagpipes, and I'm going to sing along and add a yodel mashup. I call it 'yodellsing'," said Cheddar George.

"We've practiced for weeks. It's going to be amazeballs," said Lottie.

"Oh, right. Well, you look *lovely*," said Nanny Vera.

"But smell terrible," muttered Grandad Frank as his nose got a whiff of 'burnt waffle'. "I bet Amanda Nelson hasn't had to park in a field," he moaned.

"She probably arrived in a shiny limo," said Lottie.

Amanda Nelson was a news reporter from Spotlight Isle of Wight, the local BBC news show. Lottie watched it every night after dinner and Amanda was always reporting from somewhere on the island. She lived in Alum Bay and as she was the most famous (and only) celebrity living in the area, she'd been asked to be one of the judges for the talent contest.

"I'm going to get Amanda Nelson's autograph," said Lottie.

"Good idea. And I hope Edna Biddle has her stall selling afternoon tea. I'm parched. Too much tea is barely enough," said Cheddar George.

"Well, I bet Amanda Nelson has something stronger than tea to drink," said Grandad Frank. "Nosey Rosie Saunders told me she consumes gin by the *bucketload*."

Grandad Frank noticed Nanny Vera's side eye glare and decided it was best to keep quiet about Nosey Rosie's latest gossip.

"When I was a lad, me and Harry Lambert sneaked into this field one night and he nicked a load of leeks," said Cheddar George. "Harry then tried flogging them in Shanklin market. 'Leeky Lambert' was his nickname for a while. He got called that again in later life, but for a different reason."

Nanny Vera got out the car and checked Grandad Frank had parked the Volvo to her liking.

"All hands on deck," she said and Lottie helped Grandad Frank unhitch the Oldie TT from the car's towbar.

Lottie and Cheddar George's Bavarian outfits consisted of a green hat, white shirt and brown lederhosen trousers that reached just below the knee. Long white socks and suede shoes completed the look.

"Cheesy does it. I should have ordered the next size up in the lederhosen," said Cheddar George, with a painful wince as he climbed onto the Oldie TT's tartan seat. Into the wicker basket on the front, he popped an emergency cheese sandwich wrapped in a brown paper bag and a handful of butterscotch sweets.

Lottie climbed into the sidecar and sat her bagpipes on her lap. She shoved an old C90 tape into the radio cassette player and pressed the 'PLAY' button. An

Engelbert Humperdinck tune came from the speaker.

"You can't go on stage with chocolate around your face, Lottie," said Nanny Vera. She took a hankie from her beige handbag, spitting on a clean bit and wiping Lottie's dirty cheek.

"There. That's better. Now, don't run over people's feet, Dad," said Nanny Vera, as Cheddar George and Lottie set off in the scooter, trundling at five miles an hour across the field.

"I wonder if Duncan Mackay will be his usual cheery self today," said Grandad Frank.

Duncan Mackay owned Pennywell Farm where the fete was held, and he was the most miserable man you could ever meet.

"At least he can't complain about the weather. Mind you, Heather the Weather reckons it'll rain later," said Nanny Vera as she walked arm in arm with Grandad Frank over to the entrance.

The stalls at the fete were surrounded by people of all ages enjoying the late summer sunshine. Nanny Vera had a system. She always started at the stall to the left of the entrance and made her way around the field in an anti-clockwise direction.

From the first tombola stall run by the staff from the Alum Bay Dog Rescue Centre, Nanny Vera won a bottle of orange squash (which was two years out of date), a tin of sardines and a garden gnome (with a cracked beard and missing arm).

The stall next to it was a lucky dip (Nanny Vera's favourite) and she was thrilled to win a dinner plate with a picture of the Grand Duke of Luxembourg.

Grandad Frank wasn't impressed but kept quiet.

On the other side of the field, Lottie pointed to a large brown tent owned by the scouts, with a white bed sheet tied above the entrance saying, 'The Bay's Got Talent'.

"That's us."

Cheddar George checked his trusted Timex watch. "I don't think there's time for a cuppa now, Lottie, so we'd better get over there."

He parked the Oldie TT near the entrance and as he got off, his bad knee cracked like a glow stick.

Lottie swung her bagpipes onto her shoulder, and they went inside the tent, which smelt old and musty, like Cheddar George's sock drawer at home. At one end was a low stage and wooden benches, arranged in neat rows. These were full of locals, waiting to be entertained.

A woman with a clipboard and hair she struggled to control darted over.

"I *love* your outfits. Are you performing?" she asked, blowing her long fringe away from her eyes.

"Yep. Hansel and Pretzel. Back by *unpopular* demand," said Cheddar George.

"Magnif. And what will you be treating us to this stupendous afternoon?"

"A musical number. Lottie here wanted to do a tune by either Lady Blah-blah or the Karzy Chiefs, but I persuaded her to do something more traditional, so we chose *This Little Light Of Mine*," said Cheddar George.

"Sounds perfect!" said the woman scribbling on her clipboard.

"We hope so, my dear. Tash-hag time to shine."

"Magnif. We'll be starting in five minutes. You're on after Graham the blindfolded balloon modeler and before Liz and Ashok over there, who plan to toss and catch raw eggs with their feet. Isn't *that* exciting!" said the woman, puffing again to shift her troublesome fringe.

Lottie decided there and then *not* to watch the egg tossing twosome. There was no way she wanted to see *anything* involving bare feet.

"You can put your musical gizmo behind the stage for now if you want," said the woman. She tucked her clipboard under her arm and rushed off to check that Liz and Ashok had a good supply of wet wipes in case they needed to clean up any eggy mess after their performance.

"Where's Amanda Nelson?" Lottie asked.

"Under a table with a bottle of gin if you believe Nosey Rosie Saunders," chuckled Cheddar George. "I'll find a seat," he said, as Lottie walked with her bagpipes between the rows of crowded benches towards the stage.

In front of the stage, Lottie spotted three chairs with pieces of paper pinned to the back, marked 'JUDGE'.

Duncan Mackay sat in one chair with a face you wouldn't run towards. The middle chair was empty, and Lottie guessed it was reserved for Amanda Nelson. An elderly vicar sat in the third. He turned around and smiled at Lottie and straightened the white dog collar around his thin neck.

"Afternoon, dear child. I hope you are enjoying this

glorious day."

"Can I have your autograph?" asked Lottie.

The vicar smiled again, showing his perfectly white teeth and closed a leather-bound bible he'd been reading. "I'm not famous, dear child."

"That's OK. I'm collecting autographs and can start a new list of churchy-people."

"Then of course, my dear. After all, the good book tells us that we are all 'stars' in the eyes of the Lord," replied the vicar, tapping his bible.

Lottie handed Paddy and the Duke to the vicar, and he signed 'Bless you. Reverend Maurice Mullard' on a blank page and handed it back.

"Thanks. I'm in the talent contest," said Lottie.

"Playing the bagpipes, I see. The Lord has blessed us with this glorious day and I'm sure the sun will shine in my heart, when I hear you play. I wish you the very best of luck," said Reverend Mullard.

Lottie gave the vicar a smile, then offered her pad and pen to Duncan Mackay. "Can I-"

"*No*," barked Duncan Mackay. "I won't sign anything after my wretched wife tricked me into signing over a fortune, then packed her bags and legged it to Milton Keynes."

"But it's..." Lottie began, then decided from the stern look on Duncan Mackay's face, she wasn't going to get his autograph.

She put her bagpipes at the back of the stage and sat on a bench with Cheddar George, who'd just let 'Tommy out of prison', clearing everyone from the area around them.

"I might have put too much Marmite in my spray tan mix," Cheddar George whispered to Lottie as his burnt waffle creation dripped from his top lip into his mouth. On the bench in front, the stink of 'Tommy' became too much for yet another couple and they moved away.

Suddenly, a tent flap opened, and Amanda Nelson swept in. She waved at the audience and shook hands with Duncan Mackay and the Reverend Mullard before taking her seat.

The woman with the clipboard climbed onto the stage, puffed to shift her fringe and introduced the opening act – Sophie Noble-Nuttal, who Lottie knew from Cringle Park school, (but didn't like because in the summer she almost drowned the BREW Crew on purpose).

Sophie stood on stage with Monty, her overweight Pug. Both wore white and yellow cheerleader costumes from the Alum Bay Sapphires, of which Sophie was captain. Monty didn't look happy at all about being dressed up.

Sophie got Monty to sit perfectly still on a stool and then balanced three paper cups on his flattish head. She tried a fourth, but a boy in the second row opened a bag of crisps at the critical moment and Monty suddenly leapt from the stool and charged across the stage and jumped onto the boy's lap, spilling prawn cocktail crisps over the grass. The audience applauded politely as Sophie abandoned her cup balancing doggy act and sat on a bench at the back of the tent with a face like a melted welly.

"She wasn't very good," whispered Lottie.

"Agreed indeed. It certainly wasn't a 'pawesome' performance. Two out of ten at the most," replied Cheddar George.

Graham, the blindfolded balloon modeler was the next performer. Things started badly for Graham because he got in a muddle when he pulled his blind fold over his eyes and began his act standing with his back to the audience.

"The good book says to keep your eyes on the stars and your feet on the ground," Reverend Mullard said, helping Graham to turn and face the sniggering audience.

Graham's hands were then a blur, creating balloon animals of all colours and proudly holding them aloft for all to see, but nobody could make out what they actually were. At the end of making a parrot (which looked more like a snake that had swallowed a tennis ball) he twisted the top of a red balloon to make the bird's plumage and the balloon suddenly popped, causing poor Monty the Pug to piddle over Ashok's bare feet. The terrified dog then tried to scramble under the side of the tent to escape, while Ashok stormed off in a huff with a handful of wet wipes.

"Another two out of ten. They do say you should never work with children or animals," chuckled Cheddar George.

Once the woman with the clipboard and the wayward hair cleared up the mess with paper towels, she took to the stage as if in a hurry. "Well, that was entertaining. Ladies and Gentlemen. And now we have

Hansel and Pretzel with a fine tune we should *all* know."

"Time to shine, Lottie," said Cheddar George, wiping burnt waffle off his top lip.

Lottie helped Cheddar George up the two steps to the stage and then picked up her bagpipes and held the bag under her elbow and blew into the mouthpiece. A dull drone filled the tent and Monty whimpered as if in pain. Cheddar George grinned at the three judges and then counted them in.

"A one…two…A one…two…three…four…" Lottie blew as hard as she could and her fingers flew up and down the chanter, playing the opening notes to This Little Light of Mine, (and only missing a few notes here and there). Cheddar George took a deep breath and yodellsang along.

"This little light of mine, I'm gonna let it shine.
Yodeladay-a-day-a-dee, yodeladay-a-day-a-doe.
This little light of mine, I'm gonna let it shine.
Let it shine, let it shine, yodel-a-dee.

Everywhere I go, I'm gonna let it shine.
Yodeladay-a-day-a-dee, yodeladay-a-day-a-doe.
Everywhere I go, I'm gonna let it shine.
Let it shine, let it shine, yodel-a-dee.

This little light of mine, I'm gonna let it shine.
Yodeladay-a-day-a-dee, yodeladay-a-day-a-doe…

The audience clapped along, and the Reverend

Mullard sang the non-yodelling bits. But disaster struck halfway through the third verse, when Cheddar George suddenly swallowed a large bluebottle mid-yodel and coughed so hard his false teeth shot out and clattered at Amanda Nelson's feet. Lottie carried on playing, with Reverend Mullard singing along, while Cheddar George took an age to climb down the steps, bend down and pick up his teeth, while still coughing up bits of bluebottle.

"Has anyone got a drink for the poor old chap… before he's sick all over me," called Duncan Mackay.

Lottie noticed Amanda Nelson's grip tighten on a bottle of Coke in her hand.

Reverend Mullard handed Cheddar George a paper cup. "Here you are. It's water or 'Adam's Ale' as I like to call it."

Cheddar George gulped the drink before slipping his teeth back in.

"Thank you, vicar," he said and then managed to yodelsing the final chorus from where he stood, and the crowd applauded again.

"Bravo. Bravo," said the Reverend Mullard as Lottie and Cheddar George took a bow and returned to their seats. Duncan Mackay fidgeted in his seat wearing a face like thunder and wondered how many *more* acts he was expected to sit through.

"We should have worn our roller skates. That would have made it more exciting," said Lottie.

"Never mind, darling. Up here for talent shows, down there for dancing," said Cheddar George, letting 'Tommy out of prison' again. "I'd score us five out of ten. Tash-hag nailed it."

Liz and Ashok had gone home to disinfect Ashok's feet, so there were only two more acts for Duncan Mackay to endure; a spotty teenage lad whistling bird impressions (which Monty the pug didn't like at all and barked constantly throughout) and finally, a lady, who for some reason sang I Wish It Could Be Christmas Every Day, while bashing an old tambourine on her hip.

"Christmas gets earlier every year," whispered Cheddar George as the woman got somewhat carried away during the second chorus and bashed her tambourine so hard, it shattered, showering the judges in the front row.

Sadly for the woman, this meant her Christmas started and ended early and the contest was over. The three judges brushed tambourine shrapnel off their laps and huddled together to discuss who'd won. After a lot of nodding, Amanda Nelson went on stage (still clutching her bottle of drink as if her life depended on it) and declared the winner to be Monty the Pug.

"Glad that's over," huffed Duncan Mackay and he marched from the tent ready to shout at anyone he fond dropping litter on his field.

Amanda Nelson presented Sophie with a certificate and a tiny silver cup, left over from the tug of war competition the year before, which no longer took place because the Freshwater rugby team were accused of cheating by Duncan Mackay (so they'd locked him in a portable toilet until it went dark).

Everyone clapped politely and then as the tent

emptied, Lottie put her bagpipes in the sidecar and joined the short queue for Amanda Nelson's autograph.

Cheddar George climbed onto his Oldie TT and winced again at the tightness of his lederhosen.

The Reverend Mullard walked over to them. "A very entertaining performance, sir. I always say you should sing while the sun shines."

"Thank you muchly. And I always say the Lord wouldn't have given me maracas if he didn't want me to shake them. But I'll have to buy some stronger Dent-a-fix for next year. Tash-hag suns out gums out," said Cheddar George.

"I thought you were super, but the other judges voted for the dog. We are, after all, a nation of animal lovers and it goes to show the Lord moves in mysterious ways," said Reverend Mullard.

"Ah well. There's always Glastonbury," said Cheddar George.

"I look forward to seeing you again," said Reverend Mullard.

Cheddar George tapped Lottie on her shoulder. "I've got a one-way ticket to tasty town at Edna Biddle's tent for a cuppa and slice of her famous lemon drizzle. See you there."

"OK. I won't be long. Can you get me a hot choc and two?" asked Lottie, handing her paper and pen to Amanda Nelson.

"The youngsters love to keep us on our toes," said Reverend Mullard.

"Indeed. Of which I only have nine," said Cheddar George.

"Nine toes. Bless you. That's good to know," said Reverend Mullard.

Confused, Cheddar George frowned and rummaged in his wicker basket for a butterscotch sweet and didn't notice the Reverend Mullard open his leather bound bible. Inside was a small black box the size of a mobile phone.

He hit the 'POWER ON' button. A green LED sparkled on the RC-3 beneath Cheddar George's seat and 'UNIT READY' flashed on the screen in the vicar's sweaty hand.

"Tea and lemon drizzle will have to wait I'm afraid," the vicar smirked and jabbed a red button on the remote control to activate the RC-3.

"Why is that?" asked Cheddar George, popping a sweet in his mouth.

"You'll see," said Reverend Mullard. "Godspeed!"

The RC-3 suddenly kicked in, boosting the voltage of the scooter's battery and immediately, the Oldie TT zoomed off.

CHAPTER 14 – I'M STILL STANDING.

"My old boots. What's happening?" shrieked Cheddar George, struggling to turn the handlebars or pull the Oldie TT's brake lever.

The Reverend Mullard chuckled and followed the scooter, carefully controlling the RC-3 via the remote control hidden in his bible.

Suddenly, at the cardboard sign advertising Edna Biddle's Afternoon Tea, the Oldie TT veered left, heading down a muddy lane and the Reverend flicked a switch on the remote and the scooter's speed doubled.

"G-G-G-Good grief!" said Cheddar George. As he bounced over tyre tracks made by Duncan Mackay's tractor, his knee accidentally hit the 'HOME' button on the Route Master sat nav and a loud voice added to the mayhem. "In two hundred yards, turn left onto the A316 towards Alum Bay."

"Listen, my dear. Can you tell me how to steer this thing?" Cheddar George shouted into the speaker of the sat nav while still struggling to straighten the handlebars. The Oldie TT then veered right, behind the coconut shy and headed for the car park. The Reverend

Mullard followed – walking at a speed that wouldn't draw any attention but keeping the Oldie TT within sight.

"In one hundred yards, turn right onto the B3128 towards Freshwater," bellowed the sat nav.

"Sorry, love. I can't. I need to find out how to stop this blooming thing? It's a… a Ranger 200EV. Can you gargle it?" shouted Cheddar George.

*

Sophie Noble-Nutall sat on the grass by the Golden Arrow darts stall with a group of girls, bragging about her performance in 'The Bay's Got Talent'. She flaunted her tiny winner's cup, unaware that behind her, Monty the Pug was scraping his bum across the grass to satisfy an itch.

Nanny Vera was also there, having a go at throwing three darts to pop a small balloon and win a fluffy tortoise. She'd missed by a mile with her first two darts, but the third was a fluke and somehow a direct hit. However, the noise of the balloon bursting caused Monty the cheerleading Pug to panic once again. He stopped dragging his rear-end through a clump of daisies and fled, squealing like a piglet and yanking the lead from Sophie Noble-Nuttall's hand.

The startled Pug then leapt a row of straw bales into the area where Patsy Henderson was giving rides on her pony, Jim-karna.

"Monty! Come here," bellowed Sophie, grabbing the silver cup out of a girl's hand and racing after her scampering dog (which moved surprising fast for a podgy Pug in a cheerleader's outfit).

But Monty was having none of it. He squealed again and darted between Jim-karna's hind legs, startling the old horse.

Jim-karna's eyes widened and his nostril flared as he let out a strange gurgling noise. A second later, a pint of snot flew from the horse's nose, showering Monty and then Jim-karna bolted – jumping the straw bales and crashing into Maddie Mainard in her vicar's disguise. Maddie went down like a sack of potatoes and the remote control fell from the bible on the ground next to her and was crushed by Jim-karna's large front hoof.

*

"WAAAAAHHH!" shouted Cheddar George, as the out-of-control Oldie TT tore through yards of red, white and blue bunting (left over from the Royal Wedding) and then crashed through a prickly hedge.

"In one hundred yards, bear right," said the voice from the sat nav.

"Not now, love!" screeched Cheddar George, ducking his head to avoid cracking it on a low branch.

Suddenly Spike flew from Casey in the wicker basket and circled Cheddar George as he fought with the scooter's jammed steering.

"It's got a blooming mind of its own!" shouted Cheddar George with one hand holding onto his Bavarian hat.

Spike swooped under the seat and discovered the RC-3. He snipped a red wire, hoping to disable the device, but it was the wrong wire and made the Oldie TT go even faster, bumping across a field of cabbages.

"S-S-S-S-STOP!" shrieked Cheddar George.

*

Maddie's eyes fluttered open and the first thing she saw was Lottie, Grandad Frank and Nanny Vera staring down at her. Concerned looks etched their faces.

"Keep still. An ambulance is coming, Vicar," said Grandad Frank.

Maddie sat up and quickly checked her disguise. Luckily for her, the wig, black cassock and dog collar were still in place.

"You've got a nasty bump on your head, vicar. You should put some vinegar on it to bring the bruise out," said Nanny Vera, trying to dab a lump the size of a golf ball on Maddie's forehead with her spit-wash hankie.

"I'm fine. Bless you all," said Maddie, pushing Nanny Vera's hand away and picking up the shattered pieces of the remote control as she slowly sat up.

"I have to go… I've got to get ready for the Evensong service at St Michael's."

Grandad Frank helped Maddie to stand and handed her the bible. "You don't look well at all, Vicar."

"I'll be fine," said Maddie, her eyes scanning the fields around them for Cheddar George and the Oldie TT. "Thank you and bless you all."

Maddie staggered away, still dazed and trying to work out what to do to complete her mission. Sophie Noble-Nutall ran passed her chasing snotty Monty, heading for Mr Whipster's ice cream van while Patsy Henderson finally caught Jim-karna by the lucky dip, where he'd stopped for a massive nervous poo.

*

Cheddar George was still battling to gain control of

his troublesome scooter, yanking the brake lever as hard as he could, but it was no use. The Oldie TT was now totally out of control. It tore across a muddy ditch, demolished a picket fence and hurtled into another field containing Duncan Mackay's prized bull.

"Gordon Bennett," said Cheddar George as the Oldie TT headed at speed straight for the huge animal. It stopped munching grass and looked *very* annoyed at being rudely interrupted by an orange Bavarian clinging on for dear like to a mobility scooter.

"Perform a U-turn when possible," said the voice from the Route Master sat nav.

"I wish I could, love," said Cheddar George, as the bull flared its huge nostrils and began charging across the field, straight towards the red and gold Oldie TT.

"Crikey," said Cheddar George. "That's not good."

Suddenly, Rula flew under the front of the scooter and lifted the front wheels off the ground.

"WAAAAAHHH!" shouted Cheddar George again, as his seat tipped back, and he found himself staring up at the cloudless sky.

With the front wheels no longer touching the ground, Rula could now steer the Oldie TT, turning it back the way they'd come. Cheddar George could feel the ground shaking just behind his scooter as the bull thundered after him at full speed, getting closer every second.

Penny flew behind Cheddar George's shoulders and coloured the back of his hat bright red. Ledley whisked the hat from Cheddar George's head and wafted it in front of the bull's angry eyes. The brave pencil flew away from the Oldie TT and the enraged bull followed the painted hat.

"My old boots. That was close," said Cheddar George, looking back over his shoulder at the bull, charging around the field chasing Ledley and the Bavarian headgear.

"Perform a U-turn when possible," said the Route Master.

"Agreed indeed, love. Cheesy does it," said a very relieved Cheddar George.

Rula steered the scooter back through the gap in the picket fence and finally Spike managed to snip the correct wires and totally disable the RC-3.

Rula gently lowered the front wheels to the ground and Cheddar George rolled to a halt and let out a deep sigh.

"By jimminee. I'm all for adventure before dementia, but *that* was a little extreme!"

While Cheddar George ate half his emergency cheese sandwich, Rula and Spike quickly repaired the fence before the bull escaped from its field. Ledley fluttered over the hedge and dropped the Bavarian hat back in place.

"Tickety-boo," said Cheddar George and then patted the brim of the hat and pointed at his feet. "Up here for bullfighting, down there for dancing."

*

Maddie ducked into the first-aid tent where Miss Black, the local scout leader, was smearing butter on a boy's ears in an attempt to remove a wooden hoopla ring, which he'd foolishly slipped over his head and was now firmly stuck below his earlobes.

"Keep still, Josh," ordered Miss Black, slapping another handful of butter on the boy's sore ears with more force than was probably required.

Unseen by Miss Black and 'Butter nut Josh' (who was busy picking his nose and eating it), Maddie removed the vicar's fake teeth and pulled off the dog collar and cassock. Underneath, she wore a plain blue shirt and jeans. She quickly swapped her wig for a baseball cap and a pair of sunglasses. The vicar's outfit was shoved in her duffle bag she'd hidden under a table earlier, and then Maddie left the tent.

"Where are you, George Hardwick?" Maddie muttered, rubbing the huge lump on her forehead, still hopeful of a chance of collecting her target today.

She hurried unnoticed past Lottie, Grandad Frank and Nanny Vera, who'd just won a bottle of Hot To Trot chili sauce on yet another lucky dip stall.

Duncan Mackay's gravelly voice suddenly bellowed over the public address system.

"The final of the wellie throwing contest will start in two minutes in the main arena. And make sure you take *all* your wellies home afterwards, as I have to pay for the ruddy bins to be emptied."

Maddie rushed around the field, searching every tent and stall, but there was no sign of her target.

"I can't fail again," she muttered, knowing Sir Charles Oakley would be livid if she didn't take Cheddar George to the prison ship that night.

Then Maddie spotted her target, trundling back across the field towards Lottie, Nanny Vera and

Grandad Frank, calling and waving frantically.

"Here comes Tango Tim," said Grandad Frank.

Maddie scurried away – furious she'd failed for a second time. In the car park, she drove off in a white van she'd stolen from outside Ventnor train station earlier in the day.

*

"Did you get some lemon drizzle cake?" Lottie asked.

"No, Lottie. And you'll be flabbergasted when I tell you *what* just happened!"

Cheddar George told his amazing story and then pulled the RC-3 from his wicker basket.

"Wow! What is *that*?" asked Lottie.

"Tash-hag trouble!" replied Cheddar George.

Grandad Frank decided it best to call the police. When Detective Inspector Sergeant-Constable arrived, he met them in the first aid tent where 'Butter nut Josh' was just on his way to casualty to have the hoopla ring removed.

Cheddar George sipped sweet tea from a paper cup and munched more of his emergency cheese sandwich to calm his nerves.

Detective Inspector Sergeant-Constable sat on a straw bail, notebook in hand. "More trouble, Lottie?"

"A vicar tried to kidnap Cheddar George," said Lottie.

"He nobbled my Oldie TT," said Cheddar George, pointing at the RC-3 in his wicker basket as his other trembling hand slopped tea down his lederhosen.

"Can you describe this vicar?" asked the Detective

Inspector, licking the end of his pencil and opening his notebook to a blank page.

"I got his autograph. His name was Maurice Mullard and he was… vicarish," said Lottie.

"Anything else," said Detective Inspector Sergeant-Constable, writing the vicar's name in his notebook.

"He was about five foot eight, slim and in his mid-fifties," said Grandad Frank.

"No, Frank. He was shorter and older. And did you notice his breath when you picked him? It smelled like the fish counter at Verdi's," said Nanny Vera.

"He was knocked out by Jim-karna," said Lottie.

The policeman raised an eyebrow. "I'll need to get a statement from Mr Karna. He might have got a good look at this vicar."

"That might be difficult. Unless you can speak 'Ponyish'," said Grandad Frank.

"Ah. Anything else," sighed the Detective Inspector.

"Nice teeth, but angry eyebrows," said Cheddar George, sipping his tea.

"And he had a tattoo," said Lottie.

Detective Inspector Sergeant-Constable stopped writing. "A tattoo? Where?"

"Totes. By his watch on his sleeve. I saw it when he signed my autograph book," said Lottie. "It was like… the tail of a fish."

"My old boots! That sounds *just* like the tattoo Dorothy had at the bowls club. The lady who took Gouty George."

"Are you *sure*?" asked the Detective Inspector.

"Yes. I remember it now."

"Now, Sir, this is very important. Can you think of anyone who might want to harm slash hurt you?"

"Sidney Openshaw's dad," said Cheddar George, nodding quickly.

Detective Inspector Sergeant-Constable wrote the name down in capital letters in his notebook.

"And why would that be?"

"I borrowed his car and crashed it by the Red Lion pub. It was such a hullabaloo," said Cheddar George.

"Now we're getting somewhere. And when was this?" asked Detective Inspector Sergeant-Constable.

"June… 1933," said Cheddar George, finishing his cheese sandwich and feeling much better.

Detective Inspector Sergeant-Constable sighed again and scribbled the name out. "I doubt Mr Openshaw would hold a grudge *that* long."

"Or even be alive," muttered Grandad Frank.

"Why would anyone do this?" asked Nanny Vera, tugging her spit-wash hankie from the sleeve of her beige cardigan and dabbing her eyes with a semi-clean patch.

"I'm not sure. But I intend to find out, Mrs Jenson," replied the Detective Inspector.

"Do you think someone is trying to kidnap everyone called George?" asked Lottie.

"My old boots. There's a thought," said Cheddar George.

"Should I let Georgina Atkins know at the bingo? Her husband calls her 'George'," said Nanny Vera, grabbing the Detective Inspector's arm.

"Amongst other things," muttered Grandad Frank

but then kept quiet, due to the side eye stare Nanny Vera gave him.

"You're jumping to conclusions slash assumptions," said the police inspector. "Let me run the description of the tattoo through our computers to see if that brings up anything *useful*. Stay home if you can for now and if you do leave the house slash property, make sure you're *not* alone."

Alan Barbara

CHAPTER 15 – GIME ME JUST A LITTLE MORE TIME.

Maddie sat at the back of the Coffiesta in Alum Bay facing the door to the promenade and the inviting blue-green sea beyond. She wasn't collecting pensioners today, but still wore a disguise. Today she'd dressed as a bus driver, but now regretted that decision because three pensioners had already asked her what time the one nine five bus to Newport left from outside the Post Office.

Pensioners sat at the beige tables, browsing the pages of Gardening Monthly or checking their blood pressure using the free testing equipment with the hidden microphones. A steady stream of old people waited their turn at the counter and a Cliff Richard tune from another era played gently over the stereo.

Maddie checked her watch and spooned a heap of Strawberry jam onto a Whitney-Hew-Scone that she'd treated herself to. The sweet taste was a delightful change to the Boomer's Tuna she'd eaten for months. She'd arrived early; once a Caruthers' agent, always a Caruthers' agent..

Maddie sipped her Tea-Vee-Wunda and wondered

how many of the pensioners around her she'd be asked by PCS Control to collect in the future. They were all chatting and surely, some of them were telling brave tales of wrongdoing that the PCS agents were monitoring in the office at the back.

Guz Sharma appeared from the office and started cutting a Rod-Stew-Tart into slices. He hurried over to Maddie, mumbling the secret passphrase to ensure he had it correct.

"Yo, Sister. They've Got an Awful Lot of Coffee in Brazil."

Maddie gulped her drink and gave Guz dagger eyes, not wanting to draw attention to herself. "What do you want?"

"Are ya collecting, sis?"

"None of your business," hissed Maddie.

"So you *are* collecting! Can I help? I've applied for promotion to become a Collector like you and I'm *desperate* to get crackin' and grab my first cruddy fuddy duddy. Is it that old girl over there?" asked Guz, nodding at a little old lady, sat by the door, tucking into a plate of Nat-King-Toad-In-The-Hole. "She told her friend she'd watched TV without a license for a month in the 70s. PCS are checking it out now."

"I'm not collecting," hissed Maddie.

"I bet you are, sis. When I'm promoted, I shall be known as 'Agent Zorro'. You could show me the ropes."

"Go away. You're *not* supposed to recognise me and the only rope I'll show you is one to tie you to that coffee machine," Maddie hissed, spreading more jam on her Whitney-Hew-Scone.

"I hear ya, no wuzzies. I'm stealth," Guz whispered, and he winked and began clearing cups and plates from the pensioner's table next to Maddie. They were playing Scrabble and swapping stories about how things were much better in the good old days when they still had a milkman and men wore trousers in a way that kept their underpants hidden.

The door opened and Emelia Douthwaite and Sir Charles Oakley entered. They spotted Maddie, dodged the stray Scrabble tiles on the beige carpet and sat opposite.

"Ad infinitum, et ultra," mumbled Sir Charles.

"Ad infinitum," replied Emelia and Maddie, wagging a finger as their salute.

From behind the counter, Guz Sharma recognised Sir Charles. His face was always on the news, spouting on about laws for this and that. Guz decided now would be the ideal time to introduce himself to his big boss. He straightened his Coffiesta trilby hat and rushed over to their table.

"Yo, another brother from the street. They've Got an Awful Lot of Coffee in Brazil."

"Excuse me?" said Sir Charles.

"Papa Charlie. You're the head honcho. I'm one of your gang. Part of your fam-a-lam. Agent Zorro!" he said, winking and flashing his wrist to show a new mermaid's tail tattoo (which he'd drawn himself with a felt pen). "I just gotta get a selfie with you, Papa Charlie," he squealed and ducked behind the beige sofa where Sir Charles and Emelia sat.

"Explain, do, Emelia," growled Sir Charles as Guz Sharma draped one arm around Sir Charles' shoulder and quickly took a photo with his phone.

"Agent Sharma," hissed Emelia through clenched teeth. "We have an important meeting, so if you could just do the task you were employed to do and serve food and drinks to your customers and monitor their conversations for wrongdoing, *that* would be wonderful."

"No wuzzies, Sister. I'm old news," said a disappointed Guz and he trudged back to the counter.

"Maddie, I'll come straight to the point," said Sir Charles. "You've put the cat amongst the Columbidae *again*. That's two strikes you've had at this chap…"

"George Hardwick," said Emelia.

"Yes, this George Hardwick. Does he have some kind of superpower?" asked Sir Charles, pulling his pipe from his jacket pocket and jamming it in his mouth.

Emelia tapped his elbow and pointed at a 'NO SMOKING' sign on the table.

"Puffle-huff," snapped Sir Charles and shoved his pipe back into his pocket. "I mean, Maddie. How hard can it be to grab an old codger who's *over* one hundred?"

"I had some bad luck… again," said Maddie, feeling her cheeks blush.

"We only have one more chance to nab him, otherwise he'll be the first pensioner to slip through the net with the three-strike rule. And I'm *not* having that!" barked Sir Charles. His fist thumped the table, causing a soupspoon to fly across and clatter on a table where an elderly couple had dozed off while watching a re-run of the Queen's coronation on the TV.

"I *will* take him next time. Without a doubt," said Maddie. She didn't know exactly *how* she was going to grab Cheddar George. For three days she'd been listening to the conversations in Lottie's house and all she'd heard that was the least bit interesting was the AABBCC members were planning to protest at the town hall and the Verdi supermarket were having an offer on bongos. Cheddar George was keen to buy a pair and use them to perform at the next 'The Bay's Got Talent'.

"No, Maddie. I'm going to get agent Rogers to take over the operation to collect George Hardwick and give you a rest. Take a month off," said Emelia.

"Agent Rogers? The Wicked Witch of the Vest?" shrieked Maddie.

"Yes, Maddie. Her patience and wisdom will ensure the target is collected swiftly and without a fuss," said Emelia.

"I *can* do this, Sir Charles. Trust me. Let me finish what I've started," said Maddie, seeing her dream of owning an Astronaut Roxy doll coming to an end if she didn't collect her wages for a month *and* lost her bonus payments. "I'm your best agent and guarantee George Hardwick will be collected without a problem next time."

Emelia looked at Sir Charles, who gave a reluctant nod.

"OK. Maddie. One last chance," said Emelia.

"But if you fail then we'll have to let you go. You'll

be fired from the PCS," said Sir Charles. "After all, I have the reputation of the *entire* department to consider."

"Understood," said Maddie.

"Good," said Sir Charles as he stood. "I will expect this George Hardwick fellow to be collected by the end of the week. Ad infinitum, et ultra."

More finger wagging and Latin mumbling occurred and then Emelia followed Sir Charles through the exit. As soon as they were outside, Sir Charles lit his pipe, creating a cloud of acrid smoke.

Maddie finished her cup of Tea-Vee-Wunda, put on her bus driver's coat and walked towards the door. She'd need to come up with a devious plan to capture her target. And quick.

"Excuse me," said an elderly lady who sat on a beige seat taking her blood pressure, "what bus do I need to take me to the Haven Garden Centre?"

"The number 28, my dear", said Maddie (who hadn't a clue).

Suddenly Nanny Vera and Grandad Frank came through the smoke cloud at the entrance.

"Find a table, Vera, love and I'll get the froth," said Grandad Frank.

Maddie darted between two tables of pensioners who were knitting bobble hats and disappeared behind the counter where Guz Sharma was wiping a filthy cloth over the pipes on the espresso coffee machine.

"Act normal and just serve the old guy," hissed Maddie, as she ducked and hid below the coffee machine.

"I'll have a Gerry-Raffer-Tea and a Milk-Jagger, please," said Grandad Frank.

"No wuzzies. How about a nice piece of John-Lennon-Drizzle-Cake? We have a bangin' offer today where you get free cod liver oil with any slice," said Guz.

"No thanks. I took my daily cod liver oil this morning," said Grandad Frank. "Or did I?"

Guz made the hot drinks (without making too much mess) and added a couple of Lion-All-Richtea-Biscuits on the tray for free. "Enjoy your guzzles."

Grandad Frank paid, picked up the tray and headed for the table by the bingo equipment where Nanny Vera sat. Maddie grabbed Guz Sharma's hand and dragged him into the office.

"I need to listen to the chat from that old guy's table. They might give me an idea how to nab a target I'm after."

"No wuzzies! The old birds on table 17 are about to sing to ya," said Guz. "This is so bangin'. Shall I—"

"NOW!" Maddie barked.

"OK, Sis, stay cool."

Guz Sharma clicked a few buttons on his computer and Nanny Vera's voice crackled from the hidden microphone in the blood pressure monitor on table 17.

"Harry Sniff's over there. I haven't seen him at the Burlington bingo for a while, said Nanny Vera," dunking an oval biscuit into her Gerry-Raffer-Tea.

'Smith' was Harry's proper surname, but he did an annoying and disgusting snorty-sniff every few seconds, which is why Nanny Vera tried to avoid sitting with

155

him at the bingo.

"Nosey Rosie Saunders told me he'd won the lottery and moved to Abergavenny in Wales. Just goes to show how wrong she can be," chuckled Grandad Frank and stirred his Milk-Jagger. "Is Lottie going to the club today?"

"Club? What club?" muttered Maddie, hardly daring to breathe.

"No," Nanny Vera replied, "everything is ready for the grand opening. I'll be cooking my famous canapés for all the VIPs going to the opening night."

"That should be eventful!" said Grandad Frank.

"*Come on*... tell me what club?" muttered Maddie, straining to hear every word from table 17.

Nanny Vera gave a friendly wave to Harry Sniff as he headed for the door. She could still hear him snorty-sniffing above the Vera Lynn song playing and wondered if he'd ever actually owned a hankie. "I do hope that after all their hard work the club is a success for SooTed and BooTed."

"I'm sure the Trocadero will be the talk of the town," said Grandad Frank.

"Trocadero?" muttered Maddie.

"Sis, that's the old Pavilion Theatre. Hun-percent!" Guz Sharma blurted.

"QUIET!" hissed Maddie.

"Amanda Nelson is going there tomorrow afternoon to do a news report about it reopening. Lottie's going to watch with Cheddar George," said Nanny Vera.

Grandad Frank looked concerned. "Hope he doesn't give himself another burnt waffle spray tan!"

Guz could hardly contain his excitement. "Amanda Nelson! She's that news reporter, sis."

"That's correct," muttered Maddie. "Tomorrow, old George Hardwick will be *right* under my nose!"

Alan Barbara

CHAPTER 16 – IT'S NOW OR NEVER.

In the basement of SooTed and BooTed's nearly restored Trocadero, Maddie Mainard finished applying Hush-Lush No.9 foundation to her face and tucked a strand of her hair beneath a long chestnut wig. She slipped on the jacket of a light grey suit (making sure the sleeve covered the tattoo near her wrist) and added a matching belt with a gold buckle. It had taken her four hours to complete her disguise. She stood and admired her reflection in the mirror.

"What do you think?" Maddie asked, pulling back a thick curtain. Her eyes met the terrified stare of Amanda Nelson, sitting in a chair wearing identical clothing. She had her hands and feet bound with a thin rope, expertly tied in a reef knot by Maddie. Amanda didn't reply; a dirty sock stuffed in her mouth wouldn't allow it.

"Just sit still, Amanda, and everything will be fine," said Maddie, zipping up a red shoulder bag.

All Amanda Nelson could do was let out a muffled yelp.

Maddie's disguise was perfect. She'd become Amanda Nelson's spitting image and after spending all

159

night watching recordings of Amanda's Spotlight Isle of Wight news reports, she'd also mastered her voice, her walk and everything else about the petrified woman tied to the chair before her. Caruthers would be impressed.

"I think it's my best disguise yet, to be honest," said Maddie, her voice sounding just like Amanda Nelson's. Using the phrase 'to be honest' at the end of a sentence was something Amanda did a lot and Maddie had picked up on that. Now was the time to put it all into practice for strike three of her Distract and Snatch of her target.

"See you later, Amanda. Don't wait up," said Maddie and she sneaked out the basement through her secret tunnel at the back and around to the front of the theatre. She walked boldly up the steps into the foyer.

"Kalispera, Miss Nelson," said Cheddar George.

"Ah, the bronzed yodeller and the bagpipe player! Kalispera, to you as well. It's lovely to see you again, to be honest. I heard about the *terrible* trouble at the summer fete," said Maddie in her very best Amanda voice.

"Yes, it was most odd. But exciting none the less," replied Cheddar George.

"He wants to try sky diving next," said Lottie, sitting behind the box office counter, doodling on a post-it note.

"Agreed indeed. Tash-hag adventure before dementia," said Cheddar George. "Although I'd definitely leave my teeth at home for that. Nothing dentured, nothing gained."

"Good for you, to be honest," said Maddie.

SooTed and BooTed appeared from a corridor that led to the dressing rooms. They both wore their fluorescent jackets, black drainpipe trousers and creeper boots.

"You two look great. I love the outfits," said Maddie, shaking hands with the two men.

"Happy-as. Where would you like to do the interview, Miss Nelson," said SooTed.

"Why don't we film it here in the box office. It has a certain charm to be honest," Maddie said.

"Right-as," said SooTed and cleared a pile of advertising leaflets from a leather couch.

Maddie pulled a small video camera from her red shoulder bag. "I'm afraid my cameraman called in sick at the last minute so if one of you could do the filming that would be super."

"Lottie should do it," said Cheddar George. "With my shaky hands it would look like you're reporting from the scene of an earthquake!"

"Excellent," said Maddie, handing the camera over. "Just point and press."

"Wickedoolie," Lottie said, staring into the tiny screen.

SooTed and BooTed sat on the empty couch with Maddie, while Lottie pointed the camera and practiced pressing the buttons to zoom in and out. Cheddar George trundled off in his Oldie TT to make builder's tea for everyone.

"Ready, Lottie?" Maddie asked.

"Totes," said Lottie and she pressed the 'RECORD' button and a red LED lit up on the front of the camera.

Maddie looked into the camera lens and smiled.

"Take one… In three… two… one… I'm at the old Pavilion Theatre in Alum Bay with its new owners, Thaddeus and Edward, or SooTed and BooTed as they like to be known. They've restored the theatre to its former glory, and it will open again soon," said Maddie. "SooTed, can you tell me why you bought this old theatre?"

"Happy-as. We've wanted to open our own Rock 'n' Roll club for years and in the summer when we saw the Pavilion, we knew it would be the perfect place."

"And the music you'll be singing every night is from the 1950s?" asked Amanda.

"That's right. We are huge Showaddywaddy fans and in our act, we sing all their hits and others from the rock 'n' roll greats like Elvis and Buddy Holly," said SooTed, grinning like a Cheshire cat into the camera in Lottie's hand.

"And BooTed, you've renamed the theatre?" Maddie asked.

"Yes," said BooTed. We're calling it the Trocadero, which is the title of a Showaddywaddy song."

"Wonderful. And when is your opening night?"

"Saturday the 18th of October, Amanda That gives us ten days to finish everything and we'll be live on stage at eight. Excited-as," said SooTed.

"And I'm sure there will be plenty of people here on that day to have a super time, to be honest," said Maddie. "This is Amanda Nelson at the new Trocadero club in Alum Bay, reporting for… Isle of Wight Spotlight… and CUT."

BooTed looked confused "You mean 'Spotlight Isle

162

of Wight'."

"What? Oh yes. Silly me! I'm always getting that bit wrong," Maddie said, annoyed with herself for making such a stupid mistake. "I'll do that last bit again later at the BBC news studio."

"Happy-as," said SooTed.

"When will it be shown on TV?" asked BooTed.

"Tomorrow evening at seven," said Maddie, as Cheddar George returned with a tray of mugs, all only half full of strong tea.

"Who would have thought we'd be on the tele, mate?" asked SooTed, picking up his mug of tea.

Maddie took a blue pen and a small notebook with 'BBC' printed across the cover. "I just need to ask you a few questions to get some more details from you."

"Happy-as," said SooTed and as he took a sip of his tea, Maddie grinned and clicked the top of the pen with her thumb.

CRASH

"Crikey!" said SooTed, suddenly jumping from the couch and looking up at the ceiling above the box office.

"Something's happened up in the gantry," said BooTed, also on his feet in a flash.

"That's awful," said Maddie, offering her well-practiced 'deeply worried expression'.

But Maddie Mainard knew *exactly* what had happened, because she'd planned it. Earlier in the day when the theatre was empty, she'd hidden an ADD in one of the old wooden crates in the corner of the loft above the box office. The Audible Distraction Device was the latest gadget she'd ordered from the lab at the PCS. A powerful loudspeaker, hidden in the spine of a book, had been triggered by the tiny remote control in the tip of her pen.

When she hid it earlier, Maddie had chosen 'Sledgehammer smashing wood' from the list of available noises the ADD could play, and she was delighted it now had the desired effect.

"We'd better go and check it out, mate. Soon-as," said SooTed. "In case it's the blooming rats chewing the new electrics again."

"Nik-nacks! I'll come as well," said Lottie, quickly handing the video camera back to Maddie and grabbing Casey.

"Tickety-boo. I'll look after Amanda until you get back," said Cheddar George.

"Ok. We won't be long," said SooTed, rushing with BooTed and Lottie down the corridor to the stairs that led to the gantry above the box office.

Maddie smiled at Cheddar George and slipped the pen and notebook back in her handbag. "I hope it's nothing serious."

"Agreed indeed. The lads don't want any surprises this close to opening night," said Cheddar George. "Have you ever filmed a news report about a yodelling pensioner?"

Maddie popped the camera in her handbag. "Sadly not, but I'll ask my producer. This is a fabulous place isn't it. Last year I interviewed a Professor van de Dudok for Spotlight Isle of Wight. He was a local historian and knew all about this old building."

"I missed that news report, Amanda. Must have been doing my hair. I bet this place could tell many a tale. I'm 90-11 and it's been here for as long as I can remember," said Cheddar George.

"Professor van de Dudok told me it was once owned by Lady Prudence Bagerstock who also owned Datchet Manor on the way to Carisbrooke Castle."

"I went to a party at Lady Pru-Bag's once," said Cheddar George. "Very thick carpets."

"Really! And Professor van de Dudok said during the second world war, Lady Bagerstock was *convinced* the Germans would invade the island and steal everything valuable, so she hid her famous painting behind a false wall in the basement of this very building. And poor Lady Bagerstock died just after the war and never told a soul where she'd hid it, so it *must* still be here, to be honest," said Maddie.

"Blimey," said Cheddar George, shifting on the seat of his Oldie TT onto one bum cheek to let another 'Tommy' out of prison. "Parpon me."

Maddie wafted a hand to clear the air. "It's a Lombardi!"

"Isn't that a dance?" asked Cheddar George.

"And the thing is, Lady Bagerstock had no relatives, so whoever finds the painting can keep it. It's valued at just over a *million* pounds. Wouldn't it be wonderful if we found Alberto Lombardi's painting tonight? Think of all the publicity for the new club."

"Tickety-boo," said Cheddar George.

"If you and I found it, SooTed and BooTed could claim the painting and I'd get a fantastic news story for

Spotlight Isle of Wight, to be honest," said Maddie, making sure she got the name of the TV show correct this time.

Cheddar George tapped his yellow fedora hat and pointed at his feet.

"Up here for treasure hunting, down there for dancing. Let's take a shuftie, Amanda. There's an old service lift next to the dressing rooms."

"Excellent! I'm sure we can find the lost masterpiece today," said Maddie.

"Agreed indeed. Strike while the iron's lukewarm, I say," said Cheddar George and wrote 'GONE TO BASEMENT WITH AMANDA. SEARCHING FOR OLD PAINTING' on a post-it note and stuck it on the box office counter.

"This way," said Cheddar George and he set off, trundling towards the lift in his Oldie TT with Maddie hurrying behind.

Cheddar George poked the button and the lift door slid open. "All aboard."

The service lift took them down to the gloomy basement. It was a dark windowless maze of corridors and storerooms, full of theatrical junk and lit by just a few old lamps dangling from the tall ceiling. Maddie allowed herself a wicked grin. She knew every inch of this place and it was now time to spring the trap and finally collect George Hardwick *and* get her important bonus payment.

CHAPTER 17 – DON'T STOP ME NOW.

"Professor van de Dudok told me the Lombardi *could* be in one of these storerooms, to be honest. Shall we start with this one?" asked Maddie, pointing at a battered door to her left marked 'STOREROOM 7'.

"Tickety-boo. Lead on Macduff," said Cheddar George and he trundled his Oldie TT after Maddie through the door.

"Try to find a false panel in the wall," said Maddie, making sure the door stayed open.

"This is just like an old episode of Murder By The Book," said Cheddar George, tapping the wall by the door and slowly making his way further along the wall. "This is all solid brick, Amanda."

"Keep going. It's got to be here somewhere, to be honest," called Maddie, pretending to search a large cupboard while watching Cheddar George like a hawk out the corner of her eye.

Cheddar George slowly made his way around the room, tapping and hum-yodelling the theme tune to Murder By The Book. As he reached down and tapped the wall near his foot the sound changed from a solid

THUD to a light DONK.

"This sounds different," he called.

Maddie hurried over as he tapped the wall again with his wrinkled knuckle.

"My old boots. What do you think?" asked Cheddar George. "I'm sure that's hollow. What do we do now?"

Maddie grinned. "Well done, George. See if there is a hammer in that box over there I can use to smash the wall," she said, pointing to a rusty toolbox perched on a workbench at the far end of the gloomy storeroom.

"Tickety-boo," said Cheddar George. "This is rather exciting, don't you think?"

He flicked a light switch above a shelf with boxes full of old makeup, but it did nothing. Maddie had seen to that earlier and she watched closely, biting her lip as Cheddar George stopped his Oldie TT by the workbench. As he peered in the toolbox, he didn't notice Maddie sneak up behind him in the shadows and smear superglue on the scooter's handlebars. The first stage of her Distract and Snatch operation.

"No luck, Amanda. I'm afraid it's empty," said Cheddar George. His wrinkly fingers gripped the handlebars to turn the Oldie TT around and as he did so, Maddie pounced and plunged an old cloth sack over his head. The Snatch was on.

"Good grief," squealed Cheddar George, unable to free his hands to remove the sack. He shook his head, trying to throw off the dusty sack and his hearing aid came lose and fell on the floor.

"Got you… *at last*," muttered Maddie.

"What? What are you doing, Amanda? My hands…"

But Maddie ignored Cheddar George's startled cry and sat on his lap, stamping on his foot to work the power pedal. The Oldie TT shot forward, its front wheel crushing Cheddar George's hearing aid as Maddie rode through the storeroom door and down a dark corridor. The wheels of the Oldie TT left tyre tracks in the dust as Maddie headed through the maze of twists and turns and darkness of the basement.

"My old boots! You can have the Lumbago painting… I won't say anything! Please. Just let me go!" shouted Cheddar George from under the sack.

"You've been nothing but trouble from the start, George Hardwick," shouted Maddie, weaving the Oldie TT through the corridors as fast as she could. "But you're mine now. Third time lucky!"

"Bird wine yucky? What do you mean?" asked Cheddar George, struggling to hear Maddie's voice without his hearing aid.

The Oldie TT zoomed down a ramp and veered left into the Props Department, almost tipping over. Maddie forced Cheddar George's hands to steer between two mannequins dressed as Queen Victoria and Price Albert and then she reached out and grabbed the handle of a wooden mop leaning against a wall. She swung the mop above her head and bashed a lever on the ceiling. An old oak wardrobe door at the end of the corridor sprung open.

TheOldie TT hurtled into and through the wardrobe which led to Maddie's hide-out.

"We're home already, George," she said and pulled a rope hanging down the wall without stopping the scooter. The wardrobe door clattered shut behind them and a row of old dusty costumes dropped to hang from a clothes rail, hiding a secret panel at the back of the wardrobe.

Maddie braked hard and the Oldie TT screeched to a halt. She leapt from Cheddar George's lap.

"Let me go, Amanda. I've got bingo tomorrow!" shrieked Cheddar George. "The painting is all yours," he pleaded.

"There is no painting, George. You're the treasure. The *hidden* treasure," said Maddie and quickly unlocked the door to the beer cellar and shoved Cheddar George, confused and still glued to his Oldie TT into the darkness.

"What? Where are we?" asked Cheddar George.

"Where *nobody* can find you," Maddie hissed into his ear and removed his right shoe and sock.

"Four toes. Perfect," said Maddie and yanked the cloth sack from his head.

A terrified Cheddar George looked into Maddie's eyes.

"Why have you done this, Amanda? I'm an old man of 90-11 with only a few bob to my name, not some rich millionaire!"

"I know *exactly* who you are," said Maddie, her sinister voice echoing round the beer cellar. "You're my next big fat bonus."

"Bonus… I… I don't understand?" cried Cheddar George, struggling to free his hands from the handlebars, but it was useless, they were stuck fast.

Maddie stuck a strip of Gaffa tape across Cheddar

George's mouth and left him in the dark and damp cellar, slamming the door on her way out. If he'd still had his hearing aid, he would have heard the key turning in a lock and Maddie giggling as she walked away.

CHAPTER 18 – I SAW HER STANDING THERE.

Lottie sat on the leather couch in the box office, drinking a mug of hot choc and two.

SooTed flopped into the seat next to her and popped a boiled sweet into his mouth, relieved there were no sign of rats in the gantry above.

"That was fun" he said, offering the packet of sweets around and grabbing his half mug of Cheddar George's builder's tea which was now only lukewarm.

"What was fun?" asked Nanny Vera. She'd popped in with Grandad Frank on their way back from the Verdi supermarket, where they'd bought a new shredder for all their unwanted paperwork and the bongos for Cheddar George. Grandad Frank was looking forward to Cheddar George dressing as an African tribesman and bashing out a tune with Lottie at next September's 'The Bay's Got Talent'.

"The interview with Amanda Nelson. It was amazeball. She let me be in charge of the camera," said Lottie, taking a blackcurrant sweet from SooTed's packet.

173

"We'll be on the tele tomorrow evening," said SooTed.

"Lovely. We'll have to find a tape and video it," said Nanny Vera.

"Where's Cheddar George?" BooTed asked, swigging his tea.

"No doubt causing trouble somewhere," chuckled Grandad Frank.

Lottie picked up the post-it she'd found on the box office counter. "He left this note. 'Gone to basement with Amanda. Searching for old painting," she said, handing the yellow square of paper to Nanny Vera.

"Well, I hope he's behaving himself and not letting 'Tommy out of prison'. What on earth would that young lady think?" asked Nanny Vera.

"We're ready to lock up and get some shuteye. Someone better go and grab them," yawned BooTed.

"Come on, Vera. Let's go and get 'Windiana Jones and the raider of the lost art'," said Grandad Frank.

"I hope it won't be full of spiders down there," said Nanny Vera.

"Unlikely," said Grandad Frank. "The rats will have eaten all o them."

"Don't worry. I'll ask the BREW Crew to go," Lottie said, opening the zip on Casey's back.

The Duke and Paddy rose from Casey.

"Spot of griffin?"

"It's home time and we need to tell Cheddar George and Amanda Nelson. They're down in the basement."

"We'll locate them and get a message to CG."

"Don't let Amanda see you. She'll make you

174

tomorrow night's news report," said Grandad Frank.

"Roger that."

Spike zoomed from Casey, dropped to the floor, morphed into a half inch spanner and removed six bolts from an air conditioning vent by Lottie's feet. He disappeared inside and the Duke followed.

A minute later, the sheet of Paddy paper danced in front of Lottie's eyes.

"Sitrep. We have a situation."

"What is it?" Lottie asked.

"Foul play suspected in the basement. Targets have completely vanished."

"Vanished? How?" cried Lottie.

*

SooTed knelt in the doorway of Storeroom seven and picked up the pieces of Cheddar George's shattered hearing aid. "This doesn't look promising."

"Where are they?" asked Lottie, a tear running down her cheek as her eyes followed the dusty tyre tracks down the gloomy corridor.

"Perhaps he dropped it without knowing," said BooTed in a hopeful voice.

Nanny Vera took her spit-wash hankie from her sleeve and dabbed her eyes. "He could be anywhere down here. What was he thinking?"

"Don't worry, Vera. We'll find him," said Grandad Frank, giving Nanny Vera a hug.

SooTed had his phone in his hand. "Suspicious-as. Shall I call the cops?"

Grandad Frank nodded and both Nanny Vera and Lottie burst into tears.

Three minutes later Detective Inspector Sergeant-Constable's car screeched to a halt outside the Trocadero followed by a police van. Eight police officers climbed from the van and huddled on the steps around their DI.

"Right. Listen up. We're looking for two people. An elderly gentlemen named George Hardwick slash Cheddar George. He's wearing a blue shirt, red waistcoat, green trousers, a pink cravat and a yellow fedora hat. He was last seen heading down to the basement with a woman slash female news reporter called Amanda Nelson who's in her late thirties with brown hair and wearing a grey suit. We need to locate them ASAP. There are no photos yet, but we do have this artist's sketch slash drawing of them."

Detective Inspector Sergeant-Constable handed out sheets of Paddy paper showing Cheddar George and Amanda Nelson's portraits, which Ledley and Penny had quickly drawn.

"Nobody is to leave the building until we've found them both. Any questions?"

"Amanda Nelson? Is she the reporter from Spotlight Isle of Wight, Sir?" asked a woman police officer.

"Correct," said the DI. "From what I understand slash know, Amanda Nelson told George Hardwick a tale about a painting hidden in the basement of this theatre, and they went searching for it. But after what happened at the bowls club and the fete, I suspect she led him down there for another reason. Let's find them and see what she's up to. Stay alert – we don't know what we're dealing with."

The police officers hurried up the steps and through the foyer to begin their careful search of the Trocadero.

Lottie sat on the couch in the box office, sniffing teary snot. SooTed sat with her, not knowing what to say. BooTed, Nanny Vera and Grandad Frank were driving around the streets near the Trocadero, searching for Cheddar George in SooTed's Hudson Hornet car.

Detective Inspector Sergeant-Constable finished talking on his radio, pulled up a chair and sat opposite Lottie.

"We will find them. They can't have gone far."

Lottie stared at her feet, sniffed and wiped snot from her nose with the back of a hand.

The awkward silence was ended by a DING and a light going on above the lift doors.

"Happy-as. I bet this is them, Lottie," said SooTed.

"At last," said Lottie, jumping off the couch. She wanted to be ready to give Cheddar George a big hug.

Detective Inspector Sergeant-Constable put a hand on Lottie's shoulder.

"Hang on. Wait just a moment slash second."

He nodded at two officers guarding the entrance and they hurried to the lift and waited for the door to open.

Lottie wiped away more teary snot, as all eyes went to the lift door.

The door rattled open, and Amanda Nelson staggered out and fainted into the arms of the police officers.

CHAPTER 19 – THE GREAT PRETENDER.

Amanda Nelson sat on the couch in the box office. As hard as she tried, she couldn't stop her legs shaking. Detective Inspector Sergeant-Constable sat opposite, open notebook in hand. Lottie and the Duke hid under the counter, desperate to listen to Amanda's sitrep.

Detective Inspector Sergeant-Constable made eye contact with Amanda. At this point, she was a suspect and he wanted her to know it. How she reacted to his first question might tell him otherwise. "Now, Amanda. Take your time and explain to me what happened. From the very start slash beginning."

Amanda Nelson sipped a full mug of sweet tea and stared at the floor.

"I… I had a phone call… yesterday from a woman from the group called the 'AABBCC'," said Amanda, in little more than a whisper. "They are residents from Alum Bay protesting about the council changing the bin collection day. Not much of a news story, but I agreed to interview the woman and perhaps do a report for Spotlight Isle of Wight."

The policeman's gut feeling told him the Amanda Nelson quivering before him was a victim and not a suspect. "This woman slash female, did she give you her name?"

"Mildred Mullard," Amanda said and sipped her tea.

Detective Inspector Sergeant-Constable wrote the name in his notebook and underlined 'Mullard'.

"I left the TV studio about 11 and as I went to my car, someone grabbed me from behind and bundled me into a white van."

"Can you tell me what they looked like?" asked Detective Inspector Sergeant-Constable.

"I didn't get a good look, but I think it was a tall, thin woman who definitely stank of fish," replied Amanda, her voice trembling as she relived her nightmare.

Detective Inspector Sergeant-Constable wrote again in his notebook. "Tell me what happened next."

"She brought me here, tied me to a chair and put on a disguise and became me. She wore the same suit, same shoes, same... *everything*. And then she left me in the dark. I was terrified. I waited and waited for ages and then I heard her come back."

"And then what, Amanda?" asked Detective Inspector Sergeant-Constable, not breaking eye contact with the trembling key witness.

"She put a blindfold on me, and I was finally untied from the chair."

Tears streamed down Amanda's face. The

Detective Inspector passed her a tissue.

"Then what happened?" he asked, pushing Amanda for vital information.

Amanda blew her nose. "I couldn't see... so I don't know."

"Just try. Do you remember any sounds slash smells? Anything you can recall *could* be useful," said Detective Inspector Sergeant-Constable.

Amanda took a deep breath and closed her eyes. "Well, I was prodded in the backside with something sharp and I heard squeaking and a noise like a cupboard door banging, to be honest. I remember being bundled into what could have been a tiny room. Then I was pushed some more, and it felt like curtains brushing my face."

Detective Inspector Sergeant-Constable looked up from writing in his notebook. "Curtains?"

"Yes," said Amanda, nodding, "and we came out through another door into a corridor, I think. We walked some more, then the horrid woman pulled the blindfold off. I smelt her ghastly fishy breath and she whispered in my ear 'Now go' and disappeared."

"How did you find your way to the lift?" The policeman asked.

Amanda shook her head. "I don't know. I walked around for ages. It's like a maze down there."

Detective Inspector Sergeant-Constable wrote frantically. "Now think, Amanda. Did you see this woman's face at all beneath her disguise?"

"Afraid not. Just a glimpse of her hand when she took off the blindfold. There was a small tattoo."

"Of a mermaid's tail?" asked the Detective Inspector, watching Amanda Nelson very closely.

"Yes. I think it was," said Amanda. It was her time to get answers. "How do you know that? What's going on Detective Inspector? Why was I brought here and trussed up like a chicken?"

"Miss Nelson, I believe a person slash persons unknown are trying to kidnap elderly folk on the island," said Detective Inspector Sergeant-Constable.

"Kidnappings!" cried Amanda.

The Detective Inspector stood and closed his notebook.

"Exactly Miss Nelson. Thank you for the information. You've been very helpful. I'll get an officer to drive you home."

"*Home*! I'm not going home, Detective Inspector. I'm going straight to the TV studio to write my report so it's ready for the breakfast edition of Spotlight Isle of Wight," said Amanda, wiping her eyes and tying her long chestnut hair into a ponytail.

"Miss Nelson, you must *not* report this incident on television slash radio. George Hardwick slash Cheddar George has just been kidnapped and there have been other attempts on him *and* other pensioners lately. I don't want to scare slash alarm the locals."

"Cheddar George? I think I've met him before… Yes… the talent show at the summer fete, to be honest. Poor man. And you say the kidnapper has tried this before?" asked Amanda, trying to get as much information as possible for her news report that would surely be her biggest story ever.

"Yes, Miss Nelson. And I believe he slash she will kidnap more pensioners unless I stop them. I'm at a critical slash crucial point in my investigation, so I need a total news blackout until I catch whoever is doing this."

Amanda thought for a few seconds and then her eyes lit up. "How about a deal? I'll not report any of this on Spotlight Isle of Wight if you let me be there with my camera crew when you make an arrest."

Detective Inspector Sergeant-Constable considered Amanda's offer. It would mean he'd be able to investigate the case without the hundreds of reporters and TV crews who'd swarm to Alum Bay like flies around a cow-pat if this story got out.

"OK, Miss Nelson. You have a deal."

Alan Barbara

CHAPTER 20 – SIGNED, SEALED, DELIVERED.

It was dawn the following day and Lottie lay on her bed staring at the ceiling. She hadn't slept a wink all night. After searching the streets around the Trocadero until after midnight and not finding any sign of Cheddar George, SooTed and BooTed had brought Nanny Vera, Grandad Frank and Lottie home to Rose Crescent. They'd stayed, dozing on the beige sofa in the lounge.

Lottie heard voices in the kitchen. Hoping it might be someone with news of Cheddar George, she grabbed Casey and rushed downstairs.

Grandad Frank sat at the kitchen table, staring out the window and lost in his own worried thoughts.

"No news yet, darling," he said, before Lottie could ask.

Nanny Vera sat next to him with her hands cradling a mug of cold tea. Her friendly face had aged overnight. She expected a knock at the door any moment from Detective Inspector Sergeant-Constable wearing a serious face, coming to give the worst news ever. The house felt cold and had lost its sense of fun and comfort.

The waiting and not knowing, brought back the nightmare of the day Lottie's mum went missing. That was February 9th 2007, when Lottie was just six months old. For the family living at 25 Rose Crescent, it was a day they never forget.

Nanny Vera went to blow her nose on her spit-wash hankie, but it was soaked with her tears. Grandad Frank passed her a fresh tissue.

"Any update?" SooTed asked. He stood by the door leading to the garden. He looked washed out, shoulders hunched, his shirt badly creased and in need of a shower.

"Nothing," muttered Grandad Frank.

"Useless-as. I'll put the kettle on."

Lottie sat at the kitchen table, fiddling with Grandad Frank's pen he always used to do the crossword puzzle in his Daily Mail (which he never managed to finish).

A sheet of Paddy and the Duke slipped out of Casey and fluttered on the table.

"We need to go back to the Trocadero and do our own recon around the basement."

"But the police didn't find anything," said Lottie.

"Exactly. They didn't find the location where the real Amanda Nelson was tied up while the kidnapping of Cheddar George took place. That's the mish-crit area to locate and search. Amanda said she went through a tiny room and brushed some curtains before her blindfold was removed."

"But there wasn't a room like that, or *any* curtains in the basement," yawned BooTed, who'd heard the kettle boiling and come to the kitchen in search of coffee.

"What if it wasn't a tiny room?"

"Eh?" said SooTed, spooning six sugars into a mug.

"What do you get in the basement of a theatre?"

"Rats?" said Grandad Frank, looking confused.

"COSTUMES. Which might hang in a wardrobe!"

"So, you think the kidnapper is hiding in a wardrobe?" asked SooTed.

"Not IN a wardrobe, but perhaps THROUGH a wardrobe – leading to a secret hide-out. If we carry out our own search of the basement, we might find something the police missed."

SooTed switched the kettle off. "Quick-as. I'll grab the keys to the Huddy."

*

At 6.45, the lime-green Hudson Hornet rumbled into the Trocadero carpark. Lottie sat in the front next to BooTed, who parked the old car next to an empty police van. SooTed crunched on boiled sweets in the back and now had a pocket full of empty wrappers. BooTed switched off the engine and they got out.

Rain lashed down, making huge puddles and Lottie slipped Casey under her jumper to keep the BREW Crew dry. Yesterday, Heather the Weather had predicted a sunny afternoon, so Lottie had planned to ride with Cheddar George in the Oldie TT to his bowls match and check up on Gouty George (who sadly, hadn't made it on holiday to Spain). But now, all that seemed a lifetime away.

They dodged the puddles, hurrying through the rain and ran up the steps to find blue and white tape with 'CRIME-SCENE – DO NOT CROSS' strung across the entrance. A police officer sat behind the tape, sheltering from the rain. He had five empty Coffiesta takeaway cups at his feet and was looking forward to going off duty at eight and getting some sleep after a *very* long night.

"Is there any news about Cheddar George?" SooTed asked, popping another sweet in his mouth.

The police officer shook his head. "Nothing yet, I'm afraid. The broken hearing aid was sent to the lab to test for fingerprints and DNA, but we won't hear for a day or so."

"OK. Thanks, officer. We just need to grab our jackets from the dressing room to take to the dry cleaners," said SooTed, impressed with his quick thinking.

"Sorry, sir, but nobody's allowed in. The DI would have my guts for garters if I let you trample over his crime-scene."

"But we have to get them cleaned before the opening night," said BooTed.

The police officer shook his head. "Sorry. *Nobody* in or out. The Boss was very clear about that."

"Miffed-as," said SooTed, realising the police officer wasn't going to let them inside.

"Come on," said BooTed. "A wasted trip. Let's get out of this rain and go back to Lottie's."

They hurried back to the car and watched the police officer drain his cup of lukewarm Milk-All-Jackson. As BooTed slotted the key in the ignition, the Duke scribbled on a piece of Paddy and it rested on Lottie's damp lap.

"We have to get eyes inside. Sit tight while we sneak in and recon the place."

"There might be more coppers inside," said BooTed, looking up at the row of small windows above the newly restored entrance to the Trocadero.

"Unlikely. The nightwatchman is probably the only one here."

"Be careful. And don't get soaked because you know water isn't good for you," Lottie said, trying her hardest not to cry all over the Duke's writing.

"Roger that."

SooTed wound a silver handle to lower his window an inch. Spike, Rula and the Duke flew through the gap and sneaked behind a row of thick hedging which ran along the edge of the footpath leading to the club's entrance. They waited behind the thick green hedge, sheltering from the rain. The police officer appeared on the top step. He wandered back and forth, talking on his radio, then once he'd finished updating his sergeant at Alum Bay police station, he sat behind the crime-scene tape and watched the rainwater run down the steps, adding to the enormous puddles on the path.

"Oh nik-nacks. They can't get passed the policeman," said Lottie.

"Where there's a will there's a way," said SooTed and he got out of the Huddy. "Know anything about cars, mate," he called to the police officer.

The police officer looked up. "Eh? What?"

"Cars, mate. The engine won't start," shouted SooTed, standing at the front of the Huddy, with rain bouncing off the bonnet.

"What's wrong with her?" said the police officer.

"Dunno, mate," said SooTed, shrugging his enormous shoulders and lifting the bonnet.

"That's the problem with those classics," said the police officer. "I'll take a look if you want. Used to be a mechanic in Shanklin before taking the Queen's shilling and joining the force."

The police officer stepped over the crime-scene tape and jogged over, dodging the puddles which were getting deeper by the minute.

"Kind-as, officer," said SooTed, staring at the huge engine and scratching his head.

Lottie watched Spike and Rula sneak from behind the hedge and follow the Duke up the steps and disappear inside the Trocadero.

"They're in," said Lottie, fidgeting nervously with a silver locket hanging from a chain around her neck.

"We're going to get arrested," whispered BooTed.

The rain continued to pour, and the police officer leaned over and jiggled a few wires and pipes on the engine. "Try it now," he shouted.

In the driving seat, BooTed pretended to turn the key and shook his head.

"Still dead-as," said SooTed, moving slightly to his right to a spot that blocked the police officer's view of the entrance to the Trocadero.

The police officer sniffed the top of the carburettor. "You have fuel getting through, so it's an electrical problem."

Lottie fiddled with the locket and stared at the building with thoughts of Cheddar George, spinning in her head. She began to cry again.

*

Spike, Rula and the Duke flew past the box office, through the empty auditorium and down the stairs to the basement. They headed for storeroom seven where Cheddar George's broken hearing aid had been found and then whizzed along the dark corridor, searching for any sign of the tiny room Amanda Nelson had described in her sitrep.

The Duke led the way, using his Sensitive Smell Detection System at its maximum sensitivity to try and detect the unmistaken aroma of 'Tommy', which Cheddar George would definitely have made overnight. The Duke suddenly turned left and picked up speed, weaving his way through the basement with Spike and Rula close behind.

They came across the two mannequins of the glum looking Queen Victoria and her husband, Prince Albert. The Duke came to a sudden stop by the oak wardrobe door and nodded. Rula prized open the door and they slid inside. The aroma of 'Tommy' detected by the Duke's Sensitive Smell Detection System increased.

*

The police officer double checked the battery connection and called to BooTed to try starting the engine again. Once more, BooTed went through the motion of pretending to turn the key and shook his head.

Lottie suddenly noticed Spike and Rula reappear at the window above the entrance. She nudged BooTed's knee, nodding with her teary eyes.

"It's still dead-as, mate," said SooTed, now soaked

191

to the skin by the driving rain.

CRASH

Inside the Trocadero, Rula had pushed over a pile of heavy wooden crates, hoping to create a diversion.

"The DI is going to kill me," said the police officer and dashed back to the theatre. He'd now have a *lot* of explaining to do.

As the police officer vaulted the blue and white crime-scene tape and disappeared inside, the Duke, Rula and Spike sneaked from the behind the box office counter and flew back to the Huddy, with Rula and Spike carrying an old suitcase. The Duke wrote frantically.

"Quick, round the back. We have a situation. We located Cheddar George, but he's now being evacuated."

"You found him? Thank you!" Lottie shrieked, clapping her hands excitedly as SooTed jumped in the back seat and Rula plonked the suitcase on his soggy lap.

BooTed turned the key and the engine started. "Hang on to your hats."

The Huddy's tyres squealed as the car took off, ploughing through the deep puddles.

"Where did you find him?" Lottie asked, so relieved Cheddar George had been found, but terrified he might be whisked away from them again.

"My SSDS detected Cheddar George's unique aroma near an old wardrobe in the Props Department. Inside we found some costumes and a false back panel which Spike removed, and we located the kidnapper's hideout. My SSDS traced Cheddar George to a cellar, and we saw him being taken from there and

forced through a tunnel at the rear by a woman."

"Blimey!" said BooTed, fighting to control the Huddy as it hurtled round a tight corner and the tyres struggled to grip the soaked tarmac.

"What's in here?" SooTed asked, clinging onto the old suitcase with both hands and sliding back and forth across the back seat as BooTed spun the wheel, flinging the car around the car park.

"Bits and bobs that might come in useful."

The Huddy bombed through another puddle, sending water everywhere and then turned a corner, making it to the rear of the Trocadero by the stage door. The place was deserted.

"Worried-as. Where did they go?" asked SooTed, struggling to see through the car's window.

"Still inside?" suggested BooTed.

"No. Look!" shrieked Lottie and pointed, as she spotted the back of a VW Campervan disappeared down the alley next to the Verdi supermarket.

BooTed revved the engine and they headed for the alley. "Well spotted, Lottie!"

At the end of the alley, the Huddy braked hard by the Pic-A-Pasta and turned left. They could see the VW Camper two cars ahead of them, making its way through the early morning traffic. The Huddy followed with SooTed chain-crunching his way through piles of boiled sweets.

Alan Barbara

CHAPTER 21 – JAILHOUSE ROCK.

Petrified, Cheddar George sat in the back of the VW, his hands and feet tied with ropes and his head covered once more by the old sack. Maddie was taking no chances this time.

He tried letting 'Tommy out of prison' a number of times, hoping the terrible smell would somehow cause the kidnapper to pass out and allow him to escape, but with the smell from the empty tins of Boomer's Tuna chunks littering the floor, adding the aroma of 'Tommy' to the mix did very little.

Maddie drove across the island toward Ryde, with BooTed following at a safe distance. When she reached the town, she headed for the seafront and once again turned onto the old wooden pier, chugging past the sinister 'KEEP OUT' signs. The van's wheels made their DUD-DUD-DUD noise as they rolled over the planks. The Huddy followed.

The VW crept down the pier and BooTed pointed out the CCTV cameras and the signs warning not to go any further.

"I think we should call the police."

"You're right, mate," said SooTed, pulling his phone

195

from his pocket.

"Miffed-as. No signal."

BooTed and Lottie quickly checked their phones.
No signal from either. HMS Chichester was
transmitting a blocking signal, which stopped any
unauthorised mobile phone within four hundred yards
of the huge ship.

BooTed stopped the car and sighed loudly.

"What now? We can't just follow. Anyone got an
idea?"

"Open the suitcase."

SooTed's sausage fingers flicked the catches and
lifted the battered lid to the case. "What the…."

"Find a suitable disguise."

"Handy-as," said SooTed, pulling out various items
of clothing.

He tossed aside a clown and a Roman Centurion
costume and then grinned. "Here. How about this," he
said, pulling out an old nurse's uniform. A dress with a
dark blue skirt and sleeves, and a white bib at the front.

"It's good, but way too small for you or me,"
BooTed said as SooTed held the uniform up.

BooTed was right. There was no way the old nurse's
costume would fit either of them.

SooTed looked at Lottie. "You'll have to wear it."

"Me! But… I'm too little. Nobody will believe I'm a
real nurse!" shrieked Lottie.

"Roger that. We're on it."

Sharpy and Rula whizzed a little way up the pier to
the Spooky-Wooky Haunted House. Inside, they found
a fake skeleton, covered in real cobwebs. Sharpy hacked

off both legs below the knee and Rula carried the bones back to the Huddy.

"Urgh. Gross!" shrieked Lottie, as Sharpy dropped the bones on her lap.

A sheet of Paddy wrapped around each leg bone to create the muscles and skin and Penny coloured them in, turning the bones into fake human legs with size three feet.

Rula yanked off Lottie's trainers and slipped them onto the fake feet and a length of Rob lashed the top of the bones to Lottie's ankles, making a pair of stilts. Lottie looked worried. She'd tried walking on stilts once before and it hadn't gone at all well, ending with another trip to the casualty department at Newport Hospital after she hit her head on a bird table in their garden (that Nanny Vera had won at the Alum Bay summer fete).

"Now you're taller by 18 inches."

"*If* I can walk in them," Lottie said.

"Easy-as. You'll be fine. You should wear these as well," said SooTed, pulling a curly ginger wig and thick rimmed spectacles from the suitcase.

"You can do this, Lottie. We have to find out who's taken Cheddar George and what they plan to do," said SooTed, peering out at the rain which still lashed down.

"I know," Lottie said, slipping the uniform over her head and yanking it down to hide her dungarees and odd socks.

"We can't turn up in this car either, mate," said SooTed.

"Sit tight. We should be able to sort that."

197

The BREW Crew flew into action again. Rula and Spike disappeared behind the abandoned Captain Cook's merry-go-round and returned with a trailer from an old train that used to ferry holiday makers up and down the pier. Pieces of Paddy paper grew to the size of bedsheets and were trimmed by Sharpy. Ledley and Penny drew and coloured them and Rula stuck them to the sides of the trailer with blobs of Rob eraser.

Rula and Spike then removed two old fruit machines from the Pot of Gold penny arcade and the BREW Crew turned these into fake medical equipment with screens, pipes, wires and dials. In seconds, the rusty old trailer was transformed into an ambulance.

"Wickedoolie," said Lottie, as Penny drew some wrinkles on her face, making her look much older.

SooTed's huge hands jammed the ginger wig on Lottie's head and the BREW Crew finished her disguise by making a badge reading 'NURSE L BAXTER' and pinned it on her uniform. More sheets of Paddy were coloured green, trimmed and turned into Paramedic uniforms by the BREW Crew for SooTed and BooTed to wear.

SooTed handed Lottie the spectacles. "Good-as. Are you ready?"

Lottie nodded, too terrified to even speak and trying to ignore the horrible churning in her stomach.

SooTed and BooTed got out the Huddy and helped Lottie stand on the wooden pier. She wobbled on her new stilts for a few seconds and then nodded. SooTed and BooTed let go and rushed across the rain-soaked pier. Lottie followed behind them, struggling to stay upright. The two men climbed into seats at the front of the fake ambulance, taken from a dodgem car and Lottie eventually joined them and sat in the back on an old bench, once part of Captain Cook's merry-go-round.

"We're coming, Cheddar George," said BooTed.

From behind, Rula shoved the ambulance slowly along the pier and the newly recruited medical team sat in silence, wondering what they'd find ahead.

As they passed the abandoned Pot of Gold penny arcade, they saw the campervan's red brake lights just ahead and the looming grey, fifty-five thousand tonne mass of the HMS Chichester.

"Crikey. He must be going on the ship," said SooTed.

"That's enormous," muttered BooTed as they slowed and waited behind a derelict donut stall for the VW to move.

*

Maddie had stopped at the security checkpoint. The guard with half an ear appeared out the rain, checked her ID without uttering a word and raised the barrier.

The VW chugged forward, stopping again at the gangplank to HMS Chichester and another guard appeared from nowhere.

"Passphrase and ID."

"They've Got An Awful Lot Of Coffee In Brazil," said Maddie, handing over her badge and pulling up her sleeve.

"Back so soon to the Guest House Paridiso," chuckled the guard.

"Another old codger for you," said Maddie.

"You're just in a nick of time. We sail at eight to the south to collect some more oldies from St Catherine's Point," said the guard, checking his watch and opening the van's door. He untied the ropes and pulled Cheddar George out and into the rain.

"Come on, old chap."

"Where am I? What's happening?" asked Cheddar George. His voice muffled beneath the cloth sack.

"You're off on a cruise, old timer. A very *long* cruise," said the guard, removing the sack.

Cheddar George itched his face."But I hate the water. Ever since Nobby Richardson shoved me in the pond in Bearwood Park when I was a kid."

"Shame," chuckled the guard.

"Watch out for this one," Maddie called, as the guard shepherded Cheddar George up the gangplank. "He's trouble."

"Don't worry. We'll take good care of him," said the guard, opening the heavy metal door in the side of the ship.

Maddie drove away, delighted to have *finally* completed her mission and avoid the wrath of Sir Charles Oakley. As she headed for Alum Bay, Maddie worked out in her head what the bonus payment would be for all her collections this month.

*

Rula stopped the fake ambulance at the checkpoint and the guard appeared looking suspicious. "ID."

SooTed wound his windows down and flashed his Verdi loyalty card. It showed a picture of Lottie's head and shoulders, added by Ledley and Penny just a second ago. SooTed hoped the guard wouldn't look too closely. The guard took the ID card and tried clearing the rain drops which covered his glasses to see better, but that just made it worse.

With the guard distracted, the Duke slipped out of the ambulance and over to a small security hut – the guard's shelter from the wind and rain of the English summer.

"We've had an urgent call. Nurse Baxter needs to see a patient," said SooTed.

"Mr George Hardwick. It's a medical emergency," added BooTed.

Rainwater dripped from the end of the guard's nose, and he gave up trying to check Lottie's ID. He handed the card back, marched to the back of the ambulance and opened the rear door. There sat Lottie in her nurse's uniform with a small medical kit made from Paddy paper on her lap and hidden inside were Casey and the BREW Crew. Lottie forced a smile and the guard nodded and marched back to the front of the fake ambulance.

"Can you hurry?" said SooTed, wiping a fake thermometer made from a piece of a slot machine on the green sleeve of his fake uniform.

"Nobody told me about a visit from a nurse," said the guard, his serious look showed he was in no mood to be hurried.

SooTed shrugged. "Someone called us a few minutes ago. Can't you just let us through so we–."

The guard's expression changed from serious to

absolutely deadly serious. "Nobody goes past me without orders from Captain Fletcher. *Nobody*. Stay here and let me check my paperwork."

He returned to his hut and wiped the rain from his glasses with a tissue. Now able to see properly, he picked up a clipboard and studied a sheet of paper, titled 'SITE ACCESS APPROVALS'. At the very bottom, he spotted an entry, added by the Duke just seconds earlier, approving a visit by Nurse L Baxter to a 'G Hardwick'.

The guard squinted, trying to read the badly written signature of the approver. It didn't look like Captain Fletcher's writing at all. The guard knew he should double check with the captain, but as it was nearly the end of his 12-hour shift and he was in no mood to make his day any harder, he returned to the ambulance and raised the barrier.

"All good. I'll radio ahead to let them know you're here."

SooTed nodded and Rula pushed the ambulance through the security gate.

Lottie felt her stomach doing summersaults as the Duke slid into the top pocket on the bib of her nurse's uniform.

"We're never going to get out of here again," said BooTed.

"Calm-as. Everything will be fine," muttered SooTed, searching his pockets for sweets but finding only empty wrappers (he'd scoffed five packets of boiled sweets on the drive from the Trocadero).

The second guard was waiting by the ship's

gangplank, getting details from the first about the medic's visit over his radio.

"The approval to board is for Nurse Baxter only. You two will have to wait the other side of the first security gate in the D-M-Zee. And you'd better hurry, nurse. We'll be sailing off into the sunset at the top of the hour."

"Where to?" asked SooTed.

The guard tapped his nose with a finger. "That's classified info, pal."

BooTed checked his watch and whispered to Lottie. "You have less than ten minutes."

"Quick-as. You can do this, Lottie," said SooTed.

Lottie nodded. Terror in her eyes and still unable to speak.

"We'll be waiting for you, nurse," said SooTed, opening the fake ambulance's rear door and smiling at the guard through the rain.

Lottie stepped from the ambulance onto the slippery planks. The wind gusted and her legs felt like jelly, struggling to balance on her stilts. She held her medical kit tight in her clammy hands and hoped the wind wouldn't blow her wig off.

"This way," ordered the guard.

From the fake ambulance, SooTed and BooTed watched Lottie slip twice and nearly fall into the water as she staggered like a robot up the gangplank behind the guard and disappeared inside the ship.

"Good Luck, Lottie," muttered SooTed.

BooTed checked his watch. "Eight minutes and counting," he said, and the two men poked their legs through the floor of the trailer and moved off 'Flintstone style'. SooTed turned the ambulance around and they headed slowly back along the pier. Once through the security checkpoint, he pulled over by the Pot of Gold penny arcade. In the driving rain they could just make out the stern of the ship and a deck piled high with wooden crates, no doubt full of supplies for the ship's journey.

*

Inside HMS Chichester, the guard removed his drenched coat and tapped a few keys on a computer keyboard. "He's just been checked in. Cell three hundred and two. Follow me."

The mention of the word 'cell' made Lottie feel even worse. She could hear and feel the powerful engines throbbing far beneath her stilts as she followed the guard along a narrow corridor and down a metal staircase. Her wet trainers squeaked as she made her away down the stairs on her stilts. She walked like a toddler who'd just taken their first few steps.

Halfway down, Lottie heard a sudden TWANG. The lace of one of her trainers had snapped and the shoe slipped off her fake foot.

"Oh no. Nik-nacks," she muttered, looking down at the bare fake foot and watched her soggy trainer bounce down two stairs and disappear down a gap.

The guard reached the bottom of the staircase and turned as Lottie limped down the last stair, trying to walk properly.

"You alright, nurse?"

Lottie's mouth was so dry, she couldn't speak. She

was the most terrified she'd ever been in her life, and just grinned as if in pain and nodded. The guard turned and walked quickly down a corridor, whistling a tune.

The sound of his heavy boots echoed, and Lottie's heart pounded in her chest. She was certain the guard would notice her squeaky limp mixed with the DONK from her shoeless fake foot and the game would be up. *Then* what would happen to her?

At the end of the corridor, the guard stopped whistling and turned left, passing a row of locked doors until he reached one marked '302'.

There was a metallic rattle as the guard pulled a bunch of keys from his pocket and unlocked the door.

"You've got five minutes. Captain Fletcher *won't* wait for anyone," he said, pushing open the cell door and entering.

The room, like everything else on the ship was painted battleship grey and it felt so cold and uninviting. A single bed was pushed into one corner and opposite was a toilet and a sink. A small TV hung on the wall next to a table and a wooden chair with no cushion. Lottie squeak-donked in after the guard (still walking like a badly built robot).

Cheddar George sat on the edge of the bed, a mixture of confusion and deep worry on his face, which matched the colour of the walls. His thin grey hair was soaked under his yellow fedora hat, and he stared at the spotless floor, not looking up at either of his two visitors. The guard leant against a grey wall by the cell door. His phone beeped, a text from his wife.

"Crack on, nurse," he said, taking his phone from

his pocket and tapping a reply.

Lottie squeak-donked over and knelt at Cheddar George's feet, praying the guard wouldn't spot her bony fake foot poking out beneath her uniform. She opened the lid of her medical kit and noticed the Duke's writing on a piece of Paddy.

"Pretend to treat his right foot."

Feet and eyes; Lottie's worst nightmare. She swallowed hard, forcing away the sick feeling in her throat and thankful to have missed breakfast that morning.

"I'm nurse Baxter, Ched... Mr Hardwick... I'm here about your poorly foot," Lottie managed to say, her trembling voice was loud enough for him to hear without his hearing aid.

"Foot," mumbled Cheddar George as if in a trance.

The guard was still busy texting his wife and didn't spot Lottie holding her breath, and her look of disgust as she removed Cheddar George's brown slip-on.

"Err. Are you in any pain, Mr Hardwick?"

"Pain," mumbled Cheddar George, in a daze and his top set of false teeth clunked against the lower ones.

"Yes, pain, Mr Hardwick... from wearing *your old boots*."

"My old...," said Cheddar George, his eyes flitted from the grey floor to the nurse's face and suddenly recognised Lottie behind the thick-rimmed spectacles.

"My old bootshhh!" said Cheddar George, winking at Lottie and pushing his teeth back in.

Lottie (still trying her hardest not to throw up) slid the blue sock from Cheddar George's right foot to reveal his four toes. Suddenly, an extra toe, made from a chunk of Rob and oozing fake blood, fell on the floor as if it had fallen from inside the sock. The toe rolled across the cell floor towards the guard, who took one look at the blood seeping from the hairy digit (complete with a yucky yellow crusty toenail) and fainted.

Cheddar George slapped his knee. "Tickety-boo, Lottie. Well done. Well done indeed."

Lottie hugged Cheddar George while sharpy cut the straps to remove her stilts. A piece of Paddy and the Duke slipped out of Casey.

"Let's get up to the poop deck."

"The what?" asked Lottie, certain she hadn't read the Duke's writing properly.

"Poop deck, Lottie. And it's *not* where everyone goes for a poop. It's the deck at the very top of the ship. I think it's near the blunt end," said Cheddar George.

"Roger that. SooTed and BooTed might see us from there and rescue us," said Lottie. "But we have to hurry, Cheddar George. The ship sails soon to who-knows-where."

The Duke wrote on a piece of Paddy.

"Leave that to us. We'll do what we're good at and panzernack it."

"Please be careful," said Lottie, as Spike, Rob, Rula and the Duke disappeared through a square heating vent on the wall. They followed the source of the heat down through the ship's decks to the engine room.

Cheddar George pulled on his sock and shoe and slowly rose from the bed to his upright position.

Laid out on a blanket at the end of the bed, he noticed a captain's uniform, created from Paddy paper by the BREW Crew. Cheddar George slipped on the black paper trousers and jacket over his damp clothes.

"Very cool, Cheddar George," said Lottie.

"Somewhat fetching don't you think? Now grab those keys, Lottie. Who knows how many others are locked up on this ship," said Cheddar George, pointing to the bunch of keys, still clutched in the guard's hand. "Ready to go ashore?" he asked, swapping his soggy yellow fedora hat for a gold trimmed captain's cap.

*

In the engine room, it didn't take long for Rob to plug a fuel pipe and Spike to snip a few cables between the diesel control gizmo and the fuel management system. After a few seconds, the thundering from the four massive diesel engines ceased.

CHAPTER 22 – I WANT TO BREAK FREE.

In the corridor outside Cheddar George's cell, Lottie turned a key in the door, locking the guard inside. Cheddar George felt the floor shudder as the engines spluttered and stopped. Silence followed, as if the old ship had somehow fallen asleep.

"That's the engines nobbled. Not sure how much time that will buy us. Let's check the other cells."

They hurried as fast as Cheddar George could manage to the next cell – three hundred and three. Lottie unlocked the door and shoved it open. The cell was identical to the one Cheddar George had briefly occupied.

Mrs Fish, startled from the noise made by the door flying open, lifted her head from a pillow.

"Have you got my constipation pills, nurse?"

"Quick," said Lottie. "We have to go."

"Go? But nurse, Splash The Cash is on TV in a minute and I *never* miss it. What could *possibly* be more important than Splash The Cash at this time of day?" asked a flustered Mrs Fish.

"Bingo," said Cheddar George. "It's eyes-down in two minutes."

"Bingo! Well, why didn't you say," shrieked Mrs Fish, scrambling off the bed.

"It's good to see you again, Mrs Fish. Vest on, teeth in," said Cheddar George.

"Why, Cheddar George? Is that you?" asked Mrs Fish.

Cheddar George grinned. "It is indeed. Time to go, my dear. You need to hurry to collect your dibber from Admiral Nelson and find a good seat. The prize for a full-house is ten bob and a meat hamper."

Mrs Fish was on her feet in no time. "Righty-o," she said, slipping a pink dressing gown over her long yellow nightie.

"Follow the signs, my dear. The bingo hall is up on the poop deck," said Cheddar George, taking an arm and leading a slightly confused Mrs Fish out of her cell.

"Righty-o. I'll save you a seat," said Mrs Fish, patting Cheddar George's hand and then hurrying up the metal staircase.

Cheddar George grinned at Lottie, tapped his head and pointed at his feet. "Up here for the great escape and down there for dancing."

Lottie and Cheddar George worked as quickly as the could, unlocking door after door and using the promise of a game of bingo to persuade the pensioners to leave their cells and head up to the poop deck.

*

In the stiflingly hot engine room, Petty Officer Zakazri, put on his glasses and stared in amazement at the frayed cables on the diesel control gizmo.

"Someone's hacked through the ruddy cable," he said to the captain, who stood next to him checking his watch.

"Sabotage?" Captain Fletcher scratched his chin, turned and spoke to a woman standing by a huge grey pipe that meandered round the engine room and up into the roof. "Lieutenant Parsons, sound the alarm!"

Lieutenant Parsons nodded and thumped a red mushroom-shaped button on the wall. A klaxon bellowed and a large bolt clunked to lock every door, including the rusty door leading from the gangplank.

*

"Crikey! That's not good," shouted Cheddar George above the wailing klaxon. Bulkhead lights suddenly flashed red along the narrow corridor as Lottie escorted Edith Entwistle from the very last cell and headed for the poop deck above.

"What's all that flashing, Captain?" asked Edith, popping a mint imperial in her mouth.

"We're also having a discotheque after the bingo, my dear," replied Cheddar George, giving her a nudge in the back to get he moving a bit quicker up the meal staircase.

*

SooTed and BooTed heard the klaxon blaring from the ship as they waited in the fake ambulance.

"Look, mate!" shouted SooTed, pointing through the windscreen. He could see pensioners, tottering, limping or being wheeled in chairs, spilling out onto the poop deck. All were dressed in pyjamas and dressing gowns, which flapped madly in the gusting wind. An array of walking sticks tapped a random rhythm on the deck as they hurried behind the huge wooden crates to shelter from the rain.

The thick ropes, tying the huge ship to the pier creaked as the ship lurched in the wind. Unforgiving sea water filled the hundred-yard gap between the barbed wire at the edge of the pier and the prison ship's huge rusting hull.

"How do we get them off?" asked BooTed.

"Not a clue. Useless-as," replied SooTed.

*

Spike, Rula, Rob and the Duke had now made it up to the poop deck. The Duke spotted an old anti-aircraft gun at the rear of the deck, unused for many years. He scribbled on the side of a wooden crate.

"Wind speed (WS) – 15 knots
Spike's weight (SW) – 2 ounces
Altitude Variation (AV) – 130 feet
Flight Distance (FD) – 300 feet
AAGA = WS * (SW / (AV * FD))
Anti-Aircraft Gun angle (AAGA) = 11 degrees.

Spike disappeared down the gun's four-inch barrel and Rula wound a metal handle to rotate the heavy gun and aim it at the pier. A rusty lever was nudged by the Duke to set the angle at 11 degrees and then he thumped the 'FIRE' button.

BANG.

A puff of smoke erupted from the gun's barrel and Spike shot out, tied to one end of Rob rope. The other end had been expertly knotted around a post that secured the anti-aircraft gun to the poop deck. SooTed and BooTed heard the gunfire and leapt from the ambulance.

"Whoa!" said SooTed ducking out the way of Spike's harpoon, which narrowly missed his head and thudded into a thick wooden post behind him.

DOIIINNNG.

SooTed yanked Spike out of the post. Skewered to the point of the compass was a folded note from the Duke.

"Lash the rope tight and prepare for boarders."

"The Duke has a plan," SooTed shouted to BooTed and quickly secured the rope around the bumper at the front of the fake ambulance.

BooTed's eyes followed the Rob rope back to the poop deck, where the collection of pensioners cowered in the shelter of the sodden crates. "Blimey! I know what they're going to try. We need to find something for a soft landing."

SooTed pointed at a derelict wooden building with a sign above the entrance saying OLD MACDONALD'S SOFT PLAY.

"In there, mate. Quick-as."

*

Back on the huge ship, Lottie and Cheddar George stepped onto the poop deck with Edith Entwistle. A total of 26 confused pensioners stood on the deck, drenched from head to foot. Cheddar George recognised many of the faces. They were regulars from the Burlington Bingo Hall where he went for 'eyes-down' every Friday.

Edith Entwistle watched in amazement as one end of a short length of Rob rope tied itself to the arm of a wheelchair, owned by a rather large lady called Mrs Rae. She'd been collected along with her husband by the PCS agent known as the Wicked Witch of theVest for not returning two books to Dundee library after they moved house from Scotland. On her lap Mrs Rae clutched a plastic carrier bag containing balls of wool and a half-knitted scarf (which she planned to finish while playing bingo).

"When does the bingo start, Albert?" asked Mrs Rae, looking anxiously up at her husband, while the other end of Rob rope looped up and over the longer rope which stretched to the pier.

"I *think* we're in the wrong place, sweetie," replied Albert, watching open mouthed as the rope tied itself to the other arm of her wheelchair. The BREW Crew now had a seat with the first pensioner 'locked and loaded', dangling beneath a Rob rope zip-wire, stretching down to the fake ambulance below them.

A piece of Paddy paper landed in Lottie's hand.
"Prepare to disembark."
Lottie showed the paper to Cheddar George.
"Holy Moly Roly Poly!" he muttered.
"Is this going to work?" Lottie asked.
"Well. That's how it says to do it in the book," said Cheddar George, giving Lottie an anxious grin.

Lottie jumped up on the gun platform. "Listen

everybody," she shouted. "You all have to slide down the zip-wire to get off this ship before it leaves. It's the only chance to escape."

Albert Rae stared disbelievingly at the zip-wire stretching across the hundred yards of deep water to the pier. "Surely not! There's no way my wife is going on *that!*" he said, grabbing the wheelchair and holding on for dear life.

"I'm not going either," said a woman with large pink curlers in her hair.

There was more shaking of heads and concerned mutterings from all the other elderly prisoners.

Helpless. Lottie looked at Cheddar George, not knowing how to convince everyone that the treacherous zip-wire was their only option to escape.

"Fellow islanders and Burlington bingo-buddies," said Cheddar George, climbing slowly onto the gun platform next to Lottie and saluting. "Staying on this ship means we all venture into unchartered waters. I, for one am not ready to buy-in to that journey. Our winning bingo ticket out of here is at the end of that zip-wire. We can return to the four corners of Alum Bay and to our loving families and live our lives to the full-house once more. It's time for tea."

Lottie nodded enthusiastically and thought the pensioners would be happy to escape. But she was wrong.

"What if we don't make it?" asked the woman with the curlers, her face white with fear.

"I've got a dicky-ticker and it might not stand

215

the strain. We're all past our prime," said an old man who had no hair up-top, but a carefully platted ponytail.

Others cowering against the wooden crates nodded in agreement.

Cheddar George raised his hand and put his index and middle finger up to form a 'V' sign.

"We shall Bingo on the beaches, we shall Bingo on the landing grounds, we shall Bingo in the fields and in the streets, we shall Bingo in the hills. We shall never surrender our dibbers."

"Here, here. Well said, Captain," said Mrs Fish, clapping enthusiastically.

Mrs Rae looked into her husband's eyes. "I'll go, Albert. I want to see the grandchildren again," she said, wiping a tear from her eye.

Albert Rae nodded and kissed Mrs Rae on the forehead.

"Cabin crew, doors to manual. Time to duck and dive," shouted Cheddar George and watched Rula heave the wheelchair with Mrs Rae over the edge of the poop deck.

There was a loud ZEEEEZ sound from the zip-wire, combined with an equally loud frightened scream from Gladys Rae as the chair belted down the wire with Rula tugging it along. The bag of knitting flew off Mrs Rae's lap, plopping into the murky sea below and her cream nightdress billowed around her waist.

"My old boots, Cheddar George!" said Lottie.

"Agreed indeed," muttered Cheddar George, while Mrs Rae's husband closed his eyes and muttered a prayer.

SooTed and BooTed were dragging a huge ball-pit across the wet pier when they heard Mrs Rae's terrified scream and looked back at the ship. They saw the swinging chair and the pensioner's huge purple knickers hurtling towards them.

"Crazy-as, mate. Incoming!" shouted SooTed and they heaved the ball-pit in front of the ambulance a second before the wheelchair's rubber tyres touched down with a loud CLONK on the pier.

The wheelchair aquaplaned across the slippery planks and hit the front of the ball-pit, stopping dead. The screaming Mrs Rae catapulted from her seat and somersaulted head-first into the pile of coloured plastic balls.

"We've got you, love," said SooTed wading up to his knees through the balls and helping Gladys Rae to stand. Her legs wobbled as she stumbled from the makeshift ball-pit landing area.

"That was *so* much fun!" said Mrs Rae tugging a seagull's feather from her blue-rinsed hair.

BooTed sat Mrs Rae in an old dodgem car which he pushed across the pier to the Spooky-Wooky Haunted House.

"Sit here out of the rain, my dear," said BooTed, helping Mrs Rae into a seat made from plastic skeleton bones.

"Thank you, young man. Will my husband be long?" asked Mrs Rae, pulling a soggy hankie from her sleeve and dabbing her wet face.

"I'm sure he'll be here in a jiffy," said BooTed and he shoved the dodgem back to the ball-pit, while

Rula towed the empty chair back up the zip-wire to the group of terrified pensioners up on the poop deck.

"I'm happy to go next, Captain, and help establish a base camp on the pier," said a thin gentleman, standing proudly to attention in front of Cheddar George and saluting. He was dressed in soggy blue and white striped pyjamas and held a pair of binoculars. The man was the chairman of the Freshwater bird watchers and never went anywhere without his binoculars.

"What's your name, soldier?" Cheddar George asked.

"Corporal Armstrong, Captain. From the Isle of Wight Gurkha Regiment. Service Number 71295. I fought for Queen and country and we Gurkhas don't scare easily, sir."

"Top man, Corporal," said Cheddar George, patting the old soldier on his shoulder as he saluted again. "When you reach the pier, our comrades SooTed and BooTed will be there. Get them to call the police."

Corporal Armstrong nodded and plonked himself in the seat and his bony knuckles gripped the wheelchair's arms. "Heave-ho, Captain. Ça plane pour moi, as they say!" And then he began singing the old Vera Lynn song from World War II, *We'll Meet Again*.

Cheddar George nodded and Rula tugged the wheelchair from the deck. Corporal Armstrong's singing faded as he shot across to the pier and catapulted into the ball-pit.

"Corporal Armstrong reporting for duty, sir," he said as SooTed and BooTed helped him emerge from the ball pit.

SooTed, shook Corporal Armstrong's hand. "Happy-as to have you with us, mate."

"Message from the captain, sir. He wants you to call the Old Bill," said Corporal Armstrong.

"We can't" said BooTed. "We can't get a signal."

Corporal Armstrong suddenly pointed towards the coastline.

"There's an old phone box outside the Bucket and Shade gift shop just along the road. I'll call them from there, sir."

"Good idea. Quick-as," said SooTed.

"Sir, yes sir," said Corporal Armstrong. He saluted and handed over his binoculars.

"Look after these," he said and set off down the pier as fast as his ankley-challenged legs would take him.

*

One by one, the pensioners took their turn and zip-wired down the Rob rope. For most of them, their dismount into the ball-pit wasn't at all elegant, but somehow, they managed it without breaking any bones or spectacles.

SooTed and BooTed helped the bedraggled pensioners out and ferried them in the dodgem over to the Spooky-Wooky Haunted House, where they sat shivering in their pyjamas.

"How many left?" asked BooTed, puffing hard as they returned with the empty dodgem.

SooTed peered up at the poop deck through the binoculars. "Looks like it's just Lottie and Cheddar George. Good-as."

*

Suddenly, the diesel engines burst into life and black smoke billowed from a tall funnel in the centre of the ship.

"Strewth. That's put a spanner in the works," said Cheddar George. "We'd better get a wiggle on."

"You go first, Cheddar George," Lottie shouted, as Rula returned to the poop deck once more with the empty wheelchair.

"No, Lottie. It's the captain's job to make sure he's always the last to leave his ship."

"But we don't have time," said Lottie as they felt the engine's power increase beneath their soggy feet.

"Agreed indeed. We'll go together," said Cheddar George.

The ship's horn sounded three times – the signal it was leaving port.

"Quick. Run!" shouted Lottie, hurrying to the wheelchair.

"Run?" puffed Cheddar George as he shuffled across the deck as fast as his 90-11-year-old legs would carry him. "The last time I ran, it was in black and white and Roger Bannister was in nappies."

Black smoke billowed again from the funnel and the horn sounded another four blasts. The ship began to move and the Rob rope zip-wire stretched tighter, creaking as the ship inched away from the pier.

Lottie held the wheelchair still while Cheddar George eased into it. "Let's go and get a nice cuppa."

Lottie nodded and with Rula's help, they shoved the wheelchair across the deck.

"Jump aboard, darling. Tash-hag kettle on," Cheddar George shouted.

Lottie leapt on the back of the chair just as they reached the very edge of the poop deck. She flung her arms around Cheddar George's shoulders and the wheelchair dropped over the edge of the deck and ZEEEEZ'd down the zip-wire.

The Rob rope stretched further, creaking and groaning badly as the huge ship moved further away, dragging the fake ambulance towards edge of the pier and a sheer drop into the murky water of the Solent.

"Come on. Come on. Quick-as!" bellowed SooTed. He stood in front of the ambulance with BooTed, shoving hard, trying to stop the ambulance sliding nearer to the water's edge. They knew it was pointless, but they had to do something.

Rula pulled the wheelchair even faster, using every inch of her strength.

SooTd's eyes were glued to the binoculars. "A few more seconds and they'll be clear of the water and safely over the pier."

"They're going to make it," said BooTed, his feet struggling to get any grip on the wet pier.

"I hope you're right, mate. Happy-as!"

CRACK

The zip-wire snapped, coiling like a dead snake at SooTed's feet and the wheelchair plummeted.

"My old boots! I should have worn my flip-flips and new wetsuit," shouted Cheddar George.

Lottie grabbed Cheddar George even tighter, and she could feel his heart thumping in his chest. She was a

221

good swimmer, but Cheddar George had never learnt to swim in his 90-11 years. She'd have to try and keep him afloat until help arrived. She'd learnt all about lifesaving in Mr Hugi's swimming class last year. But that had been in the shallow end of a calm swimming pool, not a deep rolling sea like the one they were heading towards.

Then Lottie realised that wasn't the only thing to worry about. If the BREW Crew were underwater for too long, it would destroy their solar-power generators. They'd never be able to recharge and would lose all their special abilities. It would kill them.

As well as trying to save Cheddar George, she'd also have to somehow hold the BREW Crew above her head to stop them getting waterlogged.

Lottie waited for the big splash, knowing it would be impossible for her to save both Cheddar George *and* the BREW Crew. She closed her eyes and waited.

PLAMP

Lottie opened her eyes. Instead of the sudden cold rush of salty seawater, the wheelchair had fallen onto something soft. They'd landed on a piece of Rob, filled with air to make a small life raft.

"That's handy," chuckled Cheddar George. "You OK, Darling?"

"Totes," nodded Lottie and delighted not to be cold and wet and putting Mr Hugi's lifesaving lesson to good use.

A length of old rope plopped in the sea next to her and SooTed and BooTed's heads appeared over the side of the pier, grinning as they looked down. SooTed held the other end of rope in his huge hand and waved it. "Grab hold."

Lottie fished the rope from the rolling waves lapping and handed it to Cheddar George. "Hold this, Captain."

SooTed pulled them to the side of the pier while Cheddar George yodelsang.

"A life on the ocean wave, a home on the rolling deep, yodel-a-dee-a-doo yodel-a-dee-a-day…"

"Try and get over to there," shouted SooTed, pointing at a wooden ladder bolted to the side of the pier and stretching upwards from the murky water.

"Roger that," shouted Lottie and used her hands to paddle, steering the liferaft slowly over to the ladder.

SooTed and BooTed scrambled down and each grabbed an arm of Mrs Rae's wheelchair and lifted Cheddar George up the ladder and safely onto the pier.

"All ashore who's going ashore. Tash-hag very moist," chuckled Cheddar George, straightening his peaked cap, soggy from the driving rain.

Lottie followed the wheelchair up the ladder and as she reached the top, they saw a police car thundering down the pier with its sirens blaring. The car slid to a halt on the wooden planks and Detective Inspector Sergeant-Constable and another police officer, Sergeant Warner jumped out. Old Corporal Armstrong had obviously made it to the the phone box by the Bucket and Spade gift shop.

"More trouble, Lottie?"

"They're getting away," shrieked Lottie as the ship, now under full power sailed out the harbour.

"Who are?"

223

"Kidnappers. Tash-hag braggarts," said Cheddar George, pointing a soggy finger out to sea.

Detective Inspector Sergeant-Constable turned to Sergeant Warner. "Get on the radio, Jackie and find out who owns that ship slash boat and *where* it is going. Pronto."

"Guv," nodded Sergeant Warner.

In the shelter of the Spooky-Wooky Haunted House, Lottie and Cheddar George told Detective Inspector Sergeant-Constable what had happened while Sergeant Warner spoke at lengths on her radio. When she finished her conversation, her face showed bitter disappointment.

"We can't get *any* details on the ship's owner or destination, Guv."

Detective Inspector Sergeant-Constable looked surprised.

"What? A ship slash boat that size must have an owner. Surely the Coast Guard can tell us?"

"Sorry, Guv. They say it's classified," said Sergeant Warner.

"Classified?" muttered the Detective Inspector. He frowned as his brain processed the information, watching through a cracked window of the Spooky-Wooky Haunted House, as the ship disappeared over the horizon.

CHAPTER 23 – SOMETHIN' STUPID.

Four days after their daring escape from HMS Chichester (which Detective Inspector Sergeant-Constable *still* couldn't find any information about), Cheddar George trundled along the promenade in his Oldie TT with Lottie next to him in the sidecar. A Perry Como tune played from the C90 tape in the forty-year-old radio cassette player.

Detective Inspector Sergeant-Constable had asked them both lots of questions in those four days, trying to piece together who was behind the kidnappings. Questions that neither could answer, so he'd made no progress in the case.

"Nosey Rosie Saunders reckons MI5 are taking over the investigation," said Cheddar George, watching a hungry seagull land on the promenade wall in front of them and peck at a piece of peppermint rock.

"Do you think she's right?" Lottie asked.

"Crikey, no. Nosey Rosie is *never* right. Hopefully the Detective Inspector will detect and inspect and get to the bottom of it. But interviewing the old folk who escaped with us will take a while.

"I can't stop thinking about it. What could have happened if we hadn't got away," said Lottie, close to tears.

"Never let thoughts of yesterday take up too much of today, darling. Tell you what, how about I treat you to a nice drink and a bun to cheer us up. Where shall we go?"

The idea of a Choc-Berry did make Lottie feel a little better.

"Can we go to the Coffiesta over there? I know you'll like it," she said, pointing along the promenade.

"Tickety-boo. I've heard a lot of good things about these new coffee shops that are popping up everywhere. Nosey Rosie Saunders reckons another one is opening in the Newport Crematorium next week. Mind you, heaven knows how they will roast the coffee beans in *that* one!"

"I want to collect a napkin from as many Coffiestas as I can and this is a good day to start," said Lottie.

"That's the spirit, Lottie. Rise and shine," said Cheddar George, heading the Oldie TT towards the coffee shop. He parked outside and both his good knee *and* bad knee creaked as he climbed off the seat. "Lead on Macduff."

Behind the counter in the bustling Coffiesta, Guz Sharma wiped his hands down the front of his filthy beige shirt and threw an empty milk carton towards the bin (but missed).

"By jimminee. This is a busy place," said Cheddar George, noticing all the old people sitting at tables, drinking and chatting excitedly to each other.

"Morning, dudes," said Guz, straightening his trilby hat.

"Kalispera, young man. Do you have Bovril?" Cheddar George asked.

"No. They don't do Bovril," said Lottie, smiling an apology at Guz Sharma.

"My new hearing aid works a treat, but my eyesight isn't what it was," said Cheddar George, squinting and struggling to read the menu on a blackboard which hung on the wall behind the counter.

"I can do you a Jimmy-Horlicks?" offered Guz.

"Thank you but no thank you, I only drink Horlicks after half-past dark," said Cheddar George.

"OK, dude. Then why not try an A-C-Tea-C?" suggested Guz.

"Goodness me, no," said Cheddar George. "Rule 43 from my 90-11 years on this earth – don't eat or drink anything that sounds like it came from a Swedish furniture store. I'll have a cup of *normal* tea and a piece of that John-Lennon-Drizzle-Cake," he added, pointing to a beige patterned plate on the counter, piled high with squares of yellow cake.

"Okey dokey. And can I tempt you to a Fred Éclair? They're for vegans."

"Sadly, I'm a Capricorn," said Cheddar George. "But thank you anyway."

"I'd like a Choc-Berry please and a piece of Flap-Jackie-Chan. It looks yummy," said Lottie.

Guz Sharma put the cakes on some plates while Cheddar George struggled to pull his wallet from the back pocket of his pink and blue striped trousers.

"Dude, that's eight pounds 50," Guz said after prodding a screen.

"Snakes alive! *Eight* pounds and ten shillings," said Cheddar George. "That was a week's wages when I drove buses! These places must make a *fortune*. It's a good job they've got an awful lot of coffee in Brazil."

Gus Sharma's eyes darted around the busy coffee shop, and he grinned and leant across the counter and lowered his voice. "Dude, you're one of us!"

"Am I?" asked Cheddar George, looking at Lottie, somewhat confused.

"Hun-percent, Old Dude. As we say, They've Got An Awful Lot Of Coffee In Brazil. Know what I mean?" asked Guz, winking.

"Of course, young man. There is a lot of coffee in Brazil," said Cheddar George, winking back at Guz Sharma. "*Mountains* of it I'd say," he added while pulling a 10 pound note from his wallet.

Guz Sharma put his hand up to stop him. "Old Dude and young duchess, as you're part of Papa Charlie's gang, drinks are on the house. Gratis."

"Young man, thou speaks with a tongue of jibber," said Cheddar George.

"What, Old Dude?"

"It's from Shakespeare. It means your choice of language is 'of the moment'."

Guz Sharma looked pleased with himself. "Yowza, yowza. I've heard of that Shakespeare dude. You know him?"

"Sadly, our paths have never crossed," said Cheddar George.

"You take a seat and I'll crank the steam kettle-o for them two brews and whiz 'em up and zippy-zip 'em over," said Guz.

"Sure. We'll *Duck and Dive* to a table over there while you *Tom Mix*!" said Cheddar George, rattling off random bingo calls in an attempt to sound 'of the moment'.

Lottie was still giggling when she sat at the only free table in the Coffiesta. She put Casey on her lap and Cheddar George eased slowly onto the beige bench next to her and opened a copy of Sea Cruising Today.

"What a pavlova. I struggled to understand a word he said."

"I bet he thinks the same after your bingo lingo. But free drinks. Lush," said Lottie.

"Agreed indeed. He thinks we're involved in some group he's part of with this 'Proper Charlie' bloke," said Cheddar George, watching Guz Sharma pour boiling milk into a mug and spilling most of it on the floor.

"Why did he keep yacking on about Brazil and coffee?" asked Lottie.

Cheddar George shrugged and noticed the Duke slip from Casey's belly and scribbled on a napkin.

"Something smells foo-foo to me. I'll check it out."

As Guz Sharma came over to them, the Duke shot under the tables and between all the pensioners bandy legs. When nobody was watching, he shot behind the counter and into Guz's office.

"Chill and relish," said Guz, sliding the tray onto their table containing beige mugs and plates with their drinks and cakes, along with a pile of beige Coffiesta napkins with red writing.

"Thank you, young man. Eight and three, *Time for tea,*" said Cheddar George.

*

In the office, three PCS agents sat at their desks wearing headphones. The Duke couldn't tell what they were doing, so sneaked over to Guz Sharma's desk and quietly searched through the drawers. When he found nothing suspicious, he emptied the contents of a bin under the desk onto the floor and checked the contents. Still nothing of interest or untoward.

Then the Duke spotted it. A black and white photo pinned to a cork notice board next to Guz's desk. The photo showed Guz Sharma with his arm draped around an older man's shoulder. What the Duke saw on Guz's arm was very interesting.

*

A minute later, from under the table, Cheddar George felt something tugging at the sleeve of his purple shirt. He glanced down at his lap to see the Duke had returned and Penny and Ledley were quickly drawing on his hand by his trusted Timex.

The Duke wrote frantically on a piece of Paddy which had settled on Cheddar George's lap.

"Show the tattoo."

"Ah well, Lottie. It must be nearly time to *duck and dive*," said Cheddar George, checking his trusted Timex and making sure Guz Sharma spotted his new tattoo of a mermaid's tail.

"Snap, Dude!" said Guz, yanking his sleeve up to reveal the tattoo he'd drawn. "We are bangin' bruvvers."

"Bruvvers?" asked Cheddar George.

"Hun-percent. We work for Papa Charlie," squealed Guz.

Lottie smiled politely (not knowing what on earth was going on). She sipped her Choc-Berry and slid one of the napkins inside Casey. It would be the very first of her new collection. She too had a new tattoo on her wrist, and no idea what it was doing there.

Guz Sharma grinned. "Hey, Duchess. Are you a *Collector*?"

"Totes," said Lottie.

"Yowza! How many have you *collected* so far?"

"Only one," said Lottie.

Cheddar George slurped his Tea-Ner-Turner.

"But I'm sure Lottie here will grab a few more in the coming weeks. When it comes to collecting, she's tash-hag *Queen bee*."

"And so bangin' young! When did ya start?" asked Guz Sharma, sliding into the empty seat opposite Cheddar George.

"This morning," Lottie said. "We're going to Yarmouth tomorrow and I'll hopefully collect another one."

"Really? Another one so soon! That's plush. Mind you, we have far too many if you ask me. No harm in nabbin' a few, is there."

"No," said Lottie, somewhat confused why the

man in the grubby uniform was so keen to know about her new hobby of collecting napkins.

Guz leant across the table to whisper, "I've fist bumped Papa Charlie *and* Maddie our bangin' Collector."

"Maddie?" asked Lottie, still totally baffled about what was going on and who these people were.

"She's known as 'Maddie the Baddie'," said Guz. "And she's a top Collector and a bangin' master of disguise!"

Cheddar George suddenly understood what Guz Sharma was talking about. He swallowed his mouthful of John-Lennon-Drizzle-Cake and washed it down with a mouthful of tea. "We've seen her in action a number of times, she's *Top of The Shop*."

"The best. She's collected loads of oldies from the island," agreed Guz.

Cheddar George leant across the table and lowered his voice. "We need to *Pick 'n Mix* your brains, my friend. Do you know where we can find Maddie the Baddie?"

"Nah. She's a nomad. Why do you need to tap her up?"

Cheddar George leant even closer to Guz. "Well, I heard she did the *Dirty Gertie* on *Two Fat Ladies* and Lottie here is desperate to find out how she did that and learn from the best."

Guz Sharma shook his head. "I dunno where she is. She's got a hide-out somewhere in the Bay, but you won't find her, Dude," he said, standing and adjusting his stained trilby. "Add-up-in-the-night-time," he said with a big grin, wagging a finger.

"What was all that about. And when did we get these tattoos?" Lottie asked, as Guz returned to the counter to server an old lady with a bowl of Soup-Waddywaddy.

"Well, from what I understand, Mr Jibber Tongue over there is involved in the kidnappings. So is this 'Maddie the Baddie'.

"We need to find slash locate her," said Lottie, sounding very much like Detective Inspector Seargent-Constable. She shoved the last piece of Flap-Jackie-Chan in her mouth and licked her fingers.

Cheddar George spat on a napkin and wiped the tattoo from his wrist.

"Agreed indeed. Something tells me we haven't seen the last of Maddie."

Alan Barbara

CHAPTER 24 – TAKE IT TO THE LIMIT.

Ridgewood Golf Club is set in one hundred and sixty acres of gentle rolling hills just outside Alum Bay. The sun, high in the sky, cast short shadows across the lush, well-watered grass. Maddie crouched behind a thick bush by the sixth green that smelt of apples. She'd been there for three hours, watching small groups of golfers walk up the fairway, all hitting their golf balls towards the yellow flagstick in the middle of the green. She wasn't enjoying the wait.

At last, Maddie saw the person she'd come to meet. Sir Charles Oakley strolled up the fairway and onto the green. He had his pipe dangling from his mouth and Emelia Douthwaite stopped pushing his golf trolley and handed him his Callaway putter. The smell of the Pierre Thabaut perfume she'd sprayed on herself on the first tee was wearing off and Emelia's nostrils now smelt the burnt pig-poo sulphur stench from her boss' pipe.

"This putt is for a five, Emelia," said Sir Charles without removing his pipe, and he tapped his golf ball hopefully towards the hole. Emelia was certain he'd taken eight shots so far on this hole (and lost at least two balls in the process) but said nothing and quickly sprayed her head and shoulders with a few more squirts of perfume.

The dimpled ball stopped an inch from the hole and Sir Charles frowned. "Close enough. Call it five," he said, puffing a fresh cloud of grey smoke.

Emelia wrote his score on a scorecard and slid the silver putter in the golf bag. Then she pushed the heavy trolley and hurried after Sir Charles as he headed for the seventh tee.

As they walked past the clump of bushes, Maddie emerged, scratching her arms, now covered in gnat bites, due to the tedious wait.

"Ah Maddie, my dear. Ad infinitum, et ultra," said Sir Charles.

Emelia Douthwaite looked shocked and wagged a finger. "Ad infinitum. Maddie, what are you doing here?"

"I asked young Maddie to come for a little chat. I have a special assignment that requires her *particular* skill set," said Sir Charles, looking around to make sure nobody else would hear their conversation. "Now, Maddie. Well done for collecting George Hardwick this week."

"Thank you, Sir Charles," said Maddie.

Sir Charles flashed a disappointed look at his caddy. "It's just a shame, Emelia, that *your* Shipping Department couldn't stop him and the other ruddy *pensioners* escaping from the Chichester. I'll be the laughingstock of the whole government if this ever gets out," he said.

It would also definitely sink his dream of becoming Prime Minister when Jammy Jarvis stepped down.

"I'll have my report on your desk by nine o'clock tomorrow," said Emelia, her cheeks blushing.

"Anyway," continued Sir Charles, puffing yet more pig-poo smoke. "George Hardwick needs to know we mean business. I want you, Maddie, to grab him *again*."

"Again? But… we're not allowed to collect him again, Sir Charles. What about the three-strike rule *you* agreed to," said Emelia.

"I've scrapped it, on *this* occasion," said Sir Charles, waving a dismissive hand. "And there's more to this collection. I've been made aware of an opportunity where George Hardwick and a few more wrinklies who've crossed me in the past, will all be together at the same place and time. And I want young Maddie here to collect them *all*."

Emelia Douthwaite stood open-mouthed, not believing what Sir Charles was actually saying.

"How many?" asked Maddie.

"Well, old George Hardwick of course, plus another four," Sir Charles said, pulling a golf club from his bag and stepping onto the seventh tee.

Emelia took a deep breath and regained the use of her mouth. "Five! A total of Five! And have they *all-*?"

"Sush, Emelia," said Sir Charles. "Can't you see I'm about to tee off."

Sir Charles took aim, swung the club and smacked his golf ball as hard as he could, slicing it into a tree to his right. The ball clattered around the branches, finally dropping at Emelia's feet.

"Puffle-huff," said Sir Charles.

Emelia Douthwaite quickly scooped the ball up and held it behind her back. Sir Charles marched over and held his hand out.

"Don't you dare count that shot."

Emelia certainly wasn't giving the ball back yet. She needed an explanation. "As I was asking, Sir Charles, have these five pensioners *all* confessed to a crime and therefore, are allowed to be taken… as per the strict PCS rules?"

"Not exactly, Emelia. But as Home Secretary, *I* make the rules."

Emelia shook her head. "You can't–"

Sir Charles jabbed a finger at Emilia. "Puffle-huff. I can and I *will.*"

"I'll do it," said Maddie. "For ten times the usual collection payment."

"Excellent. The deal is done. Now, as you know, I have my country residence near here and my dear wife is the head of the Isle of Wight Culture Club. She received an invitation to the opening of that new Trocadero club in Alum Bay. It's on Saturday and I've had a peek at the VIP guest list they sent and saw the names of some scallywags from my grammar school days – ruffians who made my life a misery. So *this* is my chance to get even."

"I don't believe it," sighed Emelia, shaking her

head. "What *on earth* did four school children do all those years ago that now makes it OK for you to have them kidnapped and locked up for the rest of their lives?"

Sir Charles puffed on his pipe and Maddie was certain she spotted a tear in his eye. "They were horrid braggarts at the Old Priory Grammar School. Called themselves the OP Gang. They got into all sorts of scrapes and did nasty things to me - like stealing my tuck shop money and putting worms in my underpants. And that was just the girls. The boys were *far* worse. One day they locked the headmistress, Fanny Falstaff, in a cold store in the kitchen block and the other teachers couldn't get her out. The OP Gang said I'd done it, so I got the blame. I can still remember the headline in the Bay News – 'Fearless Fireman Fred Farall Frees Frightened Fanny Falstaff From F-F-F-Freezer'."

Emelia frowned. "But surely, that was just a froolish, I mean *foolish* school prank?"

"A school prank which stopped me becoming Head Boy at the Old Priory. Father was so disappointed in me after that and always said I was a failure."

"I'll need equipment from PCS Control and some help on the night," said Maddie, knowing that the collection payment for this job would surely give her enough money to buy her Astronaut Roxy doll.

Sir Charles thought for a second while he puffed on his pipe.

"Emelia, get that manager from the Coffiesta in Alum Bay to assist. He's after promotion."

239

"But… this is wrong, Sir Charles. You can't collect this OP Gang, or *OAP* Gang as they would be now, with their dodgy knees and bus passes," said Emelia.

"Nonsense. Maddie, here is a list of those invited to the opening of the Trocadero. I've marked the ones I want you to collect," Sir Charles said, handing her a piece of folded paper.

Maddie's eyes scanned the list of names. Four were circled in red.

Fred Quigly
Rosie Saunders
Arthur Fry
Nancy O'Neil

Sir Charles then marched back to the seventh tee and pulled another spare golf ball from his pocket. "Ad infinitum, et ultra."

CHAPTER 25 – STRANGERS IN THE NIGHT.

SooTed and BooTed stood in their dressing room at the Trocadero. SooTed flicked a boiled sweet into his mouth and crunched. The smell of fresh paint lingered in the air. On the wall opposite the door, hung a framed poster of Showaddywaddy. It was signed by the band after a concert in Blackpool in 1985; the first of many Showaddywaddy concerts SooTed and BooTed had gone to over the years.

BooTed took a swig from a bottle of water. "Hydrate to enunciate, mate."

"Too right, buddy," said SooTed. "Well, this is it. Opening night. Nervous-as," he said, slipping on his duck-egg blue jacket and admiring himself in a tall mirror.

BooTed grinned as he combed his hair, sweeping it into an elegant quiff.

"We've waited a *very* long time for this. I only hope it all goes to plan. What if-"

"Poz-not-neg, mate, remember," said SooTed. "I'm sure it will be a blast. Which reminds me, I'm just going to check the air-con temperature after the BREW Crew fitted the new thermostat yesterday."

"OK. I'll make sure the box office is ready," said BooTed, slipping his comb into the pocket of his lilac jacket.

In the box office sat Nanny Vera and Grandad Frank. Nanny Vera's knitting needles clattered in a blur as she made herself a purple head band, like the ones she wore back in the 50s when she went dancing at the village hall in Freshwater with Grandad Frank. The splash of colour would complement her granouflage pleated skirt and cardigan (with her spit-wash hankie tucked up one sleeve).

Grandad Frank sat next to Nanny Vera, testing a new PayCheck chip and pin credit card reader. He was trying it out with his credit card and so far, had spent sixteen pounds and 83 pence of his own money and *still* couldn't get the hang of it.

Cheddar George trundled into the foyer on his Oldie TT – specially decorated for the occasion with a dozen silver cheerleader pompoms tied to the front. He wore an Elvis Presley fancy dress costume he'd bought from Verdi last year; a white jacket with huge baggy sleeves and red and gold trimmings, white flared trousers and a red shimmering cape. A black wig covered his thinning grey hair.

He rode up to the box office carrying a tray with two mugs of champagne (half full – with the rest leaving a trail on the floor from where he'd come).

"I couldn't find any glasses. But I'm sure this Asti Spew-Mandy will taste just the same from these old mugs."

"Oh lovely," said Nanny Vera. "The last time we had champagne, Frank, was at your cousin's wedding where you shouted at that woman for pushing in front of you in the queue for the buffet."

"The Vicar should have known better," said Grandad Frank, taking a mug. "Thanks, Cheddar George. Is Lottie OK?"

"Totes," said Cheddar George. "She's in that room fiddling with all those buttons and knobs on the new sound and lighting desk. That's some gizmo. I reckon it looks like something out of NASA, so I got Ledley to hang a sign up outside, saying 'Mission Control'."

Grandad Frank chuckled and spat on the back of his credit card and shoved it into the troublesome PayCheck machine again.

"I'm the official photographer this evening. Always fancied myself as a Pepperoni," Cheddar George said, checking an antique Kodak camera hanging from a brown leather strap around his neck.

Grandad Frank frowned while entering his PIN once again on the keypad. "I think you mean 'Paparazzi'."

"Oh yes, that's it, chuckled Cheddar George. "Anyway, Lottie found my old Kodak in the wardrobe with six dozen rolls of film. I hope that's enough."

"I'm sure it is," said Grandad Frank, wondering how much it would cost to get all those films developed.

"The old flash gun was a little dull, but the BREW

Crew managed to beef it up a bit," said Cheddar George.

"That's nice, dad," said Nanny Vera, finishing yet another row of knitting.

She knew with Cheddar George's shaky hands his photos would be just a foggy blur, but at least it gave him something to do and hopefully take his mind off releasing 'Tommy' from prison and ruining the atmosphere – literally!

Suddenly, the Showaddywaddy tune *You Got What It Takes* boomed from every speaker in the building, making Grandad Frank jump and spill his champagne over the credit card reader. The music stopped just as quickly as it started, and Lottie called from her seat in Mission Control.

"Nik-nacks. Sorry. Wrong button."

"No problem, Lottie. I needed to clear my ear wax anyway," Grandad Frank called back, dabbing his sleeve on the PayCheck machine to mop up the spilt champagne.

BooTed checked his watch for the tenth time in as many minutes. "Let's go over the plan once more. I'm expecting some waiters any minute to hand out the drinks and Vera's canapés. Then the Mayor and twenty other VIPs will start arriving. And then later, we'll *hopefully* get a crowd of paying punters for our big show at eight. Vera and Frank, you're in charge of selling tickets, but not to the VIPs as they get in for free."

Nanny Vera nodded and Grandad Frank gave a thumbs-up while sipping his champagne.

BooTed checked his watch again and continued.

"Good. And Lottie is in charge of music and lighting and Cheddar George…"

"I'm Elvis the pepper-whatnot," said Cheddar George. He pointed his Kodak at BooTed and pressed the button to take a picture. There was a WHUMP as the upgraded flash lit up the whole foyer as if a huge lightning bolt had struck, causing BooTed to actually go blind for a few seconds.

While BooTed rubbed his eyes, trying to regain his sight, Maddie Mainard walked confidently through the entrance, followed by Guz Sharma. Both were dressed smartly in black trousers and white shirts. Maddie wore a long blonde wig, tied in bunches and thick, tortoiseshell glasses. She'd helped with Guz Sharma's disguise – a curly black wig and walrus moustache. Guz carried a large cardboard box with 'Bay Catering' printed on the side.

"Kalispera," said Cheddar George.

Maddie recognised the greeting from the man dressed as Elvis. "Good evening," said Maddie in a broad Scottish accent. "We're the waiters you hired. I'm Audrey Robinson and this is…"

"Zak Zorro, with our waiter-job stuff," said Guz, patting the lid of the box.

Maddie's look from behind her glasses told him to keep quiet.

Nanny Vera stuffed her knitting in her beige handbag. "Ah, good. I'll take you through to the kitchen where you'll find my tasty canapés. You're more than welcome to any leftovers later."

"If you fancy a challenge," muttered Grandad Frank,

245

reading page 17 of the instruction manual for the troublesome PayCheck machine.

Nanny Vera led Maddie and Guz to the kitchen, where six large plastic tubs of her beige canapés sat on a wooden table. She'd spent yesterday making them from random leftovers from all the other tubs in her kitchen. Guz Sharma put the cardboard box on the table and began removing silver trays and wine glasses from it.

Nanny Vera pointed at the coloured lids of the tubs.

"So, I *think* in the yellow tub are my corned beef and custard tarts. Then the blue one is salmon pancakes with eggnog and chocolate sprinkles, and the orange one is Marmite and Marshmallow pies,"

"Awesome," said Guz Sharma.

"Thank you, young man. Then in the blue tub at the back are boiled egg with liquorice and sherbet dib-dabs, and in the pink one is Brussels sprout and toffee popcorn rolls. And finally, in the purple tub we have pickled onion and Haribo pies."

Maddie couldn't quite believe what Nanny Vera had just proudly described. She tried her hardest to look unconcerned, as if pickled onion and Haribo tarts were something people ate often, like sausage rolls.

"And what flavour crisps are these, duchess?" Guz Sharma asked, helping himself to a handful of odd shaped purple flakes from a bowl.

"That's lavender potpourri," said Nanny Vera. "I say you can't beat the smell of lavender on a late summer's evening."

Guz spat the potpourri flakes into his hand, which he then wiped down the front of his white shirt, causing a purple stain.

"Och aye. Your canapés sound *delicious*. We'll put them on trays, ready to serve to your guests," said Maddie.

"Perfect. I'm sure they'll go down a treat," said Nanny Vera.

"These look well-plush, duchess," said Guz, removing the lid of the purple tub and having a good sniff of the pickled onion and Haribo pies.

"Too kind," smiled Nanny Vera and left Maddie and Guz and returned to the box office to find BooTed pacing back and forth.

"What if no one comes tonight? Or we mess it up on stage?" he asked.

"Take a few deep breaths, dear. I'm sure everything will be fine," said Nanny Vera, picking up her knitting needles again.

"I find yodelling *very* good for stress. Shall we try?" asked Cheddar George, checking his false teeth were stuck to his gnarled gums with plenty of Dent-a-fix.

He pursed his lips and yodelled the first line of Elvis Presley's 'Hound Dog' but stopped when an elderly woman scurried through the entrance.

The woman was Nancy O'Neil, the Mayor of Alum Bay and the leader of the town council. She wore a long purple velvet gown that stretched to her ankles. A huge gold ceremonial chain decorated her neck, which was so heavy, it made her walk with a stoop, and she could only see the ground six feet in front of her.

"Evening, your worship," said Nanny Vera.

"Good evening, young man," said Nancy O'Neil in a

very posh voice, unable to raise her head to see who she was actually speaking to.

"It's very good of you to come, your worship," said BooTed.

"Oh, I just had to. But sadly, I can't stay long. There's an important council meeting later which I *must* attend. But when I got the invitation, I knew I couldn't miss the reopening of this wonderful theatre. So many memories."

The Mayor was *desperate* for this evening to go well after her last official engagement ended very badly. That was last December when she switched on the Alum Bay Christmas lights.

On that memorable evening, she'd stood on a windy stage outside the Verdi supermarket and made a nice speech to a large crowd and then pressed a red button to light up the town centre.

That all went very well, but as she made her way off the stage, she tripped on the frayed hem of her velvet gown, toppled forwards and spilt a pint glass of mulled wine over a mass of power plugs. The warm liquid flooded the electrics and blew the electricity to seven hundred houses (including Lottie's) and plunged Alum Bay into darkness for a week. The residents were furious and since then Grandad Frank had called her 'Nancy Night Mayor.'

"I'm *delighted* to be at the reopening of this wonderful building that's so important to our community," said Nancy Night Mayor. "And I'm amazed that you've completed this outstanding work so quickly."

"Perhaps you'd consider employing the builders who worked here to fix the streetlight in our road that hasn't worked since *you* broke it," muttered Grandad Frank. Nanny Vera gave him a side-eye glare.

Nancy Night Mayor ignored the comment. "Where are the new owners?"

"That's me. I'm BooTed," said BooTed nervously and still squinting from the effects of Cheddar George's flash gun.

"Charming," said Nancy, shaking hands and talking to BooTed's freshly-brushed suede boots.

SooTed hurried into the foyer while crunching on a boiled sweet and quickly swallowed it.

"And I'm SooTed."

He took Nancy Night Mayor's hand, peering down at the top of her bowed head and was surprised to see a few nits jumping about. "Pleased-to."

Nancy Night Mayor's face winced at SooTed's firm handshake and she thought her fingers might break. "Charmed as well. Will you show me around? I'm really looking forward to it."

"You haven't 'looked forward' for ages," muttered Grandad Frank.

"Kalispera, your worship-ness," said Cheddar George.

"Kalispera. You speak Greek," said Nancy Night Mayor. "I know a little. Yasas. That means 'hello'."

"Indeed. Nana Moskouri," replied Cheddar George. "Now, before you nip off, I must get a quick snap of your Mayor-ness for the album."

SooTed and BooTed stood either side of Nancy

Night Mayor, who summoned all the strength in her neck muscles to lift her head and smile at the camera (for only a couple of seconds). Cheddar George took the photo and another huge flash exploded.

"Tickety-boo. That will be a good one."

"Unlikely," muttered Grandad Frank.

SooTed, BooTed and Nancy Night Mayor rubbed their eyes and when they could eventually see again, they walked into the auditorium where the two waiters stood, holding glasses of Italian Villa Barilla wine.

The builders had done a stunning job, turning the dusty auditorium into the Trocadero's new dance floor, made from planks of polished wood. Coloured lights shone off a huge silver glitter-ball which hung from the roof, all controlled by an ECHO-TECH-10A sound and lighting desk (the best SooTed and BooTed could afford) in Mission Control.

Other members of the OP Gang began arriving at the box office. Fred Quigly was first. He was a small man with a thick black beard full of crumbs. He owned the Sconehenge Cafe just along the road from the Trocadero.

Next came Arthur Fry, who used to run the local fish and chip shop called The Chippy Plaice. He'd retired a year ago, but somehow he still stank of chip oil.

And finally, Nosey Rosie Saunders marched in carrying a placard which read, 'IT'S A BIN SIN'.

Rosie stomped through the foyer chanting "What do we want? Bins collected. When do we want it? THE SAME DAY AS WE DO NOW."

"Kalispera, Mrs Saunders," said Cheddar George. "Nice placard. The colours match your frock."

"Good evening, Cheddar George. Love the Elvis look," said Nosey Rosie Saunders.

Cheddar George blew his nose on a yellow polka dot handkerchief and glanced at the result before stuffing it back in his pocket. "I'm up for a dance later if you fancy one. In my day I used to love a bit of Agadoo, although with my bad knee, these days it's more Agadon't."

Nosey Rosie Saunders smiled. "That would be stupendous, Cheddar George. Tell me, is the Mayor here? Only I need to have a serious chat with her about her silly, silly plan to change the day of our bin collection. The council members are voting on it tonight and it just won't do."

"She's through there, my dear," said Cheddar George, nodding towards the twinkling lights in the auditorium.

"Give her hell," muttered Grandad Frank, giving the PayCheck chip and pin reader a wallop with the instruction manual and then switching it off and on for the *fifth* time.

Nosey Rosie Saunders marched into the auditorium with her placard held high, nearly clouting it on SooTed and BooTed's expensive glitter ball.

*

"Worried-as," said SooTed, pacing back and forth by the box office. "Only three VIPs and the Mayor have bothered to turn up."

"I know mate, I *just* don't understand. I phoned all

20 a couple of days ago and every VIP agreed to come along tonight," said BooTed.

Grandad Frank wondered if word had got out about Nanny Vera's choice of fillings for her canapés and that had put people off but decided not to mention it.

"Don't worry, dears," said Nanny Vera. "It is what it is. I believe everything happens for a reason."

Maddie Mainard *was* the reason. The day before, she'd disguised herself as the new postman (now that Owen was sunning himself on his cruise to Adapazari) and delivered notes through the letterboxes of the other 17 VIPs in Alum Bay, telling them that SooTed and Booted had caught Satnite Fever and the opening of the Trocadero had been cancelled. She was now ready for the Distract and Snatch of the five pensioners.

CHAPTER 26 – RUNNING WITH THE NIGHT.

The OP Gang stood together under the sparkling glitter ball in the auditorium, swapping chit-chat about what they'd been up to since leaving the Old Priory Grammar School many years ago.

"Now, Nancy," said Nosey Rosie Saunders, deciding it was time to get serious. She lowered her placard to the floor so that Nancy Night Mayor could read it.

"What's all this *nonsense* about changing my bin day? It's an outrage. My Neighbourhood Watch unit haven't been consulted. I hope you and the council see sense when you vote tonight. You *do* know an Olympic rower lives in my road."

The Mayor plonked herself on a chair as the weight from the massive chain around her neck gave her terrible backache. She managed to raise her eyes no higher than Nosey Rosie's belly button. "Shut it, Rosie, or I'll cut all your hair off, like I did at school."

"Humph," Nosey Rosie said. "You haven't heard the last of this, Nancy Nasty Knickers."

"Our school closed. Did you know?" said Fred

Quigly. "Furthermore, they knocked it down and built a bus depot in the grounds. And further-furthermore, that's now closed too."

"The Old Priory wasn't the same once Fanny Falstaff left," said Arthur Fry and chuckled. "Do you remember when we locked her in the freezer!"

"And furthermore, blamed Oakley!" said Fred Quigly, sniggering like a schoolboy as he remembered the incident.

"I wonder what he's up to these days?" asked Arthur Fry.

"Surely you know. He's the Home Secretary," said Nosey Rosie Saunders.

"Is he? Smoke me a haddock. I didn't realise that was *our* Oakley," said Arthur Fry.

"I'd still shove worms in his underpants," said Nancy Night Mayor.

"Canapé, Dude?" Guz Sharma asked, holding a large silver tray of beige squares under Fred Quigly's crumby beard.

"They look tasty. What's in them, young man?"

"The duchess said these ones are Marmite and Marshmallow pies," said Guz.

"Ah. Then no thank you," said Fred Quigly. "I'm not a fan of Marmite. I'd rather eat my own hair."

The silver tray was offered to the others, but having heard the unusual ingredients, they all politely refused. Guz Sharma retreated to the kitchen where Maddie had placed five of Nanny Vera's corned beef and custard tarts on another tray and was basting the beige pastry with a clear liquid.

"They all *have* to take a bite of one of these," said Maddie.

"What's that you're putting on them, sis?" asked Guz.

"It's Kacka-Lax. It was first made in World War Two and our lab got hold of the formula and made me some."

Guz leaned closer and sniffed. "Plush! What does it do?"

"Kacka-Lax causes merry mayhem in the guts as soon as it's taken, and then there's an interesting twist."

"Which is?" asked Guz, scratching his head under the curly wig.

"Exactly six minutes after it hits the stomach, Kacka-Lax reacts with the acid produced by the stomach. It slows the heart rate and knocks you out. You sleep like a baby," said Maddie, grinning and arranging the five canapés neatly on the silver tray.

"Yowza, yowza," said Guz

Maddie dropped the empty bottle of Kacka-Lax in a bin. "You bring those pickled onion and Haribo tart things and offer them first, then I'll get all five of the old codgers to eat these."

"Once they know what they're made from, you won't get *anyone* to eat this muck," said Guz, turning his nose up.

"Watch and learn, Agent Zorro. Watch and learn," smiled Maddie and picked up the tray of her very special canapés and headed for the auditorium.

The OP Gang still chatted while sipping their Villa Barilla wine. They'd been joined by Cheddar George.

He whizzed between them on his Oldie TT taking photos (all of them blurry) and causing short bouts of temporary blindness with the powerful flash gun.

Fred Quigly was boring the pants off Nancy Night Mayor, telling her in great detail how his lemon curd scones had been voted the best on the Isle of Wight. Arthur Fry, (who'd already heard Fred's tedious sconey tale), helped himself to another glass of Villa Barilla and joined Nosey Rosie Saunders and Cheddar George, who chatted about 'the good old days'.

"Life was simpler in our day, when a rectangle was called an oblong," said Arthur Fry.

"Agreed indeed," said Cheddar George.

Arthur Fry sipped his wine and gargled before swallowing. "I mean, in our day you didn't have frozen food. We cooked everything from fresh and there was no such thing as a microwave. My son found half a conker in his Slim-To-Trim ready-meal last week and was rushed to hospital to have his stomach pumped."

"I didn't know conkers were that poisonous," said Nancy Night Mayor, staring at Arthur Fry's knees.

"Weak stomachs, that's the problem with the younger generation. A lack of germs due to all the bleach they chuck around. Load of cod-wallop," said Arthur Fry.

"Agreed indeed," said Cheddar George. "Do you know, I ate raw potato peelings for a week during the war and they never affected me."

"Was that due to rationing?" Nancy Night Mayor asked.

"Oh no, my dear. It was when I forgot my wife's

birthday," said Cheddar George.

"There isn't an illness known to man that can't be cured by a Spam and chips, tea and carbolic soap," said Arthur Fry.

"Canapé?" interrupted Guz Sharma, wafting his tray under their noses. "Pickled onion and Haribo tarts."

"Certainly not," said Nosey Rosie Saunders.

Arthur Fry screwed his nose up and shook his head.

"I'm due a feed," said Cheddar George and took a closer look at the beige blobs on offer. "But I'll pass and munch my emergency cheese sandwich," he said, pointing at the brown paper bag in his wicker basket.

Guz turned on his heels towards the kitchen. "Told you," he mouthed to Maddie, who approached the group with a welcoming smile.

"Och aye. Can I tempt you all with one of these? It's a boeuf salé et crème pâtissière,"

"Ohh, *please*, young lady," said Fred Quigly, grabbing the biggest canapé from Maddie's tray.

"They sound lovely," added Nosey Rosie Saunders.

The others nodded enthusiastically, and each took a corned beef and custard tart and munched happily.

Maddie smiled again. "Enjoy the rest of your evening," she said and as she turned away, she checked the time on her watch.

Cheddar George decided after a couple of bites that he didn't care at all for the taste of the canapé and hid the rest in his wicker basket under a pile of butterscotch sweets. The OP Gang managed to finish theirs, but all took a large mouthful of Villa Barilla to get rid of the taste.

As Maddie headed for the kitchen, she tossed the empty silver tray across the auditorium like a frisbee and muttered.

"It won't be long now."

CHAPTER 27 – FOLLOW YOU FOLLOW ME.

Maddie and Guz Sharma hid behind a large Rock-ola jukebox in the auditorium. The OP Gang were still chatting and laughing with their new friend, Cheddar George, who was now munching his emergency sandwich and dropping crumbs of cheese on the polished dance floor.

Suddenly, Fred Quigly clutched his stomach and looked worried. "Back in a mo," he said and hurried towards the gent's toilet.

"Quickly, Quigly," chuckled Arthur Fry.

As Fred Quigly neared the toilet door, his hurry became a frantic dash and he barged open the door.

No sooner had he disappeared inside, when the other four pensioners all felt a strange churning in their stomachs. Wine glasses were hurriedly plonked on tables and a race for the toilets began.

Unfortunately, Nancy Night Mayor had two problems. Firstly, the weight of her gold chain meant she couldn't move at any speed and secondly, as she couldn't see where to go, she headed off in the wrong direction. Cheddar George threw his sandwich into the wicker basket and screeched up next to her in his Oldie TT.

"Hop aboard, your worship-ness. Your chariot awaits."

"Thank you, you're a life saver. And probably a knicker saver too," said Nancy Night Mayor, clambering unladylike into the sidecar.

Cheddar George stamped on the power pedal and whizzed across the auditorium, passing the other three runners, to claim first place in the 'Over 65's fancy dress 50-yard lavatory dash'.

"Worked like a charm," said Maddie, nudging Guz Sharma's elbow and watching 'Cheddar Elvis' scramble at an unbelievable speed into the toilets with the others.

"Plush! What now?" asked Guz, stuffing another pickled onion and Haribo tart in his mouth.

Maddie checked her watch.

"You head back to the Coffiesta and inform PCS Control and I'll nab all five of them before the next stage of the Kacka-Lax kicks in, which will be in… three minutes and 20 seconds. Then I'll take them to the prison ship and get paid. Job done!"

"That's bangin', sis. See you later," said Guz Sharma and he rushed off towards the box office, mumbling the PCS secret passphrase to himself.

Maddie's Distract and Snatch was working like a charm, and he'd surely get promoted to a Collector after tonight.

Maddie watched from her hiding place behind the juke box, as one by one, the shell-shocked pensioners emerged from the toilets.

"Furthermore, that was too close for comfort," said Fred Quigly, mopping his brow on a paper towel.

Arthur Fry puffed out his cheeks. "Smoke me a haddock. I think I'll call it a night."

"I think so too, but I came on the bus and I'm not sure I'd make it home without a... mishap," said Nosey Rosie Saunders.

Cheddar George eased slowly onto his scooter's tartan seat. "And I'm with Vera and Frank and they're busy in the box office. My Oldie TT's battery won't last to get me all the way home."

Nancy Night Mayor looked as worried as the rest. "I'm supposed to be at a council meeting in half an hour."

"Well, I walked here and can't possibly clench my bum cheeks for my long walk home," said Arthur Fry.

"Canapé?" asked Maddie, offering the tray of pickled onion and Haribo tarts. "Are you alright, only you *all* look a bit peaky?"

"We've just rushed to the loo to 'spend a penny', my dear," said Nancy Night Mayor.

"More like a pound in my case," said Cheddar George. "Tash-hag poonami."

"And we don't feel at all well and should be getting home as soon as we can, but don't believe that's possible, given our current... situation," said Nosey Rosie Saunders.

"I can take you home," said Maddie. "Och aye. My campervan is parked out the back *and* it has a loo."

"You're an angel," said Nancy Night Mayor (to Maddie's belly button) and she quickly climbed back in the Oldie TT's sidecar.

"I'll phone the box office when you're on the way home to let them know. It will be quicker if we go out the stage door at the back," said Maddie, as if she'd just thought of the idea.

"Lead on Macduff," said Cheddar George.

"Furthermore, pronto," added Fred Quigly, rubbing his rumbling stomach.

*

In Mission Control, Lottie sat behind the ECHO-TECH-10A sound and lighting desk. She was thrilled to be in charge of all the knobs, switches and LEDs that blinked like a Christmas tree. She turned a small silver dial which adjusted the stage lighting and then it was time to play the first tack on SooTed and BooTed's playlist for their opening night.

As she pressed a yellow button on the ECHO-TECH-10A to fade in *That'll Be The Day* - a classic Buddy Holly tune from the heyday of rock 'n' roll. As the track began to play the she noticed a red LED flashing on the CCTV security control panel to her left. She took a closer look and under the light, was a label which read 'CAMERA 6A – REAR STAGE DOOR'.

Curious, Lottie stood on tiptoe to see the screen showing the CCTV cameras that covered the Trocadero and pressed the button to zoom in on CAMERA 6A.

The screen showed Cheddar George in his Elvis Presley outfit, slowly climbing off his Oldie TT and being helped into an old campervan by one of the waiters. Lottie watched in disbelief as the OP Gang hastily followed him into the vehicle and the doors closed.

"Nik-nacks. Not again!" screeched Lottie, grabbing Casey and dashing from Mission Control.

*

"Elvis has left the building," muttered Maddie, and smiled at Cheddar George as she sat next to him. The OP Gang took their seats, looking worried and holding their stomachs.

Cheddar George's shaky hands fastened his seatbelt, and he rested his Kodak camera on his lap. "Where's the toilet, my dear? As an old Boy Scout I like to be prepared in these situations."

Maddie locked the door. "It's just behind us."

Cheddar George patted Maddie's hand. "Tickety-boo. I hope you have plenty of loo paper. Tash-hag bog-a-job."

"Can we get a little less conversation, Elvis, and get going?" asked Fred Quigly, dabbing his brow with a hankie to mop droplets of sweat. "My guts are somersaulting and, furthermore, telling me trouble is brewing."

"Sure," said Maddie. "Ready when you are, driver."

A figure sitting in the shadows in the front seat, wearing a brown flat cap, turned to face the five pensioners. Sir Charles Oakley's face showed a contented grin. "Surprise!"

"Smoke me a haddock! What the blazes are you doing here, Oakley?" asked Arthur Fry.

"You lot made my life a *misery* in one way or another, so now it's payback time," replied Sir Charles.

"What *are* you talking about, Oakley?" asked Fred

Quigly.

Sir Charles' eyes narrowed and he stared at the OP Gang in turn. "I'm getting my own back on you, after what you did to me at school. And as for you, George Hardwick, you're a wrinkly troublemaker."

"We should really be on our way, Sir Charles," Emelia Douthwaite hissed, cowering in the seat next to him.

*

As Lottie sprinted through the deserted auditorium, she opened Casey and the Duke shot out. "It's Cheddar George," Lottie blurted. "I think he's been kidnapped, *again*. Can you get a sitrep from the old van by the stage door?"

The Duke, who could move much faster than Lottie, took off, zooming through the empty Trocadero and out the exit, reaching the campervan just as its engine fired.

*

Cheddar George's stomach rumbled, and he felt he really needed to let 'Tommy out of prison' but decided right now wasn't the time nor place.

"What's happening *exactly*?" asked a very confused Nosey Rosie Saunders.

"Well. You *won't* be going home, Rosie," said Sir Charles with a wicked smile. "You'll all be locked up at Her Majesty's pleasure for a *very* long time. It will be punishment for your antics at the Old Priory and Fanny Falstaff not making me Head Boy."

"Heaven help us all," muttered Emelia.

The watch on Maddie's wrist showed that the six

minutes were up, and before the pensioners could do anything about escaping from the campervan, the Kacka-Lax twist did its job. Maddie sniggered as one by one the pensioners yawned and closed their eyes. In no time at all, they were all snoring peacefully (like they did every evening at home in front of their TV).

"I've done my part, Sir Charles. Now it's time for you to pay for my evening's work," said Maddie.

"Certainly," said Sir Charles as he put the van in gear and revved the engine. "Emelia, make the agreed payment to Agent Mainard."

"I can't believe I'm doing this," said Emelia Douthwaite, her fingers clattering the laptop keyboard perched on her knees. "Payment complete," she sighed, closing the lid sharply.

"All done, Maddie, my dear. Ad infinitum, et ultra!" called Sir Charles.

"Good. Now get us to Ryde Pier before anyone gets suspicious," Maddie said and wagged a finger in salute.

*

Lottie hurtled through the exit by the stage door and saw the campervan turn into the narrow road beside the Verdi supermarket. She leapt on the Oldie TT's padded seat and a piece of Paddy paper with the Duke's sitrep landed in her hand.

"A bucketload of griffin. Five kidnapped."

"Five! Was it Maddie the Baddie?" Lottie asked, dropping Casey in the wicker basket, now overflowing with various food and other stuff.

"Affirmative. She was helped by three other kidnappers. One works in the Coffiesta on the promenade, and I've seen a photo of

the driver in the manager's office during a recon. The third is an unknown female."

"That's not good. Did you find out where they are going?"

"Back to the pier in Ryde."

"Nik-nacks. We can't let them get on that ship again," said Lottie. "Quick, make the Paddy-sail-thingy again, so we can kite-scooter after them."

"Negative. There's no wind. The scooter needs to be lighter to make it go faster. Sit tight."

Spike unbolted the bracket holding the sidecar to the scooter and Rula heaved it aside.

"Sorry Cheddar George, but drastic times call for drastic measures," said Lottie. It was another of his favourite sayings and she *kind* of knew what it meant. She tugged the bulky fax machine from its fixings and tossed it in the abandoned sidecar, followed by the cheerleader's pompoms, the Master Route sat nav, an AA road atlas, two umbrellas, six packets of butterscotch sweets, three pairs of gloves, a first aid kit and a tartan blanket with matching thermos flask.

"That should do. Drive along the footpath and around to the front of the Trocadero. That's a shortcut and will bring us out on the road."

"Roger that," said Lottie.

Now, somewhat lighter, Lottie pressed the power pedal and set off at a decent speed. She followed the footpath down the side of the Trocadero and came out on the road by the Post Office. A hundred yards ahead of them she spotted the campervan approaching a T-junction.

*

Back in the campervan, Sir Charles slowed. "Which way, Maddie?"

Maddie peered out the window and recognised a row of shops. "Turn left by the Sherlock Combs barber shop, then just follow the signs to Ryde and find the pier," she shouted, watching the sleeping pensioners closely.

"Right you are," called Sir Charles, turning hard left at the barbers sending the five kidnapped passengers sliding across their seats.

"Nice and easy," called Maddie. "We don't want to attract attention from the cops."

"We certainly don't," said Emelia, sinking further into her seat and pulling the hood of her coat over her head.

Lottie watched the van turn as she followed in the Oldie TT. She trundled along the road at the scooter's top speed of just eight miles per hour and knew she had a big problem. "Once they get out of town, this scooter won't keep up with the van."

"Roger that. Pull over. I've got a plan."

Lottie steered the Oldie TT into the doorway of the Fifty Shades of Bay tattoo parlour and came to a stop.

Spike delved into the wicker basket and came out with the old RC-3 unit that Maddie used in her failed attempt to collect Cheddar George at the summer fete. Six coloured wires covered in butterscotch sweet wrappers dangled from the black box like a spider's spindly legs. Spike connected five of the wires to the scooter's electrics under the tartan seat, leaving the sixth unconnected (the purple one which he hoped controlled the steering).

"Now try the power pedal."

"Roger that," said Lottie, nudging the metal pedal with her right foot.

"Woooahh," she squealed, as the Oldie TT pelted along the footpath, flew off the kerb and hurtled down the road, it's speed now boosted by the added volts from the RC-3. "Wickedoolie. What do we do now?"

"Just follow the targets in their vehicle while we work out a plan to stop them. And don't let them see you."

CHAPTER 28 – LUCK BE A LADY.

Maddie checked each of the five pensioners sitting around her by pinching them on their cheek. None showed any sign of coming round from the Kacka-Lax, so she took out her phone and opened the DMRS banking app. With Emelia's recent payment for collecting the five snoring oldies from the Trocadero, her savings account showed a healthy total of two hundred and fifty thousand pounds. The most money she'd *ever* had. "Now to do a little business."

Maddie opened another app on her phone for Sotheby's Auction House. Her screen showed a view from a camera at the very back of the auction room at Sotheby's in London. The auction for Astronaut Roxy was about to take place. She recognised Mr Kumar, the old auctioneer, smartly dressed as usual, standing behind his antique oak lectern.

Rows of plush seats, arranged in a rainbow arc faced the lectern and were packed with the excited crowd, ready to bid against each other and hoping to win the doll. In the front row, Maddie recognised another face as he pushed rudely passed people and took his seat –

Lee Whitaker sat in silence. He stared at a black cardboard box, decorated with silver stars and a crescent moon, perched on a stand next to the auctioneer. The lid was open and inside stood the twelve-inch Astronaut Roxy doll. She was dressed in a white spacesuit with a matching helmet covering her flowing blond hair and twinkling blue eyes.

The doll was perfect, and it was hard to believe she'd been created over 45 years ago. Like Maddie, Lee Whitaker was a fanatical collector of Roxy dolls, and she knew he was as desperate as her to own this rare specimen that stood in the box next to Mr Kumar.

Lee Whitaker was familiar to everyone in the room. He often flew into a rage if he didn't get his own way and was known throughout the world of doll collecting as 'Angry Lee'.

Near the bottom of Maddie's phone screen was a place to enter the amount of money she wished to bid. The auction would start in precisely one minute and she was ready to bid *and win.*

In the distance, Sir Charles spotted a BP petrol station and beyond it, a set of traffic lights controlling another T-junction. "Collecting for the PCS is a piece of cake, Emilia,"

As the van approached the junction with Lottie zooming along on the scooter behind, a piece of Paddy, Ledley and Penny flew out of Casey from the wicker basket. They swept unnoticed through the petrol station and came out ahead of the van and flew up to the large signpost at the junction.

The green sign showed a road layout - Ryde to the

right and Newport to the left. The Paddy paper stretched to completely cover the sign and Ledley drew a new layout, now showing Ryde to the left. Penny coloured it perfectly and then hid behind the sign just as the lights turned red. Sir Charles came to a gentle stop at the lights and Lottie pulled off the road into the petrol station. While she waited for the van to move she wondered how on earth they could rescue Cheddar George and the others from the clutches of Maddie the Baddie.

*

Mr Kumar, the auctioneer, banged his wooden gavel on his oak lectern. The crowd hushed in an instant and Mr Kumar's serious voice rang from Maddie's phone.

"Welcome to Sotheby's Auction House, ladies and gentlemen. This evening we are offering this *very* rare Astronaut Roxy doll made by Ratello in 1975 at the very end of the Apollo space missions. These treasured dolls don't come up for sale very often and as you all know, only 11 of these Astronaut Roxy's were made. This delightful one here was actually owned by Mr and Mrs Ratello, so I expect a lot of interest. If everyone is ready, I will start the bidding at fifty thousand pounds."

The crowd sat in stunned silence, not expecting the starting price to be quite so high.

Angry Lee raised a hand and nodded confidently. "Let's get this show on the road."

"I have a bid of fifty thousand from the front row," said Mr Kumar, pointing the end of his gavel in Angry Lee's direction.

Maddie typed a bid of sixty thousand pounds on her

phone's keyboard and hit the 'PLACE BID' button.

"An online bid of *sixty* thousand has been made by Miss Mainard," said Mr Kumar and Maddie smiled, knowing Angry Lee wouldn't be happy with her being online and bidding against him.

The traffic lights changed to green, and Sir Charles checked the signpost. "Left here for Ryde," he said to Emelia and popped his pipe between his teeth and lit it. Emelia tutted and began searching in her handbag for her new bottle of Pierre Thabaut perfume.

The campervan turned left, and Sir Charles let out a huge plume of smoke, while just behind him, Cheddar George and the OP Gang slept peacefully in their seats, now snoring *very* loudly.

Lottie saw the kidnapper's van take the wrong turn for Ryde and zoomed out of the petrol station and passed the fake sign. Penny, Ledley and the piece of Paddy popped out from behind it and dropped back into the wicker basket. Lottie turned left. "I hope you know what you're doing, Duke."

*

Maddie watched the auction continue. Bids were made from others in the crowd at Sotheby's which pushed the price up and up, while Sir Charles drove steadily along the winding road and reached Afton Junction – a roundabout with exits heading to Freshwater, Sandown, Newport and Alum Bay.

Once again, the BREW Crew snuck ahead to cover the old sign and make a new one of their own, showing Ryde to the right. Sir Charles took the last exit for Ryde as directed, puffing happily on his pipe and Emelia sat in silence and sprayed herself with more perfume.

"I have a bid of a hundred and twenty thousand from Mrs Tazinski in the back row. Do I hear one hundred and thirty?" asked Mr Kumar, scanning the room and checking his monitor which displayed the online bids.

Angry Lee nodded and the crowd gasped. Maddie quickly increased her bid to a hundred and fifty thousand and squinted through the window but couldn't make out any landmarks, due to the dense Cornell tobacco smoke coming from Sir Charles' pipe.

At the back of the auction room, Mrs Tazinski shook her head. She'd offered the maximum she was prepared to pay for the doll. There were now just two bidders left in the auction - Maddie and Angry Lee.

"Where are we?" Maddie asked, her eyes not moving from the phone in her hand.

"Still heading for Ryde. It's all under control. Don't worry," said Sir Charles, puffing away.

"Excellent," said Maddie and returned to the important matter of winning the auction and claiming her prize.

Mr Kumar stared at his monitor, open mouthed. "Miss Mainard has bid one hundred and fifty thousand pounds."

Various gasps of "ooh" and "ahh" came from the crowd at Sotheby's Auction room.

"Do I have any more bids?" asked the auctioneer.

Furious, Angry Lee stood. "One hundred and eighty!" he shouted.

"A hundred and eighty thousand pounds bid by Mr

Whitaker. Thank you," bellowed Mr Kumar above the noise from the excited crowd.

Maddie wasn't going to be put off by Angry Lee's performance in front of Mr Kumar. Her finger trembled as she made a bid of two hundred thousand pounds on her phone. "That Roxy is *mine*."

CHAPTER 29 – JUMPIN' JACK FLASH.

The kidnapper's vehicle chugged along Totland Road which ran along the coast towards Alum Bay. Lottie and the BREW Crew still followed in the Oldie TT which wasn't built for such speeds and shook badly, sending painful tremors up Lottie's arms and hurting her shoulders.

Lottie glanced at the small gauge next to the speedo which showed how much power was left in the battery. The thin needle pointed at just above a quarter. "Nik-nacks. We're running out of power."

The Duke rose from the wicker basket and wrote frantically on a piece of Paddy.

"That's not good and there's more bad news. Spike's found half a canapé in the basket. I've analysed a sample and found traces of a dangerous chemical. It's likely Cheddar George and the other four have swallowed Kacka-Lax."

"Kacky-what?" Lottie asked.

"Kacka-Lax A chemical we used on secret missions in the second world war to panzernack the drivers of enemy troop trains. If they've taken it, then all five hostages will be out cold until given the antidote."

"Oh no. Don't tell me, the antidote is some fancy stuff made in a secret lab," said Lottie, as she followed the campervan around a sharp bend.

"You couldn't be further from the truth, Lottie. The Kacka-Lax antidote is a substance known as 'rennet'."

"I've heard about that in Miss Smith's Food Tech class at school. Clarissa Pendennis who knows *everything* said it's an ingredient used to make... CHEESE!"

"Exactly. And, as luck would have it, we are carrying a small supply of mature cheddar."

"In this sarnie!" shrieked Lottie, pulling Cheddar George's half-eaten emergency cheese sandwich from the wicker basket. "If we can give him some cheese and wake him up, he could help us!"

"Exactly. Just try and stick with the target vehicle while we pay them a visit."

"Be careful," said Lottie, as the Oldie TT's front wheel hit another painful pothole.

The BREW Crew flew off, with Spike holding two slices of cheddar cheese skewered to his compass point. Ledley and Penny flew either side of Spike and Rula and Sharpy flew above and below, escorting the precious cheese cargo on their mission.

It didn't take them long to catch up with the campervan, approaching low from behind to avoid being spotted. At the back of the van, Rula bent the bracket holding the bumper to the bodywork and made a small hole.

One by one, the BREW Crew squeezed through the hole and inside the kidnapper's vehicle. They drifted silently across the floor, weaving between empty tuna tins and the feet of the OP Gang who sat snoring with their heads down, dribbling on their chests.

Still with her eyes glued to her phone, Maddie's heart was racing, and she wiped a sweaty palm down her trousers. In Sotheby's auction room, Angry Lee was shouting at Mr Kumar and had just increased his bid for Astronaut Roxy to two hundred and twenty thousand pounds. It was a new world record - the most money ever offered for any toy at an auction.

Spike and Rula slid up the inside leg of Cheddar George's flared trousers, through his SpongeBob underpants and navigated their way through his troublesome string vest.

"It can't be far now, Maddie," said Sir Charles.

"Thank goodness," muttered Emelia Douthwaite.

Maddie had her eyes still locked on the phone clutched in her hand. "Very good, Sir Charles," she said, paying no attention to anything else going on around her.

While Maddie decided how much of her two hundred and fifty thousand pounds to bid next, Rula and Spike slipped out from the collar of Cheddar George's red sparkling Elvis cape. Rula prized Cheddar George's false teeth apart and Spike popped a slice of his favourite cheese in his mouth. Rula then worked his jaw up and down and Cheddar George's teeth clunked together as he chewed.

"I won't be beaten," muttered Maddie. She'd made up her mind and tapped in a bid of two hundred and thirty thousand into her phone, unaware of Spike feeding Cheddar George the second slice of cheese, which Rula helped him munch.

Maddie bit her lip and waited, as Mr Kumar announced her bid to the packed auction room there was a round of enthusiastic applause from everyone except Angry Lee. All eyes were now on him, wondering what his next move would be, all the while the rennet antidote to the Kacka-Lax began to do its job.

Cheddar George's eyes stuttered open and the very first thing he noticed through the stinking smoky fog around him was a piece of Paddy paper stuck to the top of his Kodak Camera.

"Wait for Lottie to give the order, then give them hell!"

Cheddar George covered the paper with his hand and without moving his head, took a sly look around the campervan. He gave a wry smile and shut his eyes, pretending to be still asleep and curious to know why he had the lovely taste of his favourite cheddar cheese in his mouth.

For years, he'd driven buses around the island and knew every puddle and pothole on these roads; every smell from the many pubs and takeaways which edged the streets. He felt the campervan go through a short railway tunnel and there was a metallic CLONK as a wheel rolled over a lose drain cover in the road and then his nose caught the faintest smell of fish and chips.

Cheddar George knew *exactly* where they were – half a mile from Arthur Fry's old Chippy Plaice near Salisbury Hill on the B3023. They were heading back into Alum Bay.

"This is *not* in my job description, Sir Charles. What

if we get stopped by the police?" hissed Emelia.

"Calm down, Emelia," said Sir Charles.

Emelia looked nervously out the window. "You *do* know a Detective Inspector from Alum Bay was asking a lot of questions about the HMS Chichester," she said, expecting to see a fleet of police cars with their blues and twos chasing them.

Sir Charles Oakley chuckled. "That's all puffle-huff, Emelia. Detective Inspector? More like *Defective* Inspector. I read his report. He's an idiot and hasn't got a clue."

The campervan slowed as it began climbing Salisbury Hill, the road crossing the river Thorley which flowed into the lake in Bearwood Park near Lottie's house.

Spike had to do one final daring task before leaving the kidnapper's vehicle. He sneaked under the seats to the front, darting from tin to tin of empty Boomer's Tuna and waited behind Emelia Douthwaite's feet. When Emelia shut her eyes to spray Pierre Thabaut over herself, Spike saw his chance and nipped up behind the dashboard. He squeezed his way through a gap between the speedo and heater controls and located the wiring at the back of the radio.

Spike snipped four wires, joining them together to create a new electrical circuit and then zig-zagged back through the tuna tins to the rear of the campervan where the rest of the BREW Crew waited.

Silently, the BREW Crew snuck out the way they'd come and flew down the other side of Salisbury Hill where the streetlights of Alum Bay twinkled in the distance (except the one outside Lottie's house).

On a grass verge on the edge of town was a sign saying, 'WELCOME TO ALUM BAY'. The BREW Crew altered the sign to now say, 'WELCOME TO RYDE'.

*

Lottie watched the campervan's rear lights disappear over the brow of Salisbury Hill. The scooter struggled up the hill, but just about made it to the top. Then, disaster struck. The scooter's motor died. The needle showing the battery power pointed at zero and the only noise was the rumble of the tyres on the road.

"No, not now. Nik-nacks," said Lottie, stamping her foot on the power pedal – nothing happened.

Lottie and the powerless Oldie TT rolled down the other side of Salisbury Hill towards Alum Bay. Surely now, she'd lose the kidnappers.

*

Sir Charles spotted the BREW Crew's sign. "We've made it to Ryde, Maddie," he called, still puffing happily on his pipe.

"Finally. What happens now?" Emelia asked, staring longingly at the empty bottle of perfume in her hand.

"Drive onto the pier and stop at the security gate. I'll be done soon," Maddie said.

Cheddar George never flinched as felt Maddie pinch his cheek, checking the five pensioners were still out cold.

*

As Lottie rolled down the steep hill, she was relieved to see the BREW Crew waiting for her outside the

Fishy Plaice. "The silly motor thing died. They'll get away if we stop rolling."

"Roger that. It's not much further. Keep going."

Lottie crouched down in the seat, hoping it would make the scooter more aerodynamic and roll further. Spike hovered in front of the radio cassette player, turned into a screwdriver and quickly prized off the cover to reveal the dusty innards. Sharpy snipped two wires and Spike morphed into a pair of pliers to twist the ends together and connect them to a switch. He cut another wire and ran it from the switch to a small battery.

"What are you doing?" Lottie asked.

"Establishing a communication link to Cheddar George."

Suddenly, the speakers in the radio cassette player crackled and Lottie heard a man's voice. "I told you not to worry, Emelia."

"What's *that?*" asked Lottie.

"Spike rewired their radio to transmit from inside the vehicle That's the voice of one of the kidnappers – the driver."

"Wickedoolie," said Lottie, watching Spike attach another wire to a tiny fuse inside the radio cassette.

"And that's not all. Cheddar George's new hearing aid is a RF7B. That model can pick up high-end radio frequencies. If you press the 'RECORD' and 'REWIND' buttons together you should be able to talk to him without the kidnappers hearing."

"Double wickedoolie!" said Lottie.

"Agreed. And with comms to Cheddar George, we can now execute the final stage of our own Distract and Snatch. Hopefully he hasn't dozed off again and is ready to distract the kidnappers, once Spike and Rula are in their forward position."

283

"OK," Lottie said, peering over the arched windshield as the scooter trundled silently on.

They reached the 'WELCOME TO RYDE' sign on the edge of Alum Bay and bumped over a level crossing. The scooter began to slow as the road levelled out. Spike and Rula flew back to the campervan and disappeared through the hole in the rear bumper.

"Fifteen seconds, Lottie."

"Roger that," said Lottie and her fingers pressed the 'RECORD' and 'REWIND' buttons on the old radio cassette player and she spoke into the speaker. "Yodelling man, yodelling man, this is bagpipe girl."

Cheddar George heard Lottie loud and clear in his left ear. He allowed himself the faintest of smiles, wondering what Lottie and the BREW Crew had planned.

"Yodelling man. If you can hear me, get ready to do your thing. Ten... nine... eight..."

*

"Two hundred and forty thousand," shouted Angry Lee in the auction room, to more gasps and applause from the crowd. Angry Lee grinned and took a handkerchief from his pocket and cleaned his glasses.

"Got you!" Maddie squealed, punching the air in delight. She'd studied Angry Lee at dozens of auctions and knew that when he began cleaning his glasses, he'd made his best and final bid and would offer no more. He didn't realise he did this, but Maddie had picked up on it. After all, watching people for hours and hours was a big part of her job at the PCS.

Maddie could hardly contain her excitement and was

now certain one more bid would win her the Astronaut Roxy. Her sweaty hand typed two hundred and fifty thousand on her phone. She paused with her finger hovering over the 'PLACE BID' button and she couldn't stop smiling. This was it. *Finally*, the hard work and sacrifice was totally worth it.

"Welcome home, Roxy!"

*

"NOW, yodelling man, NOW!" shrieked Lottie in Cheddar George's ear.

WHUMP

"Clickety click. Time to shine!" shouted Cheddar George as the tremendous burst of light came from the Kodak camera on his lap.

The sudden thunder flash of white light lit up the inside of the campervan and startled Maddie, making her jump. At the same moment, the campervan hit a pothole, causing Maddie's phone to fly from her hand. It clattered on the floor, bounced twice and ended up buried deep in a pile of tuna tins by Cheddar George's feet.

"No, no," cried Maddie. "My phone! My bid! My Roxy!"

Unable to see, she dropped to her hands and knees and crawled around the floor, desperately trying to find her phone and hit the 'PLACE BID' button.

"My ruddy eyes!" shouted Sir Charles. His hands were off the steering wheel, shielding his face from the intense light and the campervan swerved onto the wrong side of the road. Rula flew up from under his seat and turned the wheel to safely steer the driverless van, narrowly missing a lamp post.

From behind the campervan, Lottie saw the flash explode, lighting up the road. "I think Cheddar George got the message!"

"Top ho."

Cheddar George then did what the Duke had asked and gave the campervan's audience his version of 'hell' by yodelsinging as loud as he could.

"This little light of mine, I'm gonna let it shine." WHUMP

"Yodeladay-a-day-a-dee, yodeladay-a-day-a-doe." WHUMP

"Miss Mainard, are you there? Would you like to bid again?"

Maddie heard Mr Kumar's voice coming from her phone somewhere on the floor nearby as she blindly searched for it amongst the tuna tins. "Yes. YES. Hang on, Mr Kumar."

"This little light of mine, I'm gonna let it shine." WHUMP

"I *knew* something would go wrong," cried Emelia, her eyes stinging from the flashes of light mixed with the stinky smoke from Sir Charles' pipe.

"Shut up, Emelia. This is not the time for '*I told you so*'," shouted Sir Charles, stamping on the brake pedal.

But the pedal did nothing. Spike had sneaked under Sir Charles' feet and panzernacked the vehicle by unbolting the cable. The driverless and brakeless campervan carried on down the road with Rula struggling to keep it under control.

"Let it shine, Let it shine, Yodel-a-dee," WHUMP

Rula suddenly spun the steering wheel and the van veered left into Alum Bay High Street.

"What the puffle-huff," shouted Sir Charles with his hands still covering his eyes.

"Everywhere I go, I'm gonna let it shine." WHUMP

Every time the kidnapper's eyesight began to recover, Cheddar George fired his camera flash, blinding them again.

Maddie's hand swept the stack of empty Boomer's Tuna tins aside and at last, her fingers brushed her phone. "Yes! Finally," she said, quickly scooping it from the floor.

She held the phone inches in front of her face and squinted at the screen and could just about make out the grainy outline of Mr Kumar.

"Going… Going… GONE! Sold to Mr Whitaker for two hundred and forty thousand pounds."

"No. I want to bid again. I *have* to bid again, Mr Kumar," shrieked Maddie, jabbing the 'PLACE BID' button. But she was too late. 'AUCTION ENDED' flashed in red on her screen.

"Yodeladay-a-day-a-dee, yodeladay-a-day-a-doe," WHUMP.

Maddie flopped in her seat and a red mist of anger began to build. All her hard work for the PCS to earn the money to buy the Roxy doll had been an utter waste of time.

Rula steered right and the campervan bumped up a kerb causing the tuna tins to rattle against each other as the van rolled along the footpath outside the Weary Head Hotel. Spike retightened the bolt to fix the brake pedal and Rula pressed the pedal to finally bring the van to a stop.

The OP Gang rocked in their seats but carried on snoring peacefully. Sharpy cut the wires to the ignition and the engine died.

Furious, Maddie took a corned beef and custard tart, coated in Kacka-Lax from her pocket and shoved it under Cheddar George's nose. "Leave the camera alone, or I *will* force this down your throat and you know what happened last time."

Cheddar George sniffed the soggy canapé and knew he was beaten. He moved his hand away from the camera. "Kalispera. Maddie the Baddie, I presume. How's your belly off for spots?"

"I shall be *so* glad to see the back of you, you old codger," hissed Maddie, rigid with anger.

Cheddar George smiled. "Agreed indeed, my dear. We must stop meeting like this."

With the camera's flash no longer blinding everyone, Sir Charles eyesight was the first to recover. He turned the ignition key, trying to start the engine, but nothing happened. He rubbed his sore eyes and opened his door and his stinky pipe smoke seeped out. Maddie pinched the OP Gang, making sure they were still out cold. To Maddie Mainard, this was no longer about the money or the elusive Roxy doll. This was now about finishing the job and getting Cheddar George what he deserved – a ten by eight cell on HMS Chichester

"We can't be far from the prison ship. Go and get help from the guards at the security gate."

"Off you trot, Emelia," said Sir Charles.

Emelia crossed her arms defiantly. "I'm *not* going, Sir Charles. You and Maddie kidnapped these poor souls, so if you want to lock them up for good, then *you* go and get the guards. I told you it was wrong. *And* I've come to the decision that your PCS is a *terrible* idea."

"A terrible idea? That's puffle-huff and preposterous," barked Sir Charles. "We've kidnapped hundreds of pensioners and locked them in prison, and I won't stop."

As the smoke cleared, Sir Charles suddenly noticed the lens of a TV camera pointing at him through his open door. A group of curious people carrying placards.

"IT'S A BIN SIN," they chanted and crowded round the campervan, peering into the foggy inside.

Amanda Nelson appeared holding a large microphone and talked into the camera. "We will come back to the outcome of the council's meeting to change the bin collection day, now we bring you this breaking news story for Spotlight Isle of Wight. Seconds ago, a vehicle mounted the pavement outside the town hall in Alum Bay. Inside, Sir Charles Oakley, the Home

Secretary, just confessed on live TV to kidnapping hundreds of pensioners!"

The camera lens panned the inside of the campervan. The OP Gang still snored noisily and dribbled on their chests, Emelia cowered in her seat and Maddie just stared at her phone which showed the smug face of Angry Lee, clutching the Astronaut Roxy doll.

"Kalispera," said Cheddar George. "Does anyone have a flask of tea. Tash-hag I'm parched."

"Sir Charles. Is it true you've been kidnapping the elderly?" asked Amanda Nelson.

Sir Charles Oakley cleared his throat. "Ahem… Well… I can see it looks that way, but I can *definitely* assure you-"

"Mind out the way please!" called Lottie, as the crowd of bemused placard wavers parted and the Oldie TT rolled to a stop next to Amanda.

Lottie was off the scooter in a flash, leaping inside the campervan to give Cheddar George a hug. "It's true. They *are* kidnappers."

"Agreed indeed," called Cheddar George, wrapping his frail Elvis arms around Lottie.

"That's *very* interesting slash remarkable," said Detective Inspector Sergeant-Constable, his hand gently clearing a path through the crowd. He'd been at the town hall with the entire Alum Bay police force making sure the AABBCC protesters behaved themselves at the meeting and never expected what was happening now.

"Who are you?" barked Sir Charles.

"He's the *Defective* Inspector you said had no idea what was going on," said Cheddar George and poked his tongue out at Sir Charles.

"Well, he knows what's going on *now!*" said Lottie.

"Sir Charles Oakley, I'm arresting you for the kidnapping of George Hardwick slash a number of other senior citizens," said Detective Inspector Sergeant-Constable.

"PENSIONERS!" growled Sir Charles.

Amanda shoved the microphone under Sir Charles' nose. "Do you have anything else to say, Home Secretary?"

"Puffle-huff!" said Sir Charles as Detective Inspector Sergeant-Constable handcuffed him and led him to his car.

Cheddar George tapped his black Elvis wig. "Up here for fighting crime and down there for dancing."

Alan Barbara

CHAPTER 30 – THAT'S LIFE.

The reflection from the blues and twos danced off the shop windows and the siren echoed in the streets of Alum Bay as the police car hurtled along. In the back, Lottie sat fiddling with the heart-shaped locket dangling from her neck. Cheddar George sat beside her yodelhumming. He glanced at his trusted Timex watch. "My old boots. The boys are due on stage in just a few minutes."

"We have got to get there," said Lottie.

The late evening traffic moved aside as the police car raced through the town and finally, it zoomed past the Verdi supermarket and screeched to a halt outside the Trocadero.

"Told you we'd make it," said Detective Inspector Sergeant-Constable.

"Tickety-boo. Thanks muchly," said Cheddar George, starting the lengthy task of getting out of the police car. "You run ahead, Lottie and do an out-shout for me."

"OK. Thanks for the lift, Mr Detective Inspector," called Lottie.

"Thank *you*, Lottie. Another case slash mystery

293

solved," called Detective Inspector Sergeant-Constable, who was looking forward to his night in the cramped interview room at Alum Bay police station with Sir Charles Oakley and Maddie Mainard.

If she hadn't been in such a hurry, Lottie might have noticed the middle-aged man stood in the doorway of the Jimmy Chew's sweet shop opposite the Trocadero. He was bald with a huge spider's web tattoo on his head, hiding a deep scar. He watched Lottie race up the steps into the foyer and disappear inside.

The man smiled. "Found you, Lottie Baxter," he muttered to himself and thrust his hands into his pockets and wandered away.

"We caught the kidnappers," shrieked Lottie, racing past the box office where Nanny Vera and Grandad Frank sat, busy selling tickets to a queue of rock 'n' roll fans that stretched out the door and along the street.

"What's that, darling?" asked Grandad Frank.

"I'll tell you later, Grank. It was amazeballs. Got a show to put on," said Lottie and she disappeared through the door into Mission Control.

Grandad Frank smiled. He was very pleased with himself, as he'd *finally* mastered the PayCheck chip and pin reader (after spending 68 pounds 50 on his own credit card) and was busy taking lots of payments for the tickets which Nanny Vera handed over.

*

SooTed and BooTed stood on the stage behind a shimmering silver and red curtain. SooTed wiped a bead of sweat from his bald head. "Any second now, buddy. Happy-as. Ready for our dancin' party?" he asked, fastening a button on his duck-egg blue jacket.

BooTed grinned as he combed his hair one more time, sweeping it into a quiff.

"I can't stop trembling," said BooTed. He took a deep breath and did his usual ritual before performing; tensing his neck muscles and thrusting his tongue out like a shocked turtle to loosen his vocal cords. "We've waited a *very* long time for this. I only hope we have a good crowd in."

SooTed smiled. "Me too. *And* I hope the old Mayor and the VIPs who turned up earlier had a night to remember. All set?"

"Let's rock 'n' roll," said BooTed, shaking his friend's massive hand.

At eight o'clock precisely, Lottie pressed a button in Mission Control and the silver curtain lifted. SooTed and BooTed couldn't believe it. A huge crowd of rock 'n' rollers filled the auditorium beneath their glitter ball, cheering as Spike pressed two buttons and a rainbow of spotlights lit the stage.

The Duke flicked another switch on the ECHO-TECH-10A and Lottie leant nearer to a Vocal-Star Pro-Max microphone. "Ladies and Gents. Welcome to the Trocadero. The new home of SOOTED and BOOTED!"

The backing track to Showaddywaddy's *You Got What It Takes* blasted from the speakers and SooTed and BooTed took a deep breath and sang the first line.

Cheddar George smiled. "Tickety-boo. Time for that cuppa and to scoff the good biscuits."

Alan Barbara

A WORD FROM ALAN.

Thank you for reading Maddie the Baddie, which is my second book in the Lottie Baxter adventure series. It would be wonderful if you could leave a review on Amazon. Reviews are really important for independent authors, so please consider leaving a review if you enjoyed the book. It only needs to be a couple of lines and would really mean a lot to me.

It you'd like another adventure with Lottie and Cheddar George, then my first book called Fool's Gold is also available on Amazon here:

US - **https://tiny.one/FoolsGoldPaperbackUS**
UK - **https://tiny.one/FoolsGoldPaperbackUK**

If you'd like to know more about the man with the spider's web tattoo on his head, then I'm afraid you'll have to wait. I'm busy writing the next Lottie Baxter adventure and you can find out more about that on my website, or by signing up to my newsletter at AlanBarbara.co.uk

Building a relationship with readers is the best thing

about being an author. If you sign up to my mailing list, I can keep you up to date via a regular newsletter which has details of new releases and other snippets of news regarding Lottie's adventures.

For more information:
www.AlanBarbara.co.uk
Alan@AlanBarbara.co.uk
Facebook.com/AlanEdgarBarbara
Instagram.com/AlanBarbaraAuthor

All the best.
Alan.

Printed in Great Britain
by Amazon

21112546R00171